WHEN IT'S RIGHT

ALSO BY VICTORIA DENAULT

The San Francisco Thunder Series
Score
Slammed
Hometown Players Series
One More Shot
Making a Play
The Final Move
Winning it All
On the Line
Game On

WHEN IT'S RIGHT

A SAN FRANCISCO THUNDER NOVEL

VICTORIA DENAULT

FOREVER
YOURS

New York   Boston

Forever Yours
Hachette Book Group
1290 Avenue of the Americas, New York, NY 10104
forever-romance.com
twitter.com/foreverromance

First published as an ebook and as a print on demand: August 2018

Forever Yours is an imprint of Grand Central Publishing. The Forever Yours name and logo are trademarks of Hachette Book Group, Inc.

The publisher is not responsible for websites (or their content) that are not owned by the publisher.

The Hachette Speakers Bureau provides a wide range of authors for speaking events. To find out more, go to www.hachettespeakersbureau.com or call (866) 376-6591.

ISBNs: 978-1-5387-6312-4 (print on demand edition), 978-1-5387-6313-1 (ebook)

For my mom

ACKNOWLEDGMENTS

I dedicated this one to my mom because I drew on her a lot for Enid Braddock. My dad doesn't have ALS, but he's been sick. She's been his rock, and she's carried a lot, emotionally, for the entire family, and I can't thank her enough for that. I have lived a life I know she thinks is fairly nuts, but yet she stands by me and always supports me, so thank you, Mom.

To my husband, *je t'aime. Ton soutien signifie tout pour moi.* And yes, I'm practicing my French for our next big adventure.

Thank you to my agent, Kimberly Brower, for all that you do. You go above and beyond, and I appreciate it so much. To my editor, Leah Hultenschmidt, thank you for always finding ways to make a story stronger, and also thank you for your positive energy. To Estelle, Jodi, Monisha, and the rest of the amazing Forever team, thank you for all you do to bring these books into the world and into the hands of readers.

To all my family and friends who have been reading and promoting my books, Bev, Jenn D, Desiree, Jen O, Peter, Bunny, Mike H, Chantal, Tasha, and Matt, to name just a few, I love you all and your support means the world to me. To Jeff (Jeffie) Allen, thanks for letting me pick your brain about goalie coaches. I no longer regret having to sit next to you in journalism class back in the day.

Thank you to Paul Scheer, who decided to live-tweet *Score* and turn what could have been a bad social media moment for me into something that made me, and the romance community, smile (and laugh). Also thanks to all the other authors and readers who reached out and spoke out in support and solidarity. Extra love to the Hearties, who always have my back and who I rely on almost daily for advice, support, and laughs. You guys are just plain incredible.

As always, I am forever grateful for the readers and bloggers. There was a fairly big break between *Slammed* and *When It's Right*, so thank you for hanging on and not forgetting about the Braddock family and the SF Thunder boys. You guys are the best!

WHEN IT'S
RIGHT

Prologue

SADIE

Four years ago

It's my birthday. I'm at my favorite bar with a giant group of friends, and my favorite local country band just played the first chords to my favorite old-school country song, so right now—in this exact moment—my life is perfect. My younger sister, Dixie, lets out a loud whoop. And my older sister, Winnie, grabs her boyfriend, Ty, and immediately pulls him onto the dance floor. I jump up and down in my cowboy boots, with the twenty or so friends who came tonight, and raise my beer in the air.

"Before we start belting this out," says the lead singer, "I hear it's one of our favorite local's birthday. Sadie Braddock, get yer butt up here!"

Dixie whoops again and shoves me toward the stage. I'm not a total extrovert like her, but I'm four beers in, and it's my motherfucking birthday so, yeah, I'm going to get up there and sing "Jolene" so hard Dolly Parton would be proud. I dance my way to the front of the crowd, and the singer pulls me up on stage. My twenty-third year is starting out perfectly.

When it's over, a pair of big, strong hands reaches up to help me off the stage. They wrap around my waist the way they would wrap around a burrito, they're that big. I assume it's the bouncer, Kevin, or one of my friends, but when our eyes connect, I realize it's not. It's a tall, dark, and handsome stranger. Just when I thought the night could not get better.

"Happy birthday," he says as he dips his head so I can hear him over the band.

"Thank you," I reply with a big, bold grin. "But birthday wishes are always more heartfelt when they come with a beverage."

He laughs at that. It's a deep, nice sound. A man's laugh is essential for me. It's got to be deep, strong, and sexy, because the right guy for me is someone who will do it a lot. "I was going to offer to buy you another beer, but yours looked full."

I eye the bottle in my hand, which is only half full, then put it to my lips and down it. When I finish and look up at him, he's grinning like he just watched porn. "Looks are deceiving."

He laughs again and takes my hand and leads me to the bar.

Two hours later I've hugged and kissed my friends good-bye and now I'm doing the same to my tall, dark stranger—only with a lot tongue. It's a decent kiss. Not ovary-flipping, though, which is why I'm letting Dixie tug me away from him on the street outside Bourbon and Boots.

"Call me," he demands huskily.

"Of course," I call back as Dixie keeps pulling me down the street.

We walk arm in arm toward the subway, with Winnie and Ty trailing behind, stopping every now and then to make out. Dixie makes me tell her everything about him. "List his pros," Dixie demands. "Besides the obvious hotness."

"Pro—he's a digital producer in the film industry, which sounds all techy and smart. And he owns his own condo, so he doesn't live in his parents' basement," I explain, and she laughs but nods her head emphatically.

"Not bad." Dixie nods. Her blue eyes look up at me inquisitively. "Cons?"

"Con—he's only a year older than me," I explain, and she frowns, but I tug on her arm. "You know I like them older. And con—the blond hair. I feel like when I date blonds it looks like I'm dating my brother. No offense, Ty and Winnie."

I call that last thing over my shoulder to my older sister and her very blond boyfriend, but they're too busy sucking face again to listen. I roll my eyes and turn back to Dixie. "And he loves hockey. When he asked if I was related to Jude, he was all excited."

"Always lie and pretend you've never heard of Jude," Dixie says sternly about our older brother, who plays professional hockey for the San Francisco Thunder. "That's what I'm going to do for my internship with the team. No one is going to know I'm related to him."

"How you going to manage that?" I ask. Dixie just finished up her degree and snagged an internship with the Thunder in their PR department.

"Same way I got the job. Using my middle name as a last name," Dixie replies with a bright smile. "Dixie Wynn sounds way better than Braddock anyway. You should lie to people too and use your middle name."

"Sadie Rae sounds ridiculous to me," I reply. "Anyway, back to the dude. The kiss was okay but not OMG, which is the only reason I let you drag me away from him."

"So the fact that I flew home from school just for your stupid birthday isn't reason enough from keeping you from going home with a stranger?" Dixie asks in mock annoyance. "Wow. You're such a Jude."

I laugh so hard I snort. Our older brother is known just as much for being a giant player off the ice as he is for being a talented one on the ice. It's actually kind of embarrassing for all of us, and we spend as much time as we can teasing him about it.

"I'm honored you came home for my birthday." I smile at her and give her arm a squeeze. "But I'm not stupid. I think it was a little bit me and a lot about eating Mom's food, sleeping in my comfy guest room, and using a washing machine for free."

"That is just icing on the cake." Dixie grins. She's been spending the summer at school in New York taking classes so she can graduate earlier. I honestly don't care why she came home, whether it was my birthday or the free food and laundry. I'm just happy she's back. My siblings and I are all pretty close, no matter where any of us are living.

"Uh-huh." I roll my eyes, but I'm smiling. I might not be willing to say it aloud, but I really miss having my whole family in the same city. Jude has been gone since he was eighteen, only coming back in the summer, and even then, he's usually off doing his own thing, like tonight. He didn't want to come to the bar with us. And Winnie is madly in love with Ty and spends all her free time with him. I mean, not that I have a lot of free time because I'm an ER nurse in the biggest hospital here in Toronto, but still, I wish we had more time together, so I love when we have weekends like this.

We reach the subway entrance and come to a stop. Winnie is now being carried by Ty piggyback-style, and they look stupidly happy and in love. It makes me smile, because Winnie is such a fantastic human, and before Ty she struggled a lot with self-image and realizing her worth. She jumps off his back, and he turns and grabs her in another romantic kiss, dipping her back like they're a couple in a 1940s photo.

"Why did you agree to stay at Sadie's tonight?" Ty groans.

"Because it's my birthday. You can have sex tomorrow night," I reply for her. "Or tomorrow afternoon after the family brunch. Just not *at* the family brunch."

"That sounds like a challenge," Winnie jokes back. "Accepted."

Ty laughs. He kisses her again and then waves goodbye to all of us as he heads down into the subway and we head down the street toward the condo that I just bought.

I'm excited for tomorrow, when Jude and our parents will come over too. Then Dixie, Winnie, and I are going to the spa. It's the perfect weekend and totally makes up for the doubles I had to pull last week to get three days off in a row. Not that I minded all that much. I love my job. Even the most grueling shift is filled with a feeling of accomplishment. All I've ever wanted to do was help people.

We turn the corner onto my street, and Dixie is telling us about some disastrous hookup she had back at school with some guy who made weird noises when they kissed, when I see a shadow pacing in front of my building. I instantly recognize the broad shoulders, blond hair, and the distinct gait. It's our brother.

"What the hell are you doing here at almost one in the morning?' I call out, halting Dixie's story as her eyes turn to see Jude as well.

"Hey! Are you alone?" Dixie asks. "I didn't think it was humanly possible for you to be out past midnight without some poor, deluded girl pressing her double D's against your..."

The horrifying realization that Jude is crying hits all of us at the exact same time. It's like having your heart sucked into the turning engine of a jet plane. Quick, terrifying, and eviscerating.

"What's wrong?" I demand.

"I need to talk to you," Jude says. "He's going to tell you tomorrow, but I found out tonight and I...I can't."

"What happened?" Winnie asks, her face contorted in confusion just like Dixie's and I'm sure mine is.

"I went to see Mom and Dad tonight." He wipes angrily at his damp cheeks with the back of his hand. I'm confused again. "He went to the doctor."

"Okay, you mean Dad went to the doctor? So?" I'm beginning to piece things together, and dread fills my chest.

He looks at each of us, slowly, intensely, and I realize he is trying to capture this moment—our soft expressions, our naïveté—because it's going to leave. We're never going look so unaffected again. I know this moment, I've seen this moment happen before a doctor diagnoses a patient or a patient reveals a diagnosis to a loved one.

I feel my whole body turn to stone and yet every fiber of my being wants to move—to flee. To run away before Jude can open his mouth. I have no idea what he's about to say, but I know it's going to change everything. I can feel it.

"The doctor says he has something called Lou Gehrig's disease. Or ALS."

Dixie grabs my hand. I hear Winnie's sharp inhale and then nothing.

"What is that?" Dixie asks.

"What's the cure? There's a cure, right? Or a treatment?" Winnie demands.

"It's not serious, right? I mean it's manageable?" Dixie questions.

Dixie and Winnie assault him with questions, but he's ignoring them and looking only at me. He knows I know. He's looking at my face in desperation, wanting to see something that contradicts his own pained expression. He's hoping I know some medical information he hasn't found on Google. Something that will change the outcome he already knows is coming. He's looking for hope—even a glimmer.

But I don't have a glimmer of hope. I don't know any miracle drug or cure or anything. I can't say anything, can't do anything. My father is going to die from this. It's only a matter of when. Tears fall from Jude's eyes again, and he starts to turn away, but I grab him and pull him into a hug.

"No," Dixie whimpers, covering her face with her hands, so I reach out and pull her to me as well. Winnie is standing silently, shaking her head repeatedly, as her trembling hands start to dial her phone. She needs Ty. I'm so happy she has him.

Hours later, as the sun rises, we're all sitting silently in my living room, puffy-eyed, exhausted, and devastated. We've scoured every website on the disease, we've cursed the universe, we've had a colossal pity party, and lastly, we've made a pact. We will be there for one another—and for our parents—and do whatever it takes to make his time left on this planet as painless and stress-free and filled with love as humanly possible.

As Jude and Dixie start to doze off on the couch and Winnie disappears into the guest room, I head into my bedroom and change into sweats. Pulling my phone out of the pocket of the dress I was wearing and putting it on the dresser, I notice I have a message from the guy from the bar. It feels like a lifetime ago.

He doesn't matter anymore. Nothing matters anymore but getting the people I love, and myself, through this. I was born to help people, and now I have to help my family.

It's the only thing I care about.

1

SADIE

*B*OOM! The crashing sound feels like it shakes the whole house. I freeze in front of the mirror with one earring in, drop the other one on the dresser and rush out of my room. Winnie is already charging down the hall of the penthouse apartment we share with our parents.

"I'm okay!" My dad's voice is angry and abrupt.

We turn the corner into the master suite and find him leaning against the wall next to their bathroom. The large framed family photo that is normally on the wall has crashed to the ground, with chunks of glass scattered across the floor. And Dad doesn't have socks or shoes on. He tries to lift himself off the wall, and I jump forward.

"Don't! Stay there for a second, Dad." I turn to my older sister. "Winnie, get the vacuum."

She nods and runs back down the hall. My mom is standing half in the bathroom, half out. Her face twisted with worry and frustration. "Randy, I told you to wait until I got your walker."

"I'm just as bad with the walker as I am on my own now," he mumbles back. His speech is so slurred, it takes a minute to understand what he's saying. He has his good moments, usually early morning or late afternoon if he's had a nap, but gone are the days of regular speech. Forever.

"I'm feeling weaker than normal," he admits, which is rare for him and shocks me more than the shattered picture frame. "I think maybe I'll skip the barbecue."

My heart sinks. "Come on, Dad. It'll be fun, and you'll get to see Declan."

I try to sound casual, but the fact is he *has* to go. We *all* have to go. It isn't just a regular Sunday meal at Jude and Zoey's place. Usually mentioning his only grandchild gets him to change his mind on anything, but apparently not today. He shakes his head. "I'll just stay here and rest. Maria can stay with me."

Maria is his nurse. She comes every day now, because he needs help with everything from bathing to eating. I bend and pick up some of the bigger chunks of glass, carefully placing them in my palm. "We won't stay long," I lie.

Winnie returns with the vacuum. "I'll stay with you, Dad. I don't feel like getting dressed up for Jude's backyard anyway."

Ugh. I glance up at her, my face a mask of frustration. Why can't this family just follow orders? I want to argue with her, but she starts the vacuum, and anything I have to say would be swallowed by the loud machine. When the glass is cleared from the floor, Mom slips out of the bathroom and takes Dad's arm, helping him over to the bed. He's half dressed, in a pair of nice chinos but no shirt. Mom is still in her bathrobe, but her hair and makeup are done.

"I can stay home. I can make us something here and we can watch some TV," Mom suggests.

"Why don't we just raincheck the whole thing?" Winnie suggests, and my stress levels take off like a rocket. She turns and lugs the vacuum down the hall. When she's out of earshot, I pick up the family photo by the frame, carefully place it on top of the dresser, and remove the remaining big shards. "We are all going to the barbecue this evening at Jude's."

"Sadie, if your dad isn't up to it..." I turn and look at my mom.

"It's not just a barbecue."

"I know. It's Zoey's brother's birthday. But I'm sure Morgan won't mind if some of us don't make it," my dad says and sighs. "You can still go, and Dixie and Eli will be there."

I can't figure out how to make them come and not tell them, but this is supposed to be a surprise. It would have been a great surprise too. My mom would have teared up and Dad would have bellowed with laughter and told Jude he should have seen this coming. Jude has always been the crazy one. But now...the Braddock family doesn't get surprises. At least not happy ones. Instead we get ones like "Surprise! Your dad has ALS."

"Jude and Zoey are getting married," I say, and my parents just blink. "Tonight. In their backyard. So, I'm sorry to ruin the surprise, but you have to go."

"Oh. Oh, my goodness!" My mom starts to tear up, and I lift my hands in terror.

"Stop! Please! Save the tearful reaction for Jude," I beg. "We can still keep it from Winnie if you two can keep it under control. Jude really wanted to surprise everyone."

"Except you?" my mom asks.

I shrug and give her a wink. "Well, someone had to wrangle you people."

Mom wipes away her tears. Dad is doing nothing but smiling, ear-to-ear, like I haven't seen in months, and a selfish part of me is glad I get to see it now and have it all to myself. But he has to chill too, and I tell them that. He forces his face to relax. "That kid...always throwing me for a loop. God love him."

Winnie appears in the doorway again and takes the large pieces of glass from me and puts them in the trash bag she brought with her. Dad sits a little straighter. "I changed my mind. I want to go after all."

"We're all going," my mom adds.

Winnie shrugs and nods. "Okay, I'll go back to getting ready."

Crisis averted.

Three hours later, the ceremony is done. My brother is married and everything is perfect. My parents pretended to be as shocked as Dixie, Winnie, and the rest of the guests actually were when we got here. Zoey's dad, a retired Anglican minister, married them. Now everyone is mingling and grabbing champagne flutes and appetizers from the waiters wandering by.

Jude looks at me from where he's standing across the yard next to Zoey. Our eyes lock, and we have a moment to ourselves—in a room full of people. I give him the biggest, proudest smile and wipe away a tear. He shakes his head, kisses his wife's cheek, and walks toward me, giving me a stern look before pulling me into a hug. "None of that."

"I'm crying for Zoey," I mutter back against his ear as I squeeze him with all my might. "I'm sad she gave up and settled for you."

"That's more like it," he replies as he lets go of me, and we grin at each other. He grabs his own flute off a passing tray and walks back to Zoey.

After we all feast on a delicious catered meal, a DJ sets up in the corner and starts playing music. Jude and Zoey dance, and I feel the need to cry again. Winnie nudges me. "What's with the damn water works?"

"This is a beautiful moment, Black Heart," I snark back at her. "You know this should be making you want to finally tie the knot with Ty."

I'm kind of joking, but as soon as I say it she looks serious. "Don't do that. Don't pressure me. I get enough of that from Ty."

"I was kidding, Win," I reply and reach over and grab her hand. She pulls it away and doesn't look at me. Her eyes are on our dad, who is sitting at one of the small round tables set up around the yard with Declan asleep in his lap and our mom beside him.

"He's not going to be able to walk us down the aisle," Winnie whispers hoarsely. "He's not going to be able to dance with us. He's not going to see my kids."

I reach over and wrap an arm around her, and this time she

doesn't push me away. She leans her head on my shoulder. "Jude is lucky. I know. But Win…you could marry Ty tomorrow. You know he would do it. And then Dad could wheel down the aisle with you, and he might not be able to dance with you, but he'd watch you dance and look as proud as he does now. And as for babies…we all know you don't need a ring on your finger for that. Declan is proof."

"I could do all of that," she replies flatly. "But I would be doing it to create memories and they'd be false memories."

"Why?"

"Because Ty and I aren't Zoey and Jude," she says and pulls away from me again. "We're not soul mates. I want those memories with Dad so bad. I just don't want them with Ty."

I'm not surprised she doesn't think Ty is her soul mate, but I am surprised she's admitting it out loud. I'm trying to figure out how to respond when she gets up and walks away, rushing across the backyard and into the house. I stand up and start to follow her, but Jude steps in front of me. "Hey, Weepy. Come grab a drink with your legitimately hitched favorite brother."

"Man, I hope Dixie marries Eli soon so I have better options for this Favorite Brother category," I quip, and he gets me in a loose headlock as he barks out a fake laugh. "No wrestle mania at your wedding, douchebag."

He lets me go, but I follow him to the bar in the corner anyway. Winnie needs a little time to herself right now and besides, the conversation I probably need to have with her—about finally calling time of death on her ten-year relationship—shouldn't happen at Jude's wedding. At the bar he orders two shots of Fireball, and my eyes grow wide. "Dear God, no."

"For old times' sake," he says with a wicked grin and hands me one of the shots.

My stomach flips as soon as I smell it. "Why are you trying to make your sister puke at your wedding?"

"It's not a party until someone pukes!" he exclaims in a high-pitched girly voice. He's imitating me when I was seventeen and he got a call from one of his buddies that I was shitfaced at a house party. He showed up and dragged me out of there, and they snuck me into the house, past my mom who was watching a late-night talk show waiting up for me in the den like she always did, and then stayed up with me while I puked my guts out all night. I kept telling him it's not a party until someone pukes, apparently. I honestly don't remember a thing—except that I was drinking this cinnamon-flavored poison.

"I dare you," he says and lifts his own shot glass toward mine. Fucker knows I never back down from a dare. I lift my glass to my lips, squeeze my eyes shut, pinch my nose, and swallow it down as fast as I can. My whole body shivers in protest, and I gag, but I keep it down.

When I open my watering eyes, Jude looks like he's watching the best comedy show on the planet. "Do not make me flip you the middle finger on your wedding day in front of Pastor Quinlin."

"So..." Jude says, taking a deep breath and looking out over the small crowd. "Can you believe this is my life?"

"Honestly?" I smile. "The minute I saw you react to the news Zoey was in town I knew we'd end up here. Eventually."

"Liar."

"No, seriously," I argue back, and he turns to face me. "You heard us mention her and something about your whole face changed. That gross player face you had been wearing for like almost a decade morphed back into the sweet, kind, but inept dork capable of love." He frowns, and it makes me laugh. "Truth hurts."

"So who do you think is next?" he asks quietly as he turns back to the bartender and orders two beers.

"Out of us? I hope it's Dix." I shrug my shoulders, turning and putting down the shot glass. "I know they just started dating less than a year ago, but Eli's the one for her. I know it and I know she does too."

"Yeah. He is," Jude agrees as the bartender hands him two Coronas and he waves off the glasses he tries to hand him. "She's not that classy. Total bottle girl."

I look at the bartender and wink. "I like to wrap my lips around the shaft."

Jude groans and shudders. "What the hell is wrong with you?"

"You started it."

He sighs and sips his Corona, but when I go to lift mine to my mouth, he stops me and hands me one of the glasses on the bar. "Use this. I can't..."

I laugh and begrudgingly pour the beer into the glass. I take a sip and roll my eyes at him. "Better?"

He nods and looks back over the crowd before glancing sideways at me. "I think you should be next."

"To get married?" I snort. "To who? Please say Liam

Hemsworth. Or Chris. Or both. Is that weird? I don't even care. I'll marry both."

"I don't know who," Jude replies, ignoring my Hemsworth rambling. "But since we were kids I always thought you'd be the one to settle down first and have like five or six kids."

"Umm...hell no," I reply, horrified. "I want two. Only two. I've seen childbirth up close and personal. I know what it does to the vag. Too many births and that thing is a wreck."

"Please. Just don't go there." Jude shakes his head, pinching his eyes closed as if to block out horrible thoughts. He takes a deep, cleansing breath. "Stop trying to get me off the subject."

"Okay, let's go back to talking about me marrying the Hemsworth brothers." I give him a happy smile, but the little shit isn't having it. He wants to be serious. And I guess, because it's his wedding and I love him more today than ever, I relent. I take a big gulp of my beer, wiping some foam off my top lip. "In case you haven't noticed, I am not dating anyone right now."

"Of course I noticed," Jude says. "And in a way it's a relief because I don't have to stress out about you, or know that one of my teammates has seen you naked, which is zero fun. I mean Eli's a gentleman about it, but I still sometimes want to punch him out of principle."

"I won't date a hockey player, even when I am ready to date again, so no worries there," I promise.

"Good to know." Jude rubs the back of his neck, and we both watch Winnie emerge from the house. She looks calmer and more relaxed than when she stormed off. "And promise

me you won't date some guy you aren't actually madly in love
with. Because clearly that's garbage too."

I glance over at him and hold up my pinky toward him.
"Pinky swear."

We lock pinkies, and then he clinks his bottle to my glass.
We both take another swig. "So when will you be ready
again? And why aren't you ready now?"

"Look around you, Jude. Life isn't exactly easy right now."
I sigh and hold up my hand as he opens his mouth to argue.
"I know. It's not easy for you either, and yet you've got Zoey
and Declan and I can say, without a doubt, that bringing people into your life and your heart made life easier and better for
you and for us. I mean, look at Dad with his grandson."

We both look at our father, who is happily holding a sleeping Declan. Jude's eyes are watering, and I punch his shoulder. "Pussy."

"Fuck you." Jude laughs too.

"I can't let someone in because I'd be like Winnie. I'd take
and I wouldn't be able to give because I already give so damn
much. My job, keeping it together for Mom, keeping Winnie
positive, keeping Dixie calm, being a rock for Dad."

"You're not in this alone," Jude says quietly after a moment.

"Exactly. I'm not," I reply and sip my beer. "We are all
holding each other up here. And it's only going to get worse.
We're going to be devastated by his loss." I swallow and fight
tears yet again. "And I don't want to risk being devastated by
anything else right now. Does that make sense?"

"When it's the right person, there's no risk of devastation,"

Jude counters as his eyes move to Zoey, who is dancing and laughing with her brother and his partner, Ned.

He looks back at me, and I roll my eyes at him. "Pussy." He laughs and shoves me, and I shove him back. "Go dance with your wife."

He walks away, and I smile as I sip my beer.

I love my family. I don't need anyone else right now, and honestly...I just don't have it in me to let anyone else in.

2

SADIE

It's a slow night in the ER at San Francisco Memorial. That used to be a blessing, but now it feels like a bit of a curse. I come to work now for more than a paycheck or professional fulfillment. Now it's a place to hide. A place to get my mind off my problems and get a reprieve from my family. And when it's not busy, I can't escape—the dark thoughts in my head or the constant texts from my mom, my sisters, my brother, and my sister-in-law.

I glance at the clock above the nurse's station. Ugh. It's nine-forty. My shift only started two and a half hours ago, and I'm here until seven in the morning. I sigh as my phone dings in my pocket yet again. So far I've been ignoring it. I checked one message—the first—and it was just Winnie bitching about her boyfriend. It's gone off three more times since then, so I assume it's still her unloading all her frustration with Ty.

I glance at it now, though, just to be sure. We're not supposed to be on our phones, but they let me check it occasionally because they know my dad is sick. Just as I thought, there's more than one from Winnie, all complaining about Ty. But then there's one from Dixie. Short, in all caps:

ARE YOU AT WORK?

My heartbeat seems to stumble as I read it. Dixie, my youngest sister, does not take all caps lightly. Something is wrong, and I immediately think of my dad. The last couple of months since Jude's wedding he's been in a steady decline. I glance up. I'm the only one at the station. I can see Shelda, a friend and fellow nurse, at the end of the hall, and there's a doctor in one of the triage rooms stitching up a woman who almost chopped the tip of her thumb off cutting mushrooms. Our other patient, an elderly man who slipped in the bathtub and was brought in for observation by his nursing home, is resting comfortably in another room. I sink down into the chair and start to type back.

Yes. At work. Is it Dad?

The last time I talked to Dixie, earlier this morning, she was heading to the Thunder game to watch Jude and Eli play. Did she decide to skip the game and go visit our parents?

The doors from the ambulance bay swing open, and a paramedic pushes a gurney in with Eli on it. Holy shit! I rush around the counter.

"Oh, my God, what happened?" I gasp. My voice is not at

all that of a professional nurse, but my brain is acting the part as my eyes sweep over him looking for visible trauma. I don't see anything—no blood, no protruding bone, no laceration.

"He's a hockey player," a deep, smooth voice starts to explain, and I expect it to be the paramedic but it's not. It's a man in a nicely tailored charcoal suit. A *very* good-looking man. Tall and broad with olive skin, a roman nose, thick, dark hair, intense brown eyes, and a strong, stubbled jaw. Seriously, if I had a bucket list of male features, this man would check every one. "He was knocked out on the ice."

Eli gives me a sheepish smile. "Do you remember what happened?" I ask him.

"We were up two to one in the third, but they had a power play," he says, and I frown. He's not exactly answering my question, which means he doesn't remember being hit. Not a great sign.

"Put him in room four," I tell the paramedic, and he nods and starts to push the gurney down the hall.

"Dixie is on her way. Tell her I'm fine," Eli calls out.

The very handsome guy who came in with Eli pauses beside me instead of following him. He smells incredible—citrusy and woodsy all at once—and it makes me feel warm when I breathe it in. "Dixie is his girlfriend. She was at the hockey game, and I'm betting she's very upset."

"She is. She used all caps," I reply, and those penetrating caramel colored eyes cloud over with confusion. He looks even cuter confused.

"Dixie is my sister." I extend my hand. "I'm Sadie."

"Hello, Sadie," he says, and his full lips break into a deep, wide smile that make him so sexy I want to whistle. I bite my bottom lip to keep from cat-calling him to his pretty little face and wonder why my professional demeanor went on break early. "I'm Griffin, the Thunder's goalie coach."

"Oh, I thought Eli's coach was named Sully," I say, because I remember Eli telling our dad about his new goalie coach at Sunday dinner last week.

"That's me too," he explains. "Griffin Sullivan."

"Of course. Hockey is all about the nicknames," I reply, and he chuckles. It's a nice, deep sound that makes me feel warm again.

The doors swing open, and my little sister rushes through them, looking frantic. I glance at Griffin. "You can go be with Eli. I'll calm her down and then bring her in."

He nods and starts to walk away. I can't help but watch him go, and I feel a little delighted flutter when I see him give me an extra glance over his shoulder before he disappears into Eli's room.

I hug Dixie as soon as she's within arm's reach. "He's okay."

"He was knocked out!" she explains in a strained voice. "As in completely unconscious!"

"He was alert and talkative when they brought him in," I reply and give her another squeeze. "We'll do tests."

"Do all the tests. Whatever it takes to make sure he doesn't have a concussion or a brain bleed or an aneurysm or—" Dixie replies and pulls back from me.

"You need to stop watching medical dramas, Dix," I tell her softly. "We will do all the tests. MRIs, blood work, x-rays, hell, we'll even check his cholesterol if you want."

She almost smiles at that, but the look in her light blue eyes is still filled with worry. "I need to see him."

"Of course." I keep my arm wrapped around her waist as I guide her toward the hall leading to the rooms. "His new goalie coach came in with him. He's kind of delicious."

Dixie's eyebrows rise. "Really? He must be downright stunning if you're able to see it."

"What does that mean?" I ask as we turn the corner and make our way to Eli's room.

"You haven't noticed a guy in years," Dixie replies. "I was beginning to think your libido had died an early death or something."

"Oh, come on, it's not that big a deal," I reply a little defensively. "I just haven't exactly been getting out and meeting people."

"You work in a huge hospital. I'm sure there are hot doctors here," Dixie retorts. "Like at least one McDreamy or McSteamy."

"Again, lay off the medical dramas," I snap back. I usher her into the room. Her eyes land on Eli, and any thoughts about my lack of a love life are forgotten. She rushes to his bedside, and tears tumble from her eyes.

"I'm okay," Eli promises, reaching up and caressing the side of her face. "I swear, this is just protocol."

"You weren't moving at all," she counters softly.

"I was napping," Eli jokes and winks. "You kept me up too late last night."

"Okay, you two..." I interrupt and glance at Griffin, who is in the corner of the room looking amused. "I'd bet money you have a concussion, but the doctor will be able to tell us the degree of severity. I'll call Dr. Luongo in neuro for a consult."

"Thanks, Sadie," Eli says.

"Yes, thank you," Griffin adds, and Dixie looks up and sees him there for the first time. Her eyes do a quick sweep, and then her head immediately swivels to me and widen in approval, as if to say *You're right. He's hot.* It's about as smooth as a cactus. I'm mortified by her obviousness.

"Dixie, this is Griffin Sullivan, Eli's goalie coach," I say.

"Hi. I've seen you around, but we haven't officially met. Eli has said a lot of positive things about you," Dixie explains and walks around the bed to shake his hand. "I'm Dixie Braddock."

Griffin shakes her hand, but his eyes dart to me quickly as he adds, "Braddock? Like Jude Braddock?"

His deliciously dark eyes find mine again, and I shrug. "Yep. The Thunder's little superstar is lucky enough to call us his sisters."

Griffin laughs again. "And the plot thickens."

There's a vibe between us so strong it's electric. At least it feels that way…But maybe it's only wishful thinking. Man, he is seriously handsome. And charismatic. And sexy. I love the easy smile parting his lips and the warm glow in his eyes, the five o'clock shadow shading his strong, angular jawline, the way he is filling out that suit…

"So the tests?" Dixie's voice pulls me away from the list I'm making. "All of them? Now."

I blink, trying to ground myself in reality again, and nod.

"I'm on it. I'll send Shelda in to get his vitals while I call for the consult."

I turn and leave the room. Shelda is walking toward me. "I heard your sister's boyfriend is here?"

Of course she heard already. Shelda is that little birdie that flutters around the hospital hearing and seeing everything. She's not a gossip or busybody, by any means; she's just been working here since she was sixteen, first as a candy striper and now as a nurse, and everyone knows her, loves her, and talks to her about everything. She's my favorite head nurse in this place and a dream to work under.

"I hope that handsome devil isn't too banged up," Shelda adds, and I smile.

"He's probably got a concussion. I'm going to call for a consult. Can you go in and take his vitals?" Shelda nods. "Oh, and if Dixie gets too... Dixie-ish, feel free to kick her out. She's a bit of a bossy control freak in a crisis."

Shelda lets out a breezy laugh. "No worries, sugar. I can handle overbearing girlfriends and wives in my sleep."

She pats my shoulder as she passes by on her way to the room.

I head to the desk and call for a consult, mentioning it's also a personal favor if they can get here as soon as possible because it's a family member. Dr. Luongo shows up less than five minutes later. He's one of the first doctors I met here, and he's one of my favorites. Tall, lanky, with curly salt-and-pepper hair, a friendly smile, and a quick wit.

"Hey, Sadie, is it your dad?" he asks, concern flooding his deep voice.

"No. My sister's boyfriend," I reply. "He's the goalie for the Thunder and he got knocked out during the game."

"Ah," Dr. Luongo sighs. "That definitely sounds like a concussion, but let's see how bad it is. Room?"

"Four." I point and force myself not to follow. Although Eli's not technically family, he's close enough that I wouldn't be considered unbiased so I shouldn't get involved in his case. I'll let Shelda handle it.

I walk down the hall to check on the elderly patient in room two. He's asleep and his vitals are stable, his IV full. As I make my way out of his room, Griffin is standing in the hall outside Eli's room, his cell phone to his ear. I can't hear what he's saying, but he looks pissed. His jaw is clenched, and his brow is pinched. Still gorgeous, though. I bite my bottom lip to keep myself from laughing at my reaction. Seriously, it's like I've never seen a hot guy before.

He glances up and sees me, and I quickly wipe the smile off my face and head around the corner to the front desk. Hopefully I didn't look like a weird stalker or something, just standing there staring at him. A second later, he's standing on the other side of the desk.

"The doctor's been in there a while," he says to me, clearly concerned.

"Don't worry, he's probably being extra cautious because I told him Eli was family," I explain and smirk. "Or else my little sister is asking him a million questions and demanding a million unnecessary tests. It's probably a combination of both."

He laughs. "I think it's sweet that she's so ..."

"High-strung? Dramatic? Intense?"

He grins at me, clearly delighted by my adjectives, and I swear the room gets brighter. And I get warmer. "I was going to say in love," he says. "She loves him very much to be that concerned and it's beautiful. Eli's a lucky man."

"Huh...a sensitive, insightful hockey player." I give him a sassy wink. "Now that's a real plot twist."

Dr. Luongo turns the corner and joins us at the nurses' station. "I'm going to have him sent up for a CAT scan, and you can get him a room. He's definitely spending the night. It's precautionary, but he started getting nauseous so we should keep him here, wake him up every hour and keep him hydrated."

"Okay. Thanks, Dr. Luongo."

He leans on the desk and smiles. "I've told you before. It's Bob."

"Thank you, Bob. I owe you one."

"You can get me one of those fancy lattes next time we run into each other at the diner next door," he tells me with a grin. "I think they're ridiculously overpriced and won't pay for them myself, but I do accept gifts."

I laugh as he heads toward the elevators. I turn back to Griffin. "He's the best in city and he isn't all the worried about Eli, so you don't have to be."

He nods, but he seems like he has something more to say. I wait and watch as he dips his head a little and he rubs the back of his neck, but what comes out of his mouth isn't what I expected. "The best doctors are paid in fancy lattes. Who knew? Of course I'd take my pay in lattes too if they were delivered by you."

A blush blooms on my cheeks, and I suddenly realize I

must look so dowdy right now. I never wear makeup to work, and my ash blond hair is always pulled back into a ponytail. I smooth the sides self-consciously and react the only way I know how to a compliment, with a joke. "I should tell the Thunder you said that. They could use your salary to increase my brother's paycheck or Eli's."

"Are you a nurse or a sports agent?"

"Last time Jude signed a big contract, he took the entire family to Bora Bora, so really I'm just a selfish sister," I reply and wink.

"Well, I think—" He stops as his cell phone buzzes in his hand. He glances at the screen, silences it, and shoves it in his pocket. "I wish I could stay, but I have to get going."

"That's okay, like I said Eli is in good hands and he'll likely be fine," I assure him, but I'm disappointed he's leaving.

"I'm sure he will be." Griffin nods. "He's not the reason I was hoping to stay."

Dixie comes running down the hall. "He just threw up! All over himself."

She slaps a hand over her mouth because it must have made her nauseous too, but despite that the look in her eyes is pure fear. I step out from behind the counter. "Nausea is a symptom of a concussion, Dix. It's okay. I mean it's gross, but he's not dying. I'll go clean it up."

I head toward the supply room to grab new sheets and the plastic receptacle I lovingly call a barf bucket. I glance over my shoulder at Griffin, and he walks toward me. "I don't want to keep you, but is there any way I can get updates on him? Since I have to go. I mean, I'm not family but—"

"We can call you," Dixie offers, interjecting herself into what feels like our moment.

"Dixie will probably just spend half the night snoring by his bedside, so it's probably best if I keep you updated," I volunteer and Dixie, who was on the brink of looking offended, suddenly clues in and smiles.

"Totally. Good idea," Dixie agrees and turns to Griffin. "I'll give you her number while she goes to clean up the love of my life and then you can text her so she has yours."

"Sounds like a plan," Griffin says and looks at me again, pinning me with that lovely, intense stare of his. "I look forward to hearing from you."

I just smile and force my legs to take me down the hall. The last thing I want to do right now is clean up barf, but at least I got his number...even if it's for professional reasons...Technically.

3

GRIFFIN

Despite the fact that my star goalie is in the hospital and might be out of the lineup for a while and my ex has sent me not one but three angry texts since I left the hospital, I'm grinning. I walked into that hospital with nothing more on my mind than getting my player treated. Now my mind is filled with thoughts of a very pretty, very charismatic nurse. It's been a long time since my mind was on anything other than my work and my kid, but Sadie Braddock made one hell of an impression.

Sure, she was pretty, with her bright blue eyes, high cheekbones, and sexy curves not even her scrubs could hide, but her looks aren't why I'm still thinking about her. It was her warm smile and the effortless way she balanced being a calm, professional nurse and a concerned sister and was witty and sassy the entire time.

I pull into the marina parking lot, and my smile disintegrates when I see my ex-wife's car in one of the visitor slots. My chest instantly tightens and my jaw locks. I do not want to deal with her tonight. I jump out of my Range Rover and rush toward my houseboat. Even as I unlock the gate to the dock, I can see her silhouette standing on my front deck next to my front door.

"Lauren." I say her name as passively as possible. "What are you doing here? It's my night with Charlie."

"If it's your night, why aren't you spending it with her?" Her face, which I used to think was pretty stunning, is twisted into a tight, angry snarl.

"I had a game and she didn't want to come, so I had Hunter stay with her." I'm completely pissed that I have to explain anything to her. I don't report to her or need to tell her my plans when Charlie is with me. We have joint custody of our six-year-old daughter. Our agreement is simple, and we used to get along and work with each other, but now…the last few months, she's been like this. And I am at the end of my fuse. But I know, as much as I want to tell her to fuck off, I have to work as hard as I can at keeping things between us civil for my daughter's sake. God, it sucks, though.

"The game ended over two hours ago, Griffin," she snaps. "I'm here because Charlie had a nightmare and wanted to talk to me. I asked why she wasn't talking to you, and she said you weren't home."

"My goalie had to go to the hospital." I move past her and punch in the code for the lock on the front door. "I'm here now, so you can go."

"I'll go with my child."

The front door swings open, but I don't step inside. I turn to face her again. "*Your* child?"

"If she's yours, why are you not spending more time with her?"

"I had to work, Lauren," I say in a low voice through gritted teeth.

"You're home!" Hunter says from behind me, and I turn to see him walking toward me.

"You know he let me stand out here and knock for, like, ten minutes," Lauren complains to me and glares over my shoulder at my younger brother. Hunter gives her a dazzling passive-aggressive smile.

"I don't have to open the door. It's Griff's night. Being his lawyer and all, I am well aware of the custody agreement, but if you're confused I can print you off another copy." His smile widens, and it makes her scowl deepen.

"How's the wife, Hunter? Did she smarten up and leave you yet?"

"Nah. She believes in love and commitment, unlike you," he retorts. He winks at her. "Also most sane people consider me quite the catch."

As much as I enjoy watching my kid brother take her down a peg, I'm worried Charlie might overhear, so I put an end to it. "It's late. You should go home. Now."

Lauren just crosses her arms and glares at me from the threshold of my front door. I cross my arms too. I'm not giving Charlie over early. We have a Sunday morning apple pancake thing that I am not giving up. Hunter stops being my snarky younger brother and goes back to being my counsel. "All hate aside, Lauren, you can't legally just show up here and take Charlie on days when Griffin is legally entitled to her. You get her back at noon tomorrow, so you need to go. And if you don't go, I can and will call the police, and we will end up back in court."

She looks like she's about to have steam whistle out of her ears. I can literally see her swallow down her rage. "You know what? I'll go, but I'll see you in court anyway. This isn't working out for me."

She turns and starts stomping down the dock.

I walk over and close the door behind her, locking it, and since it's mostly just a glass pane, I also pull down the shade to block any last part of her retreating presence. "It's not about you, you selfish psycho nightmare," Hunter mutters and heaves out a sigh and rubs a hand over his face.

I lean on the peninsula part of the counter in the kitchen. "She's just venting, right? She doesn't want to drag this into court again."

"She'd be an idiot if she did," Hunter replies, walking past me and opening the fridge to grab two beers. He hands me one and twists the cap off his. "It's a fair agreement, no one has violated it, and Charlie is happy. So a judge is going to be pissed she is wasting his time if she does."

I try to relax a little and take a sip of the IPA. "I take it she's okay? Why didn't you call me?"

"Because it really wasn't a big deal," Hunter replies and drops into a chair at the small, round dining table that separates the kitchen from the living space. "She woke up a little freaked out about some dream and wanted to call her mom. I figured if I didn't let her, it would be a bigger deal. I know you're trying to keep things Zen in front of her. Plus I didn't know Lauren would show up here in evil bitch mode."

"I just wish I had been here so she couldn't find another thing to blame me for." I swallow down another gulp of beer and put the half-empty bottle on the counter. "Charlie's asleep now?"

"Yeah, she had a few tears, called Lauren, calmed down, and was out like a light again," Hunter explains, and before he can say more my phone dings.

I look down and see the number Dixie gave me and smile. I smile a lot, especially around my daughter and my family, but this one must look different, because as I glance at my brother he has an eyebrow raised. I turn my shoulder toward him so the nosy bastard can't read what's on the phone as I open the message.

Sadie here! Eli went down to neuro for the CAT scan.

He's still pukey, so we pumped him full of anti-nausea meds.

I promise not to text again unless something is wrong.

Wouldn't want to keep you up.

I type back quickly.

Thx Sadie. Please text no matter the time.

I won't mind being woken up by you… even if it's only to talk about Eli.

Also, is 'pukey' an official medical term? ;)

"Why you smiling at your phone like it's a Victoria's Secret angel?"

I look up at Hunter and decide to share because he's been bugging me lately that I need to "get back out there" when it comes to women. "Because she's hotter than those angels. And kind of a real one. She's a nurse."

"Say what now?" Hunter looks intrigued and excited. "You take your goalie to the hospital and pick up a hot nurse? I like your style, big bro. I didn't know you had it in you."

"Neither did I anymore," I admit sheepishly and walk around the counter to head to the living area. He follows, like a puppy in search of a treat. If he had a tail it would be wagging. "I didn't exactly pick her up. But I am flirting, and she seems to be flirting back."

As if to prove my point, my text alert goes off again. I look down and read the message twice. It's that good.

Pukey is totally a medical term.

Learned it in college along with icky and oogy.

Look forward to waking you up in a few hours with an update... sorry not sorry.

Okay now I'm just plain grinning. Hunter is too. "Okay, flirty you is freaking me out. It's so abnormal, you look almost...happy."

"Shut up. I haven't been that bad," I mutter and shove my phone in my pants pocket as I shrug out of my suit jacket.

He laughs. "You totally have. But I get it. It's been a rough couple of years."

"It has." Lauren and I have been divorced for two years, but to be honest it's been rough since before the divorce. The year before we both admitted the marriage wasn't working was pretty bad too. "But maybe things are changing. I mean..."

I pause. Hunter's face instantly morphs into an expression of support. People never believe we're brothers because we look really different. I have more of my mom's Italian genes, and he has more of my dad's Irish ones. My hair and eyes are dark and my skin is olive where Hunter's is very pale. He has light hazel eyes and, when he had hair, it was red. He started going bald early so he just shaves his head now. He's shorter, five foot ten compared to my six four. Our personalities are different too. I'm less goofy than he is, and he hates sports, which I love. But he gets me like no one else, so I'm not surprised when he knows why I'm hesitating.

"You want to ask her out?" he says, and I nod.

"I'm thinking about it. But is it appropriate?" I have to ask. "I mean not only is she my goalie's nurse, she is also his girlfriend's sister and related to a player on the team."

Hunter looks shocked by that revelation, but it doesn't faze him long. "I doubt it's breaking any ethics code if you ask her out. Besides you're the goalie coach, not like a real coach. No one cares what you do." He shrugs.

I slowly raise my middle finger at him. He smiles back.

"She doesn't work for the team, and you're not her patient. But you're four months into the season, and she's probably been at games to see her brother play. Honestly, it sounds like you should have run into her a hell of a lot sooner."

"I wish I had," I respond.

He laughs and rubs his hands together like some kind of

evil genius in the middle of plotting something. "Oh...I like this. I like this a lot. You are finally back in the land of the living."

"Yeah, yeah." I roll my eyes and give his shoulder a shove. "I need to go check on Charlie. You should head home to that lovely wife of yours."

"Maybe one day I can say that to you," he replies as he grabs his jacket off the hook by the front door. "I mean I have never been able to say it to you because when you were married to that witch Lauren I didn't actually want to send you home to her."

I chuckle. "Shut up. Say hi to Mia."

He nods and heads out the door. I lock up, shut off all the lights on the main floor, and head upstairs. The houseboat isn't big, but I love it. I've always loved the water—any water. I grew up on a lake in Minnesota. In the summer I would water-ski and fish, and in the winter I would play hockey. We took annual trips to North Carolina, where my maternal grandparents lived. My parents would spend every day golfing, but I spent every day at the ocean body surfing and skim boarding.

Lauren worries constantly my houseboat puts Charlie at risk of being in a tsunami. She grew up in Redondo Beach near LA but hates the ocean. It's so ridiculous. The only reason she lives in the area is because when we divorced she wanted to be near her parents. Now, she lives high up the hill in Marin, as far from the ocean as she can get.

I roll my eyes just thinking about it as I climb the metal-and-wood staircase to the second floor. I turn left and peek into Charlie's room. The space is a wash of orange, red, blue, and green color from her night light on her wooden night table, which is a globe etched with multicolored dinosaurs carved in the shape of a T. rex. She's on her left side, legs tucked up and arms tugging the covers up over most of her face. All I can see is her forehead and her mop of wavy copper hair. It's a sign she wasn't totally over her nightmare when she fell back asleep. A hard knot of guilt forms in my gut. I wish I could be here for her every minute of the day and night. I honestly do, but I know that's not healthy. And I'm not away a lot. I've denied myself any form of a life outside work and Charlie, because I don't want to take away from the time I do have with her. I don't regret it, but I didn't realize how lonely I am until tonight. Until Sadie.

I take a step into the room, but my text alert dings and I freeze. Charlie doesn't move, thankfully. I step back into the hall, pull my phone out of my suit pants pocket and bite back a smile at her number on my screen. I check the text.

Eli's CT is clear. Nothing abnormal.

Kid actually has a brain. Who knew? ;)

Pukefest should stop by morning and he'll likely be released by noon.

I feel relief wash over me and start typing a response.

Good update, about the CT. I'm betting the doc will want him off the ice for a bit. I'm guessing a week.

I wouldn't let Eli on the ice for a week at least anyway. I only stopped playing a little over four years ago, so I still distinctly remember being pushed through a concussion, more than once, and how it did me no good. I vowed when I became a coach I wouldn't do it to my players.

You're psychic! Yeah doc said 7-10 days.

Sorry. I know that's not good for the game.

So, psychic, give me some winning lottery numbers. ;)

I chuckle. Funny, getting her as Eli's nurse kind of feels like I won a lottery. I start to type back, my fingers moving quickly, trying to outrun the nervous tension spreading through my body. I can't believe I'm about to do this...

Trust me I'm not psychic. If I was I would know the answer to the question I want to ask you.

I lean against the wall outside Charlie's room and wait. Is this stupid? Is she really flirting with me? Am I flirting with her? Do I even still know how to do that? My phone beeps.

What question is that? Don't leave me hanging....

Here I go. Maybe dating is like riding a bike...even though it feels more like walking off a cliff.

I'd know the answer to whether you want to have coffee with me tomorrow afternoon?

Am I even free tomorrow afternoon? Should I have checked my calendar? Nah. I know I don't have Charlie, and fuck anything else. For this woman, I'll reschedule.

I scrub a hand over my face. It feels like the longest minute of my life, but that's all it takes for her to respond.

I'd love to.

My face explodes in a smile, and my chest releases a huge breath I didn't realize I was holding. I type back a time and a place, hoping it works. Four p.m., Saint Frank Coffee on Polk. I have no idea where she lives, but even if it's on the other side of San Francisco I will pick her up and drive her there. It's that good.

I set my phone to silent and head back into Charlie's room. Her little fists have released the viselike grip she was holding the blankets with, and she's flopped over onto her back. I can see her whole little face now; she seems peaceful. I stop at the side of the bed, lean down and smooth back her hair. She doesn't stir. Just in case she has another dream I leave the door wide open and leave mine at the other end of the short hall open too.

I put my phone on the dresser in my room and realize she responded.

See you then, Griffin.

I just lined up my first date since the divorce. I kind of wish Hunter were still here so I could high-five someone.

4

GRIFFIN

When I wake up the next morning, I instantly think of Sadie, and it puts me in a great mood. I reach over and check my phone. She's left me a new message, and I smile.

> Hey coach. Your goalie will make it. Upchucking has stopped.
>
> Pupils are back to normal. He's asking me to get him a milkshake.
>
> Should be discharged by noon.

I lean back against my headboard and type a response.

> Glad to hear it but please remind him milkshakes are not part of the Thunder meal plan. Pucks bounce off fat way too easily.
>
> Hope you get some sleep too. I'm not the most exciting date andI'd hate to have you fall asleep on me.

Maybe I shouldn't be so self-effacing, but I'm so rusty at this dating thing that I can't help joking about my insecurity. I'm not the type of guy to put on fake bravado. It used to make Lauren so mad. She always wanted me to be less authentic, which I thought was ridiculous. My phone buzzes with a text.

I think you're pretty damn compelling so I doubt I'll even yawn.

But I'll order a double espresso, just in case. ;)

I laugh.

"What's so funny, Dad?"

Charlie is standing at the door to my room in her Minion-themed pajamas, her hair all over the place. She rubs her left eye with the back of her hand. I put my phone on the night-stand. "Morning, kiddo. Come up here."

Charlie pads her way into the room and climbs up onto my king-size bed. She drops herself dramatically onto the pillows beside me, then makes a big deal about fluffing them up as she settles in next to me. "Why were you laughing? YouTube videos?"

"Not videos," is all I say and try to tame her hair. It's thick and wavy like mine, which we get from my mother, and it makes for some incredible morning bedhead. But instead of it being dark brown like mine, it's unabashedly red, which she gets from my dad, along with the freckles. Her light eyes and the dimple in her chin are all Lauren, though. "Are you ready for your favorite breakfast?"

She grins. It's my favorite thing in the world to look at. "Apple pancakes?"

I nod, and she giggles excitedly. "Can I help?"

The kid loves to cook...well, more accurately, she loves to eat ingredients while I cook, but I don't mind. In fact, I kind of love it. I nod and she scrambles off the bed, running out of my room. I stand up and throw on a T-shirt to go with the sweatpants I slept in and call for her to hold the railing going down the stairs.

I grab my phone and send one last quick message to Sadie.

I am really looking forward to seeing you again.

Then I leave my phone on the nightstand and head down to the kitchen.

Forty-five minutes later Charlie and I are both full of cinnamon apple pancakes and she's in the living room watching *Clifford the Big Red Dog* on Netflix while I clean up and drink an espresso. I'm so glad she isn't talking about her nightmare, and she didn't wake up again last night. I asked her, while we ate, if she had a good night, and she nodded and said Uncle Hunter took her for frozen yogurt, which she shortens and pronounces "frodo." She doesn't bring up the nightmare or calling her mom, so I don't either. I still wish I had been here for her, though.

I glance at the clock on the stove. I have two more hours with her before she's due back at her mom's, and I can't be late because Lauren has already proven she's in bitch mode, and I don't want to make things worse. "Charlie, how about you run upstairs and change and we go to the park before you head back to Mom's?"

"The park next to the dog park?" she asks, and I inwardly groan. She has become super obsessed with dogs, and I know when her birthday rolls around she's going to ask for one of her own. Lauren hates pets, so she'll say no, and I'm not around enough with the hockey schedule to keep a dog here for her. Ugh. This may be her first heartbreak.

"Okay," I say because that park also has a skateboard ramp, and she can easily be pulled away from watching pooches to watch skaters. She also wants a skateboard. My daughter is a big fan of anything that causes me heart palpitations and gray hair.

She scrambles upstairs, and I join her a few minutes later and change into jeans and a cable-knit sweater. Charlie does a decent job of dressing herself, which isn't always the case, so we make it to the park fairly quickly. We spend the rest of our time together goofing off on the jungle gym, watching the skaters and dogs. By the time I'm driving her back to Lauren's she's yawning, which should make Lauren happy. Last time I dropped Charlie off, Lauren complained she was "hopped up on sugar" and wouldn't go to bed on time.

She meets me at the door, her boyfriend, Cale, standing behind her in the hall, yanking on his shitty leather jacket. He looks like he just woke up and hasn't bothered to comb his greasy black hair, let alone shower. But then again, he always looks like that. He's a musician in a band named Two Dollar Bill, which is about the amount of money he's made in his career too.

"Hey." He grumbles to me as he steps through the open front door, giving Lauren a half-hearted kiss on the cheek as he passes. "Later, Chuck."

Charlie gives him a lackluster wave, and I visibly bristle. I fucking hate that he calls her Chuck. It's not a term of endearment, it's a sign he doesn't give a fuck. And it's not that I want this jackwad to be in love with my kid, but I do want him to be respectful. And he's not. My eyes meet Lauren's. She knows what I'm thinking and instantly rolls hers. She sings Cale's praises every chance she gets. I want better people than this idiot named after a vegetable in my daughter's life.

Charlie clammers through the open door, and Lauren tries to smooth her hair. "Does Daddy forget to brush your hair?"

"I brushed it," I say quietly. "We were at the park and it got messed up."

"You know you should put it in braids or pigtails when she's at the park," Lauren chides.

"Okay. Next time." I give her an overly large smile.

Charlie turns and wraps her little arms around my leg. "Bye, Daddy. See you soon."

"Bye, Charlie." I bend and kiss the top of her head. "Call me tonight, okay?"

She nods and disappears into the house. I nod at Lauren and start down her front walk. "Griffin!"

I turn to face her. I feel an overwhelming sense of dread. I say nothing, waiting for her to speak. She looks oddly uncomfortable. "Are you going to work now?"

My brow furrows. "Yeah. Why?"

She shrugs. "Nothing. I just was wondering. You still want her on Wednesday?"

"I want her every day," I reply, trying not to sound as annoyed as I am. She frowns, deep and hard, and huffs before turning around and shutting the front door. Luckily, she didn't slam it, but I know she wanted to. At least she's keeping up her end of our pact not to fight or be hateful to each other in front of our daughter. I'll take that as a win.

I try not to dwell how much Lauren's attitude annoys me as I drive to the rink. Instead I start thinking about Sadie again. I've only been with the Thunder since the start of the season, but I'm surprised I haven't seen her before. Her brother Jude is not just a star for the Thunder, he's a superstar in the league. I had hated playing against him, although as the backup goalie on most teams, I didn't face him often. I think only twice. I remember him being talented yet devious. He didn't mind crowding your crease and was the king of trash-talking on the ice. Working for the team now, I see him differently. He's hardworking and loyal to his teammates, with a sharp sense of humor, which I now know is clearly a family trait, as are the blond hair and blue eyes. The whole team was aware of his family because Dixie was always hanging around and attending games and fund-raising events as Eli's significant other, and I'd been told she used to work for the Thunder. Jude's a very vocal advocate for ALS, and I'd seen his dad at games in a wheelchair. I just didn't realize he had more than one sister. How the hell had I missed that?

I get to the arena, and my mood shifts dramatically. I'm never in a bad mood when I'm around a rink. From the time I was a kid until right now, everything about hockey, the rink, the ice, makes me feel at peace. Joyful, even. The Thunder's head coach meets me at the door to our offices, which are tucked in just past the training rooms. "How's Casco?"

"He'll be okay, but he's going to need about a week off at least," I reply.

Coach swears under his breath. "We're playing the Saints tomorrow. Do you think Carling is ready for them and fucking Westwood?"

I nod firmly. "I'll make sure of it."

I spend the next two hours with Noah Carling, the team's former starter and now backup goalie. Eli stepped in when Noah needed surgery last year, and despite a rocky start, Eli helped the Thunder earn a Cup last year, so he earned the starting position. Noah has been a little shaky since his return, and maybe a little bummed he lost his spot, but as we work together I know he's going to be fine against the best team in the league right now.

As I leave for the day, I'm excited to see Sadie again. I dig in my pocket for my phone—all my pockets...I can't find it. Did I leave it in the car? In my office? I start to mentally walk through my day.

"Excuse me?"

I realize there's a young guy standing in front of me. I wonder if he's a fan of the team. Sometimes they wait in the parking lot to get autographs and selfies with players after practice. "Players already left for the day. Sorry."

"Are you Griffin Sullivan?" he asks.

"Yes," I reply, and he shoves an envelope at me.

"You've been served," he says, and abruptly turns and walks away. I stand there in the empty parking lot feeling like I've just been sucker punched. And then I open the envelope, and I feel like I've just been dropped into an abyss.

It's a summons to family court. Lauren wants full custody.

5

SADIE

When I wake up, there's a lump beside me in the bed, hogging all the covers. I rub the sleep from my eyes and stare at the blond head. It's Dixie. Typical. I give her a nudge and yank back the blankets she stole. She groans and rolls over to face me. "I was comfy."

"Of course you were," I reply. "But it's my bed. Go be comfy in your own apartment."

"My bed isn't as nice," she replies and sits up, running her fingers through her wheat blond hair. "And Levi is at our place being the overprotective big brother. He needs to see for himself Eli is doing okay, so I can't nap."

"I still don't understand why you two don't get a real apartment," I say as I sit up and yawn. I glance at the clock on my bedside table. It's just before two in the afternoon. I've been asleep five hours. Sadly, it felt like two. Working until seven in the morning and then forcing myself into bed while the rest of the world starts their day isn't easy, but it's part of the job. "Eli makes a kajillion dollars a year. You can afford something bigger than that shoebox you live in. Like something with a proper bedroom."

She shrugs. "We like my apartment. It's cozy and has sentimental value. It's where we first got together."

"So what? You're going to get married and have babies and raise them in four hundred square feet? There's sentimental and then there's stupid." I stretch, and she uses the moment to yank the covers back over her tiny body. I grab them and pull them back, leaving her bare. She's wearing leggings and an oversize sweatshirt, so she doesn't need my covers.

"We're not getting married or having babies," Dixie replies.

I lift an eyebrow. "Ever?"

"No, I mean... not now." She looks down at her hands in her lap. "I don't know if he's thinking about that yet."

I laugh. "Are you kidding me?"

"No. I mean... well, it's just we haven't even talked about that," Dixie explains, and her big blue eyes are wide with insecurity. "I know he loves me and I love him, but marriage might not be his thing. I don't know. I mean, we talk about the future, but not in those definitive terms."

I shake my head. "I'm not surprised. You guys never talked about moving in together either. He just got the full-time contract with the Thunder and moved his stuff into your place. Everyone thought he was staying there while looking for his own place, but that never happened."

"We did talk about that... eventually. Well, he left me a note before a road trip and said he wanted to stay instead of getting his own place so it's official now," Dixie replies almost defensively. "I was never going to ask him to leave because I didn't want him to."

I smile at her. "No one expected you to ask him to leave. You two are perfect for each other. Even Mom isn't concerned about how fast you guys got together, and you know she would tell you if she was. Hell, Ty and Winnie have been dating since high school, and Mom warned her to think twice when she was thinking about moving in with him."

I get out of bed and walk over to my dresser. Dixie sits cross-legged on the bed, grabbing my pillow to stuff behind her back. "Yeah but Winnie and Ty were only, like, twenty-one when they talked about it."

"Now she's almost thirty, and I swear Mom would still tell her to think twice." I grab some gray velvet sweats and tug them on as I glance up at Dixie. "Wouldn't you?"

"Hell, yes," Dixie replies easily.

"And no one is telling you that because you and Eli work. Hell, you more than work. You are soul mates, just like Jude and Zoey," I say confidently. I knew from the minute I met Eli Casco that he was exactly what my sassy, OCD, tough-as-nails little sister needed. Even more so, he was what she deserved. He's wild, kind, confident, respectful, and is protective of her. If things didn't work out between them, I would be as devastated as she would.

Dixie's uncertain expression falters and is replaced with a confident, radiant one. "He is my soul mate, and between you and me I want to marry him one day. And have babies. But until then, our apartment is fine."

My stomach grumbles. The bowl of cereal I ate before falling into bed wasn't enough. I rub my stomach, as if trying to placate it. Dixie notices, or heard the grumble, and looks at me seriously. "You're not eating enough."

"I know." I've lost some weight in recent months. It's partly stress about my dad and partly too many overnights at work. I use all my breaks for cat naps instead of meals. "Not on purpose. Come on, let's get food."

I walk to my closed door and she follows. "Wanna go out? We could grab sushi or burgers and shakes. My treat!"

"I can't. I have plans later and have to get ready," I say. I think about all the texts I've shared with Griffin, and butterflies take flight in my gut. I try to ignore them as we make our way down the hall toward the kitchen.

Winnie is in the dining room, sitting at the head of the table with a giant bowl of spaghetti and meatballs. I stop. "Carbo-loading before your next big fight with Ty?"

She tries to obliterate me with her eyes. Dixie giggles behind me, which only intensifies Winnie's death-stare. We wander into the room, and both Dixie and I grab forks out of a drawer in the buffet and sit down on either side of Winnie. She ignores us and lifts a forkful of pasta to her mouth as we both dive in with our own forks. Dixie goes for a meatball and I twirl some pasta onto my fork.

"I thought you weren't working tonight?" Dixie says to me.

"I'm not," I say, confused.

"Oh...but I thought you said you had plans."

I swallow my pasta and stare at her. Winnie uses the moment to pull her pasta dish closer to her and farther from us, but it stops nothing. As soon as she lifts her fork to her mouth again, Dixie leans over and grabs another meatball.

"I can do things other than work, Dix," I remind her.

"You don't, though," Dixie counters, without an ounce of remorse.

Winnie nods. "She's right. You don't."

"You two are assholes," I say.

"Says the woman eating my damn lunch," Winnie shoots back.

"We aren't being cruel, just being honest," Dixie tells me as she pops the last of the meatball into her mouth. "You don't even look at men like they're men, you know what I mean. They all might as well be statues. The only time I've even seen you do a double take in the last year was last night when..."

Why can't I have stupid siblings who don't know how to put two and two together? Why couldn't I get all the brains in the family the way Winnie got all the culinary abilities and Jude got all the athletic talent? Dixie slaps her palm on the oak table so hard it makes the plate of spaghetti rattle. "Do you have plans with Sully?"

"Who is Sully?" Winnie asks.

"Griffin Sullivan." Dixie is buzzing with excitement. "He's Eli's goalie coach and he's tall, dark, and delicious."

Winnie wrinkles up her nose. "Aren't coaches like a hundred?"

"Not this one," Dixie says. "Thirty-something. Eli says he's a nice guy. He's the quiet and mellow type, which Eli says makes for a great coaching style."

"You told Eli I liked him?" I ask, ready to stab her with my fork.

"Oh, so you *do* like him?" Dixie says slyly and wiggles her eyebrows. "And no, I didn't say a word to anyone. I'm just telling you what Eli has said about him in general."

"It's good Griffin is quiet," Winnie replies. "Because Sadie won't have to worry about shutting up. She can keep doing all the talking."

"Ha. Ha," I reply with zero humor.

"Is he your plans?" Dixie asks me as Winnie finishes the last of her pasta. "Please say he's your plans."

"It's just coffee." I relent, because as much as I don't want to make this a big deal—yet—I like talking to my sisters about good stuff...and he is good stuff.

I stand up and walk out of the room. I'm barely two feet into the hall when I hear their chairs slide back and their feet stomping across the hardwood floors. They're chasing me. I pick up the pace. I make it to my room at the end of the hall and start to close the door behind me, but those wily bastards manage to slip in before I can. Ugh. Here we go. I knew I shouldn't have said anything.

"You have a coffee date? With Sully?" Dixie repeats for clarification as she drops her ass onto my bed. "I need all the details."

"I offered to give him texts updates on Eli." I shrug, feeling ridiculously self-conscious. "And while we were texting, he asked if I wanted to meet him for coffee."

"And you said yes?" Winnie seems so blown away it's comical. "Who is this wizard that he can turn you back into a red-blooded woman?"

I roll my eyes and walk over to my closet. What the hell do I wear? I spend most of my time in scrubs at work or at home in sweats and yoga pants with my family. Ugh.

"Holy shit." Winnie gasps, and I spin to see her face buried in Dixie's cell phone. "He is so delicious."

"Who?"

"I pulled up pics of Sully." Dixie smiles deviously. I jump across the room and lunge for the phone, scooping it out of Winnie's hand. The picture on the screen is him in a suit walking behind some players in the arena. It must be prior to a game because they're all in suits. Man, he was born to wear suits. Jude is also in the picture, but I ignore him and make the image bigger so I can get an unobstructed view of Griffin.

"I can see how he was able to pull you out of your self-imposed manbatical," Winnie says and reaches for the phone. I let her take it, and she stares at him again. "Those are some seriously kissable lips. And those eyes are the definition of bedroom eyes, all sultry and..."

"Smoldering," I finish for her, and she nods without taking her eyes off the screen. "Everything about his looks are smoldering, but it's his personality that had me agree to the date."

Both my sisters look up now, and I almost flush under their curious stares. "He's charming and just made me feel...relaxed."

"No bullshit," Winnie says with a sincere grin. "I'm happy for you."

"It's just coffee," I repeat, trying to convince both her and myself. "Now can you two skedaddle so I can get ready in peace?"

I start to push them off my bed, and they make their way to the door. "Don't you want our advice on what to wear? How to do your hair? You are actually going to do it, right? Not just shove it into a ponytail like you're a gym rat or an overtired mom of colicky triplets like you usually do."

"Out," I demand, and once they're in the hall I shut the door and lock it.

I manage to find something to wear that doesn't make me feel frumpy. Just a pair of dark skinny jeans and a pale gray, fuzzy, soft off-the-shoulder sweater Zoey got me for Christmas that I never had any reason to wear. I tug on some charcoal gray bootics and actually do a pretty decent job with my makeup, even though the cosmetics are so old they should probably be thrown out. I dart into Winnie's room on the way out and grab her cranberry colored MAC lipstick and manage to sneak by the den, where Dixie and Winnie have joined our parents, and get out of the house without having to say goodbye to any of them or answer more questions about the date.

The coffee shop he picked is a forty-minute walk away, but I'm early enough that I can do it, and the weather is too perfect to ignore. San Francisco is very different from where I grew up. In carly March in Toronto it's either raining or snowing and too cold to stroll the streets in just a sweater. But San Franciscans' idea of cold is mildly chilly to me, and they get pockets of days all winter long, like today, where it's sunny and downright balmy. I pull my sunglasses out of my bag, slip them on, and start my walk.

I get to the coffee shop with ten minutes to spare...I wait outside, not wanting to take up a table without a beverage, and waiting to order until he gets here seems like the thing to do. But twenty minutes later, he's still not here. I glance at my phone—he hasn't called or texted. I start to pace in front of the coffee shop window and then glance inside to make sure I didn't somehow miss him and he's already there. He isn't.

After another ten minutes I start to get worried. Is he okay? Was there an accident? I walk inside and order a chai tea so I can sit down, because after the walk and waiting around, my feet are killing me. These booties are not even close to as comfortable as the sneakers I wear at work. As I sit at a small table in the corner by the window and sip my tea, I can't help but entertain the startling and humiliating possibility that I'm being stood up.

My cheeks turn pink at the thought. Would he really do that to me? Why? This was his idea. What the hell...I glance at my phone and realize it's been forty-three minutes since we were supposed to meet. Do I text him and ask if he's okay, or do I assume the worst and send him a fuck-you text? I don't know what to do—except leave. It's time to leave.

I stand and walk to the garbage, tossing my now lukewarm tea in the trash. I push open the door. My phone rings. I freeze and pull it out of my back pocket. It's Griffin.

"Hello?"

"Sadie, I am so sorry," he says, his words a rush. "I was at work, and something came up—an emergency—and I was going to call you immediately, but I forgot my damn phone at home and I don't know your number by heart. I even went back into the arena to see if I could find Jude and get your number from him, but he'd already left."

"Are you okay?" I ask instantly because I can tell by his tone, remorseful and pained, that he isn't making this up. Something happened.

"I'm fine; it's a...family emergency," he replies, and I think of my dad being sick and wonder if someone in his family is ill. "And it'll be fine. I just had to meet my brother, though—like immediately—to sort this out. I...I know that makes me an asshole. I should have gone home first and gotten my phone, but I really had to get to his office. I was thinking of you, though, and how upset you'd rightfully be, and I don't blame you if you want to tell me to fuck off right now."

"I won't do that," I reply and lean against the wall outside the coffee shop. "I believe you that this was an unexpected, unavoidable stand-up."

"Still, I am so sorry."

"It's fine," I say because I am starting to feel bad for him. "Is there anything I can do to help out with your emergency?"

"I wish," he replies and sighs heavily. "I've just got... Well, my life is more complicated than I originally thought when I made the date...which is why I can't schedule a do-over just yet."

Wait...what?

Suddenly I feel like he's changed his mind about me. My heart sinks, and the burn of rejection stings me, turning my cheeks red. "Oh. Okay."

"I sincerely wish I could, Sadie."

Is he sincere? I don't know him well enough to recognize if he is or if he's just good at acting like it. But my gut says this is an excuse.

"No problem," I reply, and that burning feeling of rejection sparks my self-preservation instincts. I just want to end this call and put this failed attempt at dating behind me. "Maybe I'll see you around a game. Take care, Griffin. It was nice meeting you."

I hang up.

There is no point listening to him apologize or blow me off again. I don't know what happened in his life, and he sounds like he is legitimately regretful that he can't reschedule, but a blow-off is still a blow-off. It still sucks. I delete his number from my phone before calling a Lyft. And that's that.

6

SADIE

When I open the front door to the apartment, my goal is to slip stealthily back into my room the same way I slipped out. But the place is filled with the sound of family —plates and glasses clanging, laughter, talking and baby giggles. And the smell of my mom's roast chicken and scalloped potatoes makes my mouth water and my stomach roar.

I glance into the kitchen, where Mom is standing at the stove, Zoey's tossing a bowl of salad, and Winnie is slicing up chicken. Jude pops his head out of the dining room, sees me and walks into the hall. He's got a smiling, gurgling Declan in his arms. I hate that my heart explodes when I see this—every time—and I want to hug Jude. Braddock siblings show love by annoying the crap out of each other and teasing each other mercilessly. This kid has thrown off our natural dynamic.... But he's too damn cute to be mad at.

"Give me that chubby-cheeked nugget," I demand and drop my purse on the floor as I reach for him. Jude hands Declan over, and I immediately nuzzle my face into the crook of his neck, inhaling his perfect baby smell and the silky feel of his baby skin on my cheek. Declan giggles.

"Why are you here?" Jude asks.

"Because I live here, genius," I snark and make a silly face at Declan.

"Yeah, but Dix said you were out for the night," Jude replies, and I glance over his shoulder and into the kitchen. Dixie is staring back at me with disappointment.

"I was hoping you'd be gone all night," she says with melancholy in her voice.

"You thought I was going to go from coffee to nudity in one night?"

"I would," Winnie adds as she walks by us in the hall and into the kitchen. I follow, frowning.

"Do not start talking about your love lives in front of—"

"Declan is too young to understand," I interject.

"I was going to say in front of me," Jude replies.

Zoey laughs at him and runs a hand over her son's head as I pass by with him and head into the dining room to sit down. "Who were you on a date with?"

My eyes fly to my sisters, and I give them the loudest DO NOT SAY A WORD glare I can. They both snap their mouths shut at the same time. "Just someone I met at the hospital. It was no big deal. Not really a date. Super casual. Anyway, he had a thing and ended up having to cancel."

The energy in the room shifts so fully and completely, like air being let out of a balloon, that I can feel it. Every face staring back at me is wearing various degrees of disappointment. "Jeez, family, it's not the end of the world. Don't worry, you'll marry me off one day. Jude has enough money to pay someone to take me."

"Oh, honey. Chill," my mom says, and it makes the rest of her kids snicker. "We don't want to marry you off. It's just nice to think you're getting out and meeting new people. You used to be such a social butterfly in Toronto. All you do now is work and hang out with us. We're boring."

"Yeah, you are," I reply but grin at her and wink. "I'm not bored or lonely. It's fine. Now can we talk about something else, or better yet, stop talking and eat? Everything smells delicious."

"Eli! Dad!" Dixie calls down the hall.

Everyone sits around the table except Jude, who waits until Eli appears with my dad and helps him get his wheelchair pushed up to the table. Dad has trouble holding his utensils now, so Mom sits next to him and helps him. It's still so painful to see, which makes it hard to look away. But if I do look at him for too long he gets frustrated, and also I lose my appetite because my heart starts to ache.

Everyone sits down and starts to fight over the food, as always. My dad chuckles. "Never . . . changes. Relax, kids. Mom always makes enough."

The words come out slow, slurred, but we know what he's saying mostly because it's the same thing he's been saying since we were preteens. And just like always, we ignore him and all dive in at once, scooping up chicken, potatoes, and salad off the serving dishes in the center of the table.

"Eli, grab something now or you'll starve," Zoey advises as she snags a juicy piece of chicken breast before Jude can.

Dixie grabs a chicken leg and drops it onto his plate. "I got you, baby."

I laugh. "How are you feeling, E? Headaches? Nausea?"

"Nope. None of that," Eli says and takes the scalloped potatoes dish from Winnie, before she was finished serving herself.

"Atta boy." Zoey smiles.

"Good. It sounds like you're recovering nicely." I fight the urge to text Griffin and give him an update. I'm sure Eli will be meeting with his coach soon and can tell him himself.

"Yeah, but Sully is still going to make me take a week off, I'm sure," Eli grumbles, his green eyes clouded with frustration. "The league is really anal about head injuries."

"Fo goo reasss...on," my father comments. He's saying "for good reason," and luckily Eli understands.

"I know. I just want to play," Eli replies.

"Speaking of Sully, how's that going?" Jude asks, and I'm elated we're still talking about Griffin, even though I shouldn't be. Winnie and Dixie meet my eyes across the table, but I look away and give all my attention to the potatoes I'm scooping onto my plate.

"Great. He's a way better coach than the last one." Even I can hear the relief in Eli's voice. He butted heads with his last coach since he started with the team. "Sully is so close to the game because he was in the league just a couple years ago. He's easygoing but focused, and he's got these new exercises and stretches that are really improving my reach in net. He's also super chill, which is what I need. Like last night at the hospital, he stayed calm and just made sure I was okay, whereas the last coach would have been super annoying and made the situation worse."

I shovel potatoes into my mouth to keep from asking questions, because they wouldn't be hockey-related and it would seem weird. Winnie, on the other hand, isn't worried about looking weird. She takes a sip of water and asks, "So where is he from? What teams did he play for? Did you ever play him, Jude? Where does he live?"

The table falls silent. People don't even continue eating. My mom's hand is frozen, a chunk of chicken on a fork hovering in front of my dad's mouth. But he's not paying attention to it either. Everyone is just stunned by Winnie's sudden onslaught of invasive questions. Jude gives her a confused look. Ah, shit...If he asks her why she's so nosy and Winnie says a word, I'll die.

"He played for a couple teams, mostly as a backup goalie," Jude answers. "Los Angeles and Vegas. I played him when he was with Vegas during my rookie year. Didn't score on him, though."

Winnie nods, eating up all this info and making Jude look more confused and Eli look like he's been concussed again. Mom and Dad have at least continued eating, but they too are clearly perplexed. Dixie is trying not to snicker, so I kick her lightly under the table.

"He was drafted by the Thunder, but only played for the Storm," Eli adds and spears a potato with his fork.

"Where does he live?" Winnie asks.

"I think he lives in Marin," Eli replies. "He mentioned something about picking up his kid there."

I freeze. My mom notices. I blink and swallow down the chicken in my mouth, almost choking because I didn't chew it enough. I grab my water glass. Dixie snickers. I kick her again—harder this time. Winnie coughs.

"How many kids does he have?" Winnie asks.

Jude and Eli exchange baffled looks, and then Eli answers slowly, cautiously, like he's just realized he's dealing with a lunatic. "Umm...one...I think. At least he's only mentioned a little girl...Why all the questions about my coach?"

Winnie shrugs. "You're a part of our family now, Eli. Being invasive and getting all up in family business is what I do."

"We all have roles to play," Dixie adds with a grin. "It's how we keep this family running like a well-oiled machine."

"Yeah, your role is designated freeloader," Jude tells her. "You had breakfast at my place and dinner here. Have you ever even cooked in your own apartment?"

"I don't cook," Dixie responds, "because then I would have to clean."

"Is he married?" I ask, my voice almost hoarse from trying to hide the tension in it. My brother and Eli turn their confused stares on me now. "Winnie and I work in tandem on this invasive thing."

"I assume that a wife or girlfriend or some female of significance usually comes with a child," Jude says with snark, and I stick my tongue out at him because giving him the finger at the dinner table would be rude. Meanwhile, my brain is reeling. Is he married? Like legally? Is he a cheater? Was he going to cheat with me?

When I look across the table, Dixie and Winnie are asking me the same questions with their eyes. We've always been able to read each other's thoughts without a word. It drives Jude nuts, and even my dad thought it could get creepy. They both look as worried and borderline horrified as I am because it's a real possibility. Griffin Sullivan might be married, and in that case—I just dodged a bullet.

7

GRIFFIN

I walk through the bustling concourse slowly, absorbing the happy energy the fans are filling the air with. I don't always walk through the public parts of the arena on game days, but today, I needed the pick-me-up. I've been in a bad mood since I got served, and I need all the help I can get to shake it. The happy energy the fans have normally helps me relax, but today, it's not helping much. I don't think anything will. I turn a corner, my eyes focused on two kids in Thunder jerseys who are bouncing with excitement as their parents walk then through the arena, but then something in front of me catches my attention instead. It's a quick blur of teal jacket and brown hair moving violently downward. I instantly reach out, my hands grabbing onto her a little roughly, but I manage to keep her from hitting the cement floor.

"Oh, my God, thank you!" she says in a gasp, and I realize I just caught Trish, one of the Thunder's PR team.

"You're welcome," I reply and help her to her feet. I look

down and see a bright orange blob of nacho cheese sauce smeared across the floor and on the edge of her high heel. "Some sloppy nacho eating fan almost killed you."

"That would make for a nifty headline," Trish replies wryly. "Hockey team employee killed by nacho cheese. As a publicist I can't thank you enough for keeping that headline from becoming a reality."

She lets out a little laugh and squeezes my arm. I pat her hand reassuringly. "It's all good."

I wave over an arena employee. "We have a spill here. Can you call someone with a mop?"

"Sure thing," the employee says and gets on his walkie-talkie immediately. Confident he is going to stand there until it's cleaned up, I thank him and start back toward the doors that lead to the staff area. Trish follows along beside me.

"Since I have your attention, I was going to ask you about the goaltending situation. You know it'll be the press's first question," Trish says as I hold the door open for her. "How is Eli?"

"He appears fine, but we're keeping him out as a precaution," I explain. She nods and types something into her phone as I come to a stop at the elevator and punch the up button. "I'm heading up to the team box to watch the warm-up."

"Thanks again for saving my ass—literally," she says with a laugh. "Go Thunder!"

She turns to walk down the hall as I step into the elevator.

Ten minutes later I'm watching Noah in net during warm-up. He looks good, stopping the majority of shots his teammates are taking on him. His movements indicate he's a little stiff. But I'm not worried. I have watched him enough in practice scrimmages to know he'll loosen up the longer he is out there.

As he leaves the net to skate around a little, I let my eyes drift around the arena. The super-fans, as I like to call them, are gathered down around the boards, watching. I remember the rush of their cheers and the funny signs some of them would bring. I used to love to find the youngest kid and toss him or her a puck over the boards.

But as I search for that young wide-eyed fan pressed up against the glass, I spot someone else instead. Sadie Braddock. She looks like a sexy, free-spirited hippie country girl—which is weird for a nurse from Toronto, Canada—and hot as hell. She reminds me of those country-loving Carolina girls I used to meet on summer vacations with my parents. Only Sadie's better.

I know it was my decision to stop things before they started with Sadie, but just seeing her makes me want to talk to her again. And I shouldn't. This custody thing with Lauren isn't going away any time soon, so I shouldn't make my life any more complicated than it is. And dating is always complicated, especially as a single dad. I need to leave it alone right now or I'll screw it up. Again. So I just take this secretive moment, while no one will notice, to drink her in. She's standing next to Jude's wife, who passes Sadie the baby in her arms. He's wearing a tiny Thunder jersey with BRADDOCK on the back. I loved when Charlie wore a little version of my jersey when I played.

She takes the little boy into her arms and lifts his chubby

arm, helping him wave to his dad. Jude skates to a stop in front of them, makes a goofy face at his son, and I can see Sadie say something. Jude rolls his eyes at his sister, but he's smiling and his wife is laughing. Sadie looks down at the child and nuzzles his cheek. It makes him giggle, and she grins. She's perfect. The thought floods me.

I tear my eyes away from her as the horn sounds, signaling the end of the warm-up. I force myself to leave the box without looking back at her. I make my way down to the locker room and talk over some strategy with Noah and try to gauge his nerves. As soon as we're on the same page and he's feeling confident, I leave. I turn to walk toward the elevators, trying to focus on the game ahead and not my personal issues. It feels like an impossible task. And as if the Universe is trying to prove my point, Eli's voice booms down the cavernous hallway.

"Sully!"

I turn and find Eli, in a suit, standing next to Dixie. And next to her is Sadie. She's staring back at me with those beautiful light blue eyes. Her expression is indifferent, though, and that kind of stings. I don't know what I expected; after all, I shut us down before we even began.

"Hey, Eli." I nod. "Coming up to the box? Hello, Dixie. Sadie."

Dixie waves. Sadie pauses a moment. "Hi, Griffin."

Eli's dark brown eyes pinch for a minute, but then he smiles. "Right! You met Sadie at the hospital."

"Yes," I reply, and my eyes move back to her. The air is heavy between us with unsaid things, and Eli seems to be picking up on it as his brow furrows again. Sadie snaps the tension with a simple shrug of her shoulders. "I'm going into the lounge. Later!"

Dixie kisses Eli's cheek, waves at me again, and follows her sister.

I stare after them until I can't see Sadie anymore. Eli, still looking confused, says, "Ready to head upstairs?"

I nod because, whether I like it or not, that's all I can do. Following Sadie into the family lounge, pressing her up against the bar, and kissing her isn't an option.

Three periods later, the game is over, and San Diego is going home with the win. Overall, though, it wasn't a bad game. At least not from my perspective. Noah let in only one goal. Our offense didn't score any. That's on them, not the goalie. I kept wanting to head down to the lounge between periods and talk to Sadie, but I forced myself not to. It wouldn't do any good.

In the elevator on my way down to the players' level, I get a text from Lauren. She's complaining that Charlie keeps asking for a dog, and she accuses me of letting her think she might get one. I take a deep breath and hold it as long as I can without suffocating. Is this woman for real? I call her as the elevator opens and I step out. She answers on the first ring.

"What?"

"I haven't been encouraging the dog obsession. But you know how focused she gets," I say as calmly as I can. "I promise I'll explain to her why it's not a good idea."

"And stop taking her to the dog park."

"It's a regular park next to a dog park, and it's the closest one to the boat," I tell her. "We can walk there, and she also likes watching the skateboarders on the ramps there."

"That only encourages her to want a skateboard. You have to discourage that too, Griffin," Lauren lectures. "She's only six."

"Lauren, you're being a bit..." I search for a word that won't send her into a fit. "Much."

"You want co-parenting? This is co-parenting," Lauren snaps.

"No, this is you micromanaging your ex-husband," I shoot back. "You didn't even do that when we were married. What the hell is going on with you?"

"I'm annoyed, Griffin," Lauren complains. She pauses, and I think we might actually be getting somewhere. "I'm divorced, but yet you're still in my life almost daily. How can I move on when you're always around? It's frustrating."

Okay, even though I have zero romantic feelings for her, that stings. We promised each other when we decided to divorce that we'd make sure we both stayed in Charlie's life. I accepted that meant that Lauren stayed in my life as well to a small extent, but, clearly, she hasn't accepted it—at least not anymore, and that makes me feel shitty.

"Okay, well, I can't do anything about that," I say flatly. "Charlie is both of ours and will always be."

"But she'll be happier when I'm happier, and that means changing this agreement," Lauren replies, and my whole body is buzzing with anger.

"She's perfectly happy now. If you're not, figure it out," I snap.

"I am. See you in court!"

The line goes dead. Frustration twists my stomach and turns my blood hot. Why is she doing this? I could list a ton of Lauren's personality faults, as she could mine, but being irrational or mean for the sake it was never one of them.

I'm storming down the hallway now, still staring at my phone screen in a blind, confused rage, so I don't see someone opening the door and stepping into my path. "Whoa!" is all I hear seconds before I feel someone collide with me. She grabs my jacket lapels as she teeters backward, and I instinctively grab her elbows, my phone clattering to the ground between us.

I realize it's Sadie, and suddenly instead of letting her go when she regains her balance, I keep my hand on her elbow. When she takes a step back, it slips to her wrist and then, for a brief moment our fingers tangle, but then all contact is gone.

"Sorry. I wasn't watching where I was going," I tell her.

"Yeah. It's fine," Sadie replies curtly. "Later."

"How are you?" I ask as she's about to turn to leave. She doesn't move except to lift her head to bring her gaze to mine.

"You look fucking spectacular in a suit," she tells me, and I'm shocked by her candor. "It's like you're Giorgio Armani's muse or something. Does he have you stand in his studio and design that thing for you specifically or what?"

"No." I smile. "But I'm flattered."

"You're hard not to notice...whether I like it or not."

"You're pretty hard to miss yourself," I tell her. "I couldn't take my eyes off you during warm-up when I should've been watching the players."

Her eyelashes flutter. "I'm not even wearing Armani. My outfit is Target."

She's trying to make a joke, but I'm not in a laughing mood.

"It's more than what you're wearing. I noticed the way you let your nephew play with your hair without worrying if he messed it up. The smile on your face as you said something to Jude through the glass." I pause and watch the words really sink in. And just in case that isn't enough to make her blush, I tell her more. "You remind me of a wildflower. Beautiful, delicate, but strong and wild."

Her whole face explodes into a shade of pink that I wanted. It somehow makes her even more beautiful. But she won't hold my gaze, instead staring at the small space of blue concrete floor between us. "I should go."

"I know. I should too," I reply, but I don't move and I don't want her to either. Her hair is creating a veil so I can't see her face, so I reach out and let my fingers graze it in an attempt to brush it back. It feels incredible against my skin, but the contact causes her to step back. There are footsteps coming toward us, and we both look over as some executives march by.

Sadie drops her gaze again to the floor, then leans down and picks up my phone. She seems to freeze for a second, her head looking toward the screen. Then she stands up and shoves it at me. Her shoulders are rigid, her expression tense.

"I have a lot going on right now too. I'm sure you've heard my dad is dying," she tells me as I take the phone from her. "And I am strong and wild just like you think I am. But not wild enough to date a married man and not strong enough to handle additional drama right now. Later, Griffin."

She pushes past me. I'm so stunned I feel like the wind has been knocked out of me. I look down at the phone. The screen still has Lauren's contact information showing. Lauren *Sullivan*.

She must think I'm still married. That has to be why she's been so cold. She must think that's why I bailed on our date. Oh, God. I turn and watch her walking away. Maybe it's better if she doesn't know the truth. Telling her I'm divorced will serve no purpose except to open up a door I can't bring myself to walk through right now. But...I hate lies...even if they seem to be helping a situation, they aren't. I start to follow her down the hall.

"Sadie," I call out, but she doesn't stop walking. I pick up my pace and catch her as she reaches the elevator bank and aggressively punches the button.

I come to a stop in front of her, blocking her way to the elevator even if the doors open. "I'm divorced."

"That's what any cheating guy would say."

I lift up my left hand for proof. "No ring."

She looks at it and then back at me. She bites her bottom lip as she thinks that over. "Cheaters take their rings off all the time and stick them in their pockets or whatever."

I lift both arms, holding them out like I'm getting ready for a pat-down. "Check my pockets. Frisk me. You won't find a ring. I threw it in the ocean the day the divorce was final."

She blinks. "That's dramatic."

"Divorces tend to get the emotions going pretty good." I

give her a quick, playful smile. "But please frisk me anyway. It'll be the most action I've had in a long time."

She laughs. It's such a great sound, and it knocks the tension right out of the space between us. The elevator dings, but she doesn't get on. She just stares at me, smiling, while the doors close behind me. She bites her bottom lip. "I think I'm disappointed you're not married."

"Why?"

"Because if you're not married, then that's not why you canceled our date," she confesses, and her cheeks start to turn pink. "The only other reason I can think of is that you just aren't interested, which is totally your right but...sucks."

"That's not true," I reply and sigh. "You're the only person I've been interested in since my divorce. All I've been doing is thinking about you."

The blush on her apple cheeks deepens. I take a step toward her, take her hand in mine and pull her to the side of the hall, out of view of anyone who might glance this way. I don't want to be interrupted. "My divorce isn't new, but it's still complicated because we have a daughter. The most incredible little girl in the world. And as much as I can't get you out of my head, and don't want to, I need to focus on that right now."

I stop short of telling her the dirty details because I'm still processing them myself. And besides, she is going through a lot with her own family. I don't need to dump my shit on her too.

She nods slowly. "I understand putting family first more than anyone."

"I'm sorry," I say in a low, rough voice still choked with attraction. I just admitted to her that I can't be with her, but my body is still reacting to her. My pulse is galloping, my blood is getting warmer, and my dick is getting hard. I lick my lips, and her pretty eyes follow my tongue.

"Don't be," she replies, but her voice lacks conviction. "It's best for both of us if we don't start something we can't finish."

"Okay then," I say and take a step back.

She sighs and takes her own step back from me. "Thanks for being honest."

"Thanks for being understanding," I reply.

She starts to walk back to the elevator. I watch her punch the button, but then she slowly turns around to face me again.

She takes a couple hesitant steps toward me, like she's fighting her own actions. So I close the rest of the space between us. "What are you thinking?"

"I'm thinking that even if nothing else can happen, that this should," she says and then she puts a hand on my shoulder, lifts herself onto her toes, and presses her lips to mine.

Her lips are soft and tentative, like she's worried I might stop her. She doesn't need to be. As soon as our mouths connect, I know I need this kiss as much as she does. I reach down and grip her hips, pulling her flush against me. Her body feels so good against mine I groan. Her arms wrap tightly around my neck, and as her lips part, my tongue slides against hers and everything inside me roars to life. Every second of the kiss is passionate, desperate, and perfect—but it's over in an instant. We both pull back at the same time, and the startled look on my face is echoed in hers. She touches her lips with her fingertips. "I've never had a first and last kiss at the very same time."

"Neither have I," I say as my pulse races.

"I guess it makes it memorable." She smiles, but it's almost melancholy.

"Even before that kiss, you, Sadie, are someone I could never forget."

The elevator doors open and she almost runs inside. She smiles at me as the doors start to close, and I fight every single muscle in my body to keep myself planted where I am and not follow her inside. But I have to let her go.

8

SADIE

After dropping my dad off at his doctor's appointment, I head over to the diner across the street and wait. He's got to get a few tests done, and I know from experience, it's easier both for the hospital and the patient not to have family hovering around.

I sit at the counter, and while I wait for the waitress to notice me, someone else does—Dr. Luongo, who is sitting at the other end of the bar holding a menu. "Sadie! What a surprise. I thought it was your day off."

"Hi, Bob. It is my day off," I explain and try not to look surprised he knows my schedule. "But my dad has to see Dr. Lack."

"You should probably just have your mail delivered to the hospital with the amount of time you spend here," he quips. Sadly, he's right. He points to the empty stool beside me. "May I join you?"

"Of course," I reply, and he walks over and sits beside me. "Are you on break?"

"I'm grabbing lunch before I start my shift," he says and

lowers his voice to a whisper. "I'm not a great cook, so I eat here way more than I should."

"I don't cook either," I say with a sympathetic smile. "The last thing I want to do after a twelve-hour shift is stand around the kitchen for hours making something. I just want to stuff something down my throat and go to sleep."

He laughs. "Sounds like your life is as full and exciting as mine. My condolences."

The waitress comes over, and I order a latte and a piece of cherry pie, since I already ate at home and am just snacking to fill time. Bob orders an omelet and a double side of bacon. He catches the look on my face and winks. "I'm a neurologist, not a cardiologist."

I laugh and turn back to the waitress. "He'll also have a vanilla latte, but put it on my bill."

He smiles. "You remembered."

We talk about work stuff for a few minutes while we wait for our food. And then we start talking about our lives.

"I know you've been in San Francisco for a while now, so I have to ask, are enjoying it?" he asks me with a friendly smile.

"I love it here," I tell him as the waitress brings us our lattes. "I loved living in Toronto, but now that I'm here, I don't see myself moving back to Canada."

He lifts his latte. "Well, we're lucky to have you."

He takes a sip and smiles. "It's delicious. But you really didn't have to buy it for me."

"It's not a problem."

"So that goalie I treated is your brother-in-law?" he questions.

"Sister's live-in boyfriend, so close enough." I watch him as he nods and sips his latte again. A little foam sticks to his lip, so he picks up his napkin and wipes it away. I don't think anything of it. But I know if that was Griffin Sullivan I would want to lick it off his lip myself. It would be an instantaneous urge as soon as I saw it. Why can't I feel that way about Bob? He seems to be interested.

"Is he doing okay now?"

"Yeah." I nod as the waitress puts our food in front of us. "He's been following up with the team doctor, and he's cleared for practice and expects to be back in games soon."

His phone buzzes, and he pulls it out of his pocket and groans. "Shit. They need me in early for an emergency consult."

"Bummer," I say, but I'm kind of glad. This feels kind of like an accidental date, and I don't like it. I mean he's nice and I like him, but I don't want to lead him on.

He asks the waitress for a to-go box and packages up the remainder of his meal. "Thanks again for the latte."

"My pleasure."

"I'd like to do this again sometime," he says, and I start to panic. "Somewhere that isn't fifty feet from work."

Sadie, come on. He's the closest thing to a real-life Mc-Dreamy you're ever going to find. He's attractive and charming and despite the bacon-fest he ordered, he's fit and everything like Griffin Sullivan, but he's also the one thing Griffin isn't: ready for something. You should totally say yes to him. Do it now.

"I'm not dating right now," I blurt and instantly feel relief.

"I think you're great, but I've got too much going on with my dad and I'm just not in the right place."

"Even for one date?"

I nod. He looks disappointed. "I really hope this doesn't make working together too weird."

"Of course not. I appreciate your honesty and understand where you're coming from," he assures me with an easy smile that seems genuine. "But if you change your mind, you know where to find me."

He passes my mother on his way out without knowing it. He holds the door open for her as she comes in. She sees me and heads over, taking the stool Bob just vacated. "That was a handsome doctor."

"Yup," I agree and sip my latte. "And he just asked me out."

"Really?" Her hazel eyes spark with excitement but dim again as soon as she sees my face. "You turned him down?"

"Yup," I say again and put down my now empty latte mug. "I wanted to force myself to say yes. He's charming and good looking and everyone at the hospital likes him, so I know he's a genuinely good guy. But..."

My mom sighs, but it's not in disappointment, it's in solidarity. "The heart wants what the heart wants. And it doesn't want the sensible choice."

I nod. "I mean not that there's a choice. It's basically Bob or nothing right now."

"That doesn't mean it should be Bob," she replies, and I'm so grateful she's not one of those mothers who pushes her kids for husbands and babies. She reaches over and takes my fork, digging into the half-eaten cherry pie slice in front of me. I push it closer to her. "Your dad was the absolute worst choice ever."

She pops a forkful of pie into her mouth and chews while I laugh at that announcement. "He was just some random hottie I met on vacation. He didn't live near me. He wasn't in college. He literally lived in his parents' basement. That's like the kiss of death, even now."

"Hey, lady, back off. I live with my parents."

"Not in the basement, sweetheart," she reminds me. "Anyway, I knew I was going to be considered crazy when I started dating him, but I couldn't stop myself. He was so wrong, but yet so right."

"You two have ruined me forever," I say to her in mock anger. "I mean how am I ever going to find a love story that great?"

"Jude and Dixie both managed. You will too," she replies. "I just hope Winnie can."

She looks genuinely concerned when she says that, and I wish I could make her feel better, but I've got nothing good to say when it comes to Winnie's love life. I decide to change the subject. I pull out my phone and look at the time. "Dad should be done soon. Want to head over?"

She nods. I pull my wallet out of my purse and leave some cash on the counter for my food and the coffees. We walk across the parking lot back to the hospital, and I realize how accurate Bob's joke was. I spend way too much time here. It feels like I don't do anything but deal with illness. So why can't I talk myself into doing something more, like dating Bob?

Because you're still hung up on Griffin, I remind myself sternly. *That kiss made you feel alive and incredible and made it impossible to forget him anytime soon... or maybe ever. So you screwed yourself because you're going to have to forget him.*

We head up to neurology, and sure enough, Dad is waiting in the area outside Dr. Lack's office. He smiles at us, but it isn't relaxed and jovial like it should be. Mom bends down and kisses his cheek. Dr. Lack opens her office door. "Come in, everyone."

I feel like I'm going to the firing squad. Mom wheels Dad in, and I follow. Mom takes the chair, while Dr. Lack sits behind her desk and sighs. This isn't good. She starts to tell us the test results. Dad's mobility, muscle strength, swallowing, and breathing have all deteriorated from his last test three months ago.

"Nothing extreme, except I'm a little worried about the swallowing and want to do a follow-up test much sooner than three months, say maybe in a month?" she explains. "And it's definitely better to use the wheelchair as much as possible now."

I'm so glad I can't see their faces, because I know my parents are devastated. This is really bad news. He's quickly losing all the freedom he has left. But like always, my dad just nods stoically. Dr. Lack hands my mom a piece of paper. "I want to try this new prescription. It might help a little bit with muscle strength."

Again, Dad nods. "Thanks, Doc."

"See you in a month."

Mom gets up and wheels him out, and I follow. In the hall

she puts on a brave face. It's just about the only face I see lately. "I'm going to run to the pharmacy in the building and fill this now," she says. "I'll meet you two at the car."

"Sure thing, honey." Dad nods, and I take over behind his chair. As we walk to the elevator bay and she heads the other way toward the emergency wing, he turns his head a little to look up at me. "Well, that sucked."

"Definitely," I agree.

We get in the elevator. He doesn't say anything again until I'm wheeling him across the parking lot toward the car. "She's crying right now."

"What? Why would you think that?"

"Because I know Enid better than I know myself," he says, and there's such a deep sadness emanating from him it's painful. "She cries every time we get bad news. She tries to hide it, but I know."

I help him stand up and then put the wheelchair in the trunk while he leans on the side of the car. I open the passenger door to their car and carefully help him in. It's fairly easy right now because he still has some use of his legs and can balance a little bit. I say the first thing that always seems to come to my mind. "What can I do to help?"

I stand in the open door as he fumbles for his seat belt, but I don't help. He can still do this on his own, even though it's a struggle, and I don't want to take it away from him. When he's buckled up he looks me straight in the eye. "I asked Dr. Lack to share future test results with you first. You're good at looking at this professionally, and I'm going to need you to help me ease them into accepting what's coming."

"We all know how this ends, Dad," I remind him softly. "Dixie works for the ALS Foundation. Jude has done more research that a neurology student and—"

He holds up his hand so I stop mid-sentence, and then he reaches out and grabs my hand and gives it a small squeeze. "Pumpkin, we both know that knowing things figuratively and seeing them happen in reality are different. You've seen that yourself with patients' families, I'm sure."

He's right. I have. I've watched wives of brain-dead husbands try to rationalize that they only need more time. I've watched parents argue with doctors when they're told their kids are gone. I've seen it all.

"Sadie, I'm going to be making decisions that they won't like, but I need you to stay strong and back me up. I need you on my side," he tells me. "And to help them cope."

"Okay," I say because I knew this day would come. I knew he'd need to count on me. He's been the person I've always counted on, so I am not going to let him down. Even if the idea of it makes me feel like I'm suffocating. What I'm agreeing to means standing by his decisions. Standing by him could mean not only going against my siblings, but against my own selfish heart that wants him around as long as possible, by any means possible.

"Give me a hug, pumpkin." I lean into the car and let him wrap his arms around me. I close my eyes and absorb every second of it, burning it into my brain, the same way I have since he was first diagnosed.

My phone starts to buzz in my back pocket as I let go of him. I pull it out and am startled to see a text from Griffin.

I glance up at my dad and step away from the car. "I'll be a sec." I turn my back to him and open the message.

> I'm at the coffee shop where our date never happened. Made me think of you. I just wanted to say, hope you are doing well.

I smile but it's bittersweet. His timing would be perfect if he was my boyfriend because, shit, I could use someone to lean on. I bite my lip and text him back.

> Today is a rough one. Nice to have a friendly message. Hope you're well too.

I glance up and see my mom walking toward the car, so I close my dad's door and move to hop into the back seat.

"Can you drive home, honey?" she asks as she walks around the back of the car to hand me the keys.

"No problem." It's the easiest request I've gotten today by far.

My phone buzzes again as I'm about to slip into the driver's seat. I pause to read the message from Griffin.

> If you need to talk, you can call me. I might not be dating material, but I can be friend material.

Oh, if only that were true. I sigh. I want to lie to both of us and say sure, we can hang out as friends, but I would only be giving myself false hope. I feel like trying to deny our attraction or push it aside would become torture really fast. And I'm going through enough right now. I don't need to add self-inflicted wounds. That was why I didn't want to date anyone to begin with.

My mom looks at me impatiently. "Sorry. Just a second."

She gets into the back seat, and I respond to Griffin's text.

People who kiss like you do are dangerous friends. But I do appreciate the offer. Take care.

I toss my phone into the center console and get behind the wheel. As I pull out of the parking lot and start our journey home, my parents chatter about inconsequential things. I keep stealing glances at my mom in the rearview mirror. Now that my dad has tipped me off, I see the signs. She's got a crumpled tissue tucked into the sleeve of her sweater. Her eyes look a little too glassy. Her nose is the slightest bit red. I would have blamed it on the chilly weather, but now I know better. And I have to help my dad help her and everyone else through this latest obstacle. I have to focus on that, which is why it's a blessing in disguise that my timing with Griffin is off. I can't give my heart to someone when it's already about to be broken by something else.

9

GRIFFIN

I see my brother approaching the dock from where I'm sitting on my upstairs balcony, stewing in my thoughts and nursing a neat whiskey.

He's in his typical attire when he doesn't have to be in court—ratty jeans with holes in both knees, a T-shirt, and flip-flops. He's been out of school for almost four years, but you'd think Hunter was a permanent student if you judged him on his fashion sense, or lack thereof.

"Hey!" he calls, pulling his aviators up to rest on top of his head. "Thought I'd swing by and see my favorite girl."

"She's not here," I call back, and his expression gets hard fast. "She's at her friend Jennica's at a play date. I'm picking her up in a couple hours."

Hunter looks instantly relieved. "Oh, okay. I thought that maybe Lauren was screwing with the custody before the hearing."

"Nah. I haven't heard a thing from her," I say as I watch

him step onto the boat. "She didn't even hand Charlie off to me when I picked her up. She had that asswipe she's dating meet me at the door, and he had a written note with instructions."

Hunter halts on the deck below, shielding his eyes as he looks up at me, his face twisted with fury. "Are you kidding me? What did the note say?"

"It was a list of things I needed to remember," I explain. "Bedtime, when to feed her, and what food she likes and doesn't. It's like I was some new nanny or deadbeat dad who hadn't spent any time with their kid. I haven't gone more than three days without seeing my daughter since the divorce."

Hunter shakes his head but says nothing as he uses his key to open the main door to the houseboat. A few seconds later he's walking through my bedroom to the deck I'm on. "The note was handwritten or typed?"

"Typed. Why?"

"She's creating documentation, that smart bi—"

I glare at Hunter before he can finish his expletive. He knows I don't tolerate calling Lauren names. Out loud. She still gave me Charlie, and I worry if we get used to calling her names when Charlie's not around, we might slip and do it when she is. I don't want her to hear her mother called a bitch . . . even if she is one. Hunter stops mid-word. "She's doing this so that when she lies and says you take bad care of Charlie, she will have 'proof.'"

He makes air quotes as he says "proof," and my jaw drops along with my stomach. "A written list she claims you need in order to take care of your child, because you are too inept or distracted to remember Charlie's schedule. It's fake and I'll argue that, but it's her word against ours, and the list, typed up, seems hard to disprove."

"Are you kidding me?"

"Nope. But the good news is most family court judges know all the tricks," Hunter explains as he walks over to the bar on the deck and grabs the whiskey bottle off the top. I hand him my glass.

"Take mine. I'm not thirsty anymore," I tell him and Hunter grabs my tumbler and takes a sip before dropping down in the chair I was in before he arrived. I sigh and sit in the other one and try to relax, but I can't.

"Please don't worry," Hunter says, tilting his head up toward the dipping sun.

"You've said that a million times."

"And I'll say it a million more…until you stop stressing," my brother replies. "Lauren is not taking Charlie away. Not even for a second. In fact, by the time this is done, I'm hoping to get you more time."

"I don't want to take Lauren's time from Charlie either," I reply, and I mean it. Lauren isn't a bad mother. Charlie needs her and loves her. "But this bullshit has got to stop. I don't know why, after years of things being fine, she suddenly wants a change and is implying I'm unfit."

"I bet it's the boyfriend," Hunter suggests and sips the whiskey again. "He's the only thing that's changed since the divorce."

"That makes no sense. We've been divorced for two years. I'm sure she's been involved with other people," I argue back.

"You haven't," he remarks.

"Touché," I reply. "But it's not like this Cale guy is demanding my kid be around even more. Hell, he barely bothered to learn Charlie's name, and I'm guessing if anything he would rather she spent more time with me so Lauren would be free to follow him around all the shitty gigs he does. She can't spend all her nights in a dive bar when she's got a child at home."

Hunter sighs. "Let's talk about something better. What's happening with the hot nurse? Have you gotten to the sponge bath portion of the relationship?"

I laugh because he is ridiculous, but the fact is the whole situation is far from funny. It's a damn tragedy, and Hunter's going to kick my ass when I tell him. "I haven't rescheduled our date. And I'm not going to anytime soon."

"Okay, now *I'm* going to call her," Hunter replies, leaning toward me. "Maybe she can recommend a doctor, because clearly there's something wrong with you."

"Hunter, my life isn't set up to include a girlfriend right now," I remind him. "I work a lot, and the times I am home I have Charlie most days. Plus it's baggage enough to have an ex-wife and kid, but to also be dealing with custody issues...Sadie doesn't need that."

"Sadie," Hunter repeats her name, smiling as he pushes his sunglasses back up on his head again. "We have a name. How about a last name?"

"You don't need to know that."

His light eyes glint with mischief. "Okay, Sadie the Naughty Nurse it is."

"Don't be a cheap asshole, Hunter."

"You wouldn't care what I called her if you weren't still hoping to see her again," he replies, pausing to finish the whiskey in his glass.

"What I want and what's going to happen are two different things." I rub a hand over my chin as I think about how she turned down my offer of friendship. "Her dad is really sick, and she works twelve-hour shifts. She has a lot on her plate too. It's not just me that thinks this isn't the right time."

"Fuck. That's hard."

"Exactly," I say, feeling like he's finally getting it and siding with me. I pause and steady myself for his reaction because I know he's not going to like my last confession. He swirls the whiskey left in his glass for a moment before downing the rest of it.

"You know what I think?" he says, standing up and putting his empty glass on the table beside me. He waits a second for me to respond, but I don't because he's going to tell me what he thinks, whether I want him to or not. "I think you're looking for excuses. I think you're too much of a pussy to go after...well, pussy."

I cringe. "Hey, frat boy, rein it in. You kiss your wife with that mouth?"

His grin is almost blinding. "I do a hell of a lot more than just kiss her with it."

I do not need the visuals he's putting in my head. I shake them out. "If you think this doesn't suck for me, trust me, you're wrong. She's the first woman I've been interested in since Lauren. Hell, I'm more than interested. But seriously,

Hunter, I couldn't even handle an attempt at a first date without it blowing up."

He seems to seriously consider my words. I had already explained to him how I fucked up with the cell phone and didn't call her to cancel the date until she was already there. Even he winced at that when I told him. He sighs. "Okay, man. I get it. I'll stop bugging you for now. But as soon as we settle the Lauren drama once and for all, you're seeing this Sadie girl again...even if the only way I can get you to do it is break your nose and send you to her hospital."

I laugh at that. "You should have been a comedian. The career goes better with your wardrobe too."

"Zing!" Hunter calls as he walks back into the houseboat. "I'm heading home to my amazing woman. You should get one. You'd like it."

I don't respond. I just laugh. My kid brother is a jackass, but he's my jackass. He appears on the first level a few minutes later, and as he heads down the dock he calls out. "Tell Charlie I said hi!"

After watching his car disappear, I head back inside and start to prep dinner. I promised Charlie we could make mini pizzas. It's her favorite thing, and I don't mind it because I make a cauliflower crust and she loves to pile veggies on it. She's the only six-year-old I've ever met willing to eat brussels sprouts. I turn on the big screen in the living room to watch the Thunder game and angle it toward the kitchen, then I pull out the ingredients to start the crust. The Thunder are in Seattle playing the Winterhawks, and it's just starting.

I'm so glad goalie coaches aren't required to go on most of

the road trips. The travel was my least favorite part of playing, especially after Charlie was born. My cell phone buzzes as I'm chopping veggies. It's Jennica's mom. "Hi, Anne. Is it time to…"

Anne starts talking fast, and as I absorb what she's saying, my blood runs cold. "I'll be there in a minute. Don't panic. Don't let Charlie panic."

I hang up, grab my keys, and rush out of the boat.

10

GRIFFIN

I'm trying not to freak out, but it's not easy. When Anne told me that Charlie had stuffed raisins up her nose and there was one stuck, I was horrified and honestly a little pissed. She's a smart kid, and this was stupid. I'm fairly certain a raisin up her nostril won't kill her, but I can't help considering all the worst-case scenarios. Maybe she could aspirate it into her lungs or something? Was that even possible? I get to Anne's place in record time, and she opens the door, looking even more distraught than me.

"I am so sorry. Jennica's brother dared them to do it," she confesses. "Trust me, he's in trouble. Big trouble!"

Charlie is standing in the hall behind her, big hazel eyes wide and scared. I'm not sure if it's the thing trapped in her nostril that has her freaked out or if she's scared of the trouble she might be in. I give Anne a small, reassuring smile and motion for Charlie to join me. "Kids are kids. Thanks for calling me. I'll take her home and fix her right up."

"I think you're going to need professional help," Anne recommended. "I tried to snag it with tweezers but I couldn't."

Fuck.

I smile again. "Okay. It's not a big deal. Don't beat yourself up." I look down at Charlie and her little lip trembles. "Thank Mrs. Kesler for having you over."

"Thank you. And I'm sorry," Charlie says in a shaking voice.

Anne bends and pats her head. "It's okay, Charlie. I hope you get it out."

We head down the front path to the car. As soon as I have her buckled into her booster seat in the back, she bursts into tears. Now I'm worried the snot will loosen the thing and send it shooting down her throat, choking her. I hug her. "It's okay, sweetie."

"Is it going to be in there forever?" she asks, panicked. "Is it going to get all gross and stinky? Is it going to make my nose rot?"

"No, honey." I try not to laugh at her questions. "Does it hurt?"

She shakes her head no. I kiss her forehead. "I'm going to take you to a doctor, and they're going to remove it. It's going to be fine."

"Will it hurt then?" she asks, voice still shaky.

"I hope not," I say, which is the only honest answer I can give. I close the back and as I walk around the car, I quickly text Sadie.

Are you at work? I'm heading to the hospital now.

My kid has a raisin stuck in her nose.

I don't get an immediate response, so I hop in the car, but before I can pull out of Anne's driveway, she texts back.

I'm here, so I'll see you soon. Try not to panic.

It's more common than you think and an easy fix. Promise.

I put down the phone and let out a sigh of relief.

"Don't worry, Charlie. I just texted my friend who works at the hospital and she said she will get it out, easy-peasy."

My daughter gives me a wobbly smile. She's still scared as hell. Poor kid.

I try not to speed as I head toward the hospital. Charlie, thankfully, has stopped crying, but she's sniffing now. I dig around my console and pull out a small pack of tissue. "Try blowing, sweetie. I don't want you to sniff too hard."

I hand it back to her and I hear her blow. "It didn't come out," she reports.

"No worries, kiddo. We'll get it out."

"Will your hopsital friend laugh at me?" she asks nervously, and I bite my lip to keep from laughing at the way she said "hospital." She's started to develop self-consciousness lately, and it makes me sad. I don't remember having those worries at her age and I wonder if it's a gender thing. I hate it. It's not fair. I want her to be carefree and confident forever, even though I know that's completely unrealistic.

"No, Charlie, nurses and doctors will have seen this type of thing before. A lot," I reply soothingly. "I promise you're not a weirdo."

I glance in the rearview mirror and watch her stare despondently at the tissue in her tiny hands. "Cale laughs at me sometimes."

My blood turns to ice in my veins. Stay calm. Stay calm... "What do you mean, Charlie?"

My voice is soft and calm, but I'm griping the steering wheel so hard I could probably rip it out of the car right now. We stop at a red light. She shrugs her delicate shoulders. "I spilled my drink last week and he laughed really loud and people looked at me."

"Where was Mommy?" I'm going to fucking kill this dude.

"She was there. She told him to stop and helped me clean it up and the lady brought me a new drink," she explains. "But I cried and that made him mad."

"Well, he was wrong," I say firmly but still calmly, because I'm scared if I show her how enraged I am it'll scare her or, worse yet, make her hold on to this shitty moment even more. "He wasn't nice. You had an accident. It happens. No one should be made fun of for accidents."

"That's what Mommy said later," she says, her voice getting a little stronger and a timid smile on her lips.

Later? Lauren should have said it immediately. And then thrown Charlie's new drink at him.

The hospital is visible now half a block up, and I push my anger at Cale aside and concentrate on the problem at hand. "Try blowing again, nugget."

She does. "It didn't come out."

"Okay. No worries," I reply and pull into the parking lot.

The nurse at the desk is the friendly blond lady Sadie sent in to check on Eli. I tell Charlie to sit in the plastic chair nearest the counter and walk up. I smile. "Hi. How are you tonight?"

"I'm doing okay. Thank you for asking." She seems surprised I asked. She smiles and glances past me at Charlie. "Your little one under the weather?"

I shake my head. "No, she stuck a raisin up her nose and we can't get it out."

The blonde, whose name tag says *Shelda*, doesn't even blink. "Right. Sadie just told me you'd be coming in. We can handle that. You know my kid once wedged three marbles up his nose."

I chuckle. "Is there a support group for parents who go through this? Because I could use it right about now."

Shelda laughs. "I wish."

She asks for my insurance card and gives me some paperwork to fill out. I sit down next to Charlie and fill it in. Charlie looks nervous again. I rub her back. "It's okay. This place is big and smells funny, but the people are really nice and they'll get rid of the raisin. The nurse told me her son shoved marbles up his nose."

"Really? I wouldn't do that. They're too big!"

"Why did you do this, Charlie?" I ask without condemnation.

She shrugs and looks sheepish. "It's so embarrassing..."

I open my mouth to talk her into telling me, because eventually I'm going to make her. This is a life lesson we need to talk out so it doesn't happen again. But she looks so ashamed I worry she might cry again if I push her right now. I tell myself we can talk it out after the raisin is removed. Instead I finish the paperwork and bring it back to the counter. Shelda gives me a big, soothing smile. "I'm going to slide you into room two. Sadie will be in to help you right away. She's the best nasal extractionist we have. She's also every kid's favorite."

"Thank you so much."

Five minutes later, as Charlie sits on the edge of the bed swinging her legs, the curtain is pulled back and Sadie is standing there. She's in pale pink scrubs that give her porcelain skin tone a healthy glow. Her blond hair is pulled back in the same low ponytail it was in last time I was here, and her wide, light eyes are free of makeup. She looks gorgeous. Our eyes meet and she gives me a bright, confident smile and reaches out and pats my shoulder. "I got this. Don't stress."

My tension instantly dissipates. She drops her hand from my shoulder and turns and waves at Charlie. "Hey. You're Charlotte?"

"Charlie," she corrects quietly.

"Charlie is a cool name," Sadie replies. "I'm Sadie."

"I have a friend at school named Sadie," Charlie offers.

"Awesome!" Sadie smiles, and it's soothing even to me. "I hear you got a raisin stuck. I want to help unstick it. Is that okay?"

Charlie nods profusely. Sadie directs her to lie back on the bed. She grabs some instrument with a light at the end and angles it up Charlie's nostril. She looks over at me. "This is going to be over in no time, Charlie. I promise."

Charlie looks at me. "Can we keep it secret, so Cale won't laugh at me?"

I can feel my expression darken. "I won't tell Cale."

Sadie doesn't miss the shame on Charlie's face, and she handles it like a hero, in my opinion. "This isn't anything to laugh at. It happens to tons of kids, Charlie. I promise. My brother once shoved a Lego up his nose to keep my sisters and me from playing with it."

"A Lego would hurt!" Charlie exclaims. Sadie nods emphatically.

"It did. And he cried a lot, but I never laughed at him," Sadie replies. "And nobody is going to laugh at you."

She turns to me. "This is going to look scary to her," she explains quietly. "You might want to hold her hand."

I nod and stand up and walk over to the side of the bed as Sadie grabs a long metal tong-looking thing with bent, pointy-looking ends. Yeah, I would freak out at seeing that thing at Charlie's age. I watch her eyes flare. "Daddy…"

"It's okay, Charlie," Sadie says and puts the thing down on a sterile paper on the movable tray table. "First, I'm going to swab your nose with something. It's going to feel cold and wet, but it won't hurt."

"O…kay," Charlie says cautiously. I squeeze her hand.

Sadie glances at me but looks away. "It's a wee bit of numbing cream. The extraction shouldn't hurt, but this will make sure of it."

"Thanks."

She nods without glancing back up at me. Charlie squeezes my hand as Sadie works, but she doesn't cry and she doesn't wince. Sadie talks throughout the whole thing in a smooth, easy tone. She's incredible with kids, that much is clear, and it only makes her even more attractive to me. Within a minute the smushed raisin is in a little disposable cup.

"Okay, all done!" Sadie announces as Charlie sits up and looks into the cup. "Your nose is a raisin-free zone. Promise me you'll keep it that way."

"I will. Promise!" Charlie replies, and without me having to remind her she adds, "Thank you."

Sadie tosses the raisin into the garbage along with her gloves and turns to a computer station in the corner. She starts to type stuff up while glancing at Charlie. "Charlie, can I ask you why you put the raisin up there? I promise I won't laugh."

"Because Kevin said he could shove seven raisins up his and that we couldn't beat him because we were girls."

Charlie's attitude and competitive spirit leave no doubt she's my kid. I bite back a smile and look up to see Sadie doing the same.

"Kevin was wrong," I tell Charlie. "Sometimes when people say stuff like that you have to walk away knowing they're wrong and you don't have to prove them wrong. Especially if it's something that could hurt you."

Charlie looks up at me and then to Sadie, who hides her smile easily. "Your dad is right."

"Okay."

Shelda walks into the room. "Everything okay?"

"Raisin has been evicted," Sadie announces, and Shelda smiles. "Just finishing up the report. I can forward to your local pediatrician if you'd like."

My face drops, and Shelda notices. "I...umm...It's just..."

Sadie glances up at me. Shelda motions toward Charlie. "No sense in you sitting around this stuffy room. Would you like to sneak up to the cafeteria with me? They have some yummy oatmeal cookies tonight."

Charlie looks up at me, and I pull out my wallet and hand her a five-dollar bill. "No soda, though, Charlie. Apple juice or milk only."

"Okay." She nods. "And I won't put anything in my nose."

"Atta girl!" Sadie smiles as I try not to laugh. Shelda takes Charlie out of the room, and I walk to the door and watch them go. As soon as they are out of sight I collapse against the wall in relief and run my hands through my hair. "Holy shit, this kid thing really does kill you slowly."

Sadie laughs. "She is absolutely adorable. And by the way, please feel free to tell Jude's teammates about the Lego incident and make fun of him mercilessly."

My eyes narrow on her. "You did laugh at him when it happened, didn't you?"

"Cackled for days," she replies with an evil grin that is still somehow sexy as hell.

She finishes typing on the computer and turns her head toward me. "So you don't want the file sent to your pediatrician? You don't have to do it. We just generally offer as most parents like to keep all the records with one physician."

"No. I'd rather not," I reply and move around the bed so I can stand closer to her. She doesn't notice or at least she doesn't react. "That Cale person Charlie referred to is my ex-wife's boyfriend. If I keep this from my ex, I keep this from him, which means I won't have to punch him in the face for laughing at her over it."

Her eyes hold mine for a long moment. I can't read her expression so I get worried she doesn't think I'm doing the right thing. "Does that make me a bad parent?"

She blinks. "Of course not. Charlie is not going to need any follow-up care from this and there's no possibility of a side effect or anything, so it's not a big deal. Don't worry. Oh, and for the record, even the fact that she shoved the raisin up her nose isn't your fault and doesn't make you a bad parent. And also for the record, your ex is dating a dick."

"Yeah. She is," I say.

"You can finish up at the desk when Shelda gets back. She'll print out a copy of the report, for your records," she says and moves the computer out to the side.

"You're a great nurse," I say.

She reaches out and squeezes my arm. "You're a great dad."

I know it's probably not appropriate, but I give her a hug. "Thank you."

She hugs me back, squeezing me as tightly as I'm squeezing her. I meant it as a friendly gesture, but it feels like much more. Seeing how incredible she was at her job, and most importantly with my daughter, has only made my feelings for her stronger.

"I know this sounds crazy, but I miss you," I confess. She breaks the hug and takes a step back. "I miss all the time I never got to spend with you."

"I feel that way too."

"So let's hang out. As friends," I suggest, and it sounds as impulsive as it feels. "We can finally grab a coffee or maybe a few drinks or something."

"Griffin…" She shakes her head. "I think the only thing that would make my life more complicated than dating you would be being around you but not dating you."

I know the minute she says it that she's right. "I like you."

"I like you too," she whispers. A slow, unbelievably sensuous smile spreads across her face as her cheeks get pink. She has this way of looking angelic and sly the very same time, and it's making my dick hard. I can't remember the last time I had such an intense reaction to a smile. I don't know if I ever have. We're standing as close to each other as we can without touching. "But are you attracted to me?"

"So much I can barely stand it," I admit in a rough whisper.

"Me too." She gently bites her bottom lip before she blinks, steps away from me and the sexy-as-fuck, wicked smile disappears, and her professional smile is back. "And that's why we can't just be friends. I understand, Griffin, why the timing is off and I accept it. Honestly I'm dealing with a lot in my life too, and all my emotions and energy should be directed at my family right now, so this is probably for the best."

She says out loud what I've been telling myself every day since I bailed on our date. It should make me feel better, it should validate my decision… Why doesn't it? She steps back behind the computer.

"Shelda should be back with Charlie by now," Sadie explains, and then her expression softens a little. "It was good to see you again, Griffin...and to meet Charlie, even though it wasn't the best circumstances. She seems like a great kid."

"She is" is all I can think to say because everything else running through my mind goes against what we just mutually established—this isn't the right time for us.

"Take care." I take one last, long look at Sadie's beautiful face and leave the room to find my daughter.

11

SADIE

I yawn as I grab my coat and purse out of my locker in our nurses' lounge. Shelda is at her locker next to mine, pulling on her own jacket and primping her short honey blond hair in the small mirror she keeps in her locker. "I am way more exhausted than usual," I tell her.

"Yeah, that makes sense," Shelda says airily. "Fooling yourself takes a lot out of you."

"Oh, my gosh, teasing me for the last five hours wasn't enough?" I ask, and she firmly shakes her head no.

"Honey, it's not teasing. I'm trying to make you see the truth," she explains as she grabs her purse and shuts her locker. "That there is no right time for the right man. When he shows up, you make it work. The end."

I made the mistake of confiding in Shelda about everything that has happened with Griffin—from the text flirting, to the non-date, to the fact I thought he was married, to his confession he isn't. I hadn't intended on telling her, but for some reason, after he left with Charlie, I was all mixed up inside and needed to talk to someone. The chemistry between us when we're in the same room is so real and strong it's like its own entity. But we keep trying to ignore it, and it's beginning to feel like more work than just giving in to it. But he isn't offering to give in to it. In fairness, I didn't offer to either, despite the overwhelming urge I had to grab him by his jacket, shove him down on that hospital bed, and do a hell of a lot more than kiss him.

"But he can't make it work," I argue back, because that's the truth. I can't make him date me and he said he's "unready." "Plus you're being dramatic. You don't even know him. I don't even really know him. You can't call him the right man."

"Sadie, I have known you for almost a year, and in that time you haven't so much as talked about a hot celebrity, let alone had your face light up like a firework when someone walks by." Shelda grins and points at me. "But you did when you were talking to that man the first time he was here, and you did it again this time. That's the right man. At least right now."

I laugh, and she winks at me and wiggles her eyebrows. "When was the last time you had some hanky-panky?"

"Stop!" I laugh louder as we exit the lounge together.

"Well?" Shelda demands, clearly not letting this go.

"It's been a long time," I confess quietly and feel a flush hit my cheeks. "Too long."

We both wave goodbye to the new shift and head toward the exit. Shelda zips up her coat. "That is a tragedy, honey.

You're young, you're beautiful and smart, and you should be having all the fun the world has to offer."

I laugh. "I have a lot going on, Shel. You know that."

"I do, but that's even more reason to get some," Shelda says, and her smile gets softer, sympathetic and filled with understanding. "Life is short and it can be hard, so never turn away a chance at good hanky-panky...or better yet, true love."

"Oh, Lord, now you've gone too far!" I warn her because, hell, I don't even know this guy...I mean not really. I just really, really wish I did.

She pushes open the doors, and we step out into the crisp, early-morning air. It may be spring, but someone forgot to inform mother nature today. I glance up, and my feet stop moving as soon as I see him. He's leaning against the side of a dark green Land Rover. He's wearing a white cable-knit sweater and a pair of dark jeans, and he hasn't shaved. Ray-Bans cover his sexy eyes and a smile spreads those delicious, wide lips when he sees me. I feel like I'm in a romance movie and some uplifting music should start playing, or angels should sing or something. Because damn, this is a moment.

"Oh! Girl..." Shelda grins at me and nudges me toward him. "If you don't reconsider I'm calling the psych ward for an immediate assessment of your mental health."

"See you on Friday, Shelda," I reply and wave her off.

Griffin is walking toward me now, since it's clear I'm not moving. I notice a piece of paper—it looks like purple construction paper—in his hand. He stops about a foot in front of me. His smile widens, and I'm mesmerized by the sun glinting off the salt in his salt-and-pepper stubble. I have never, in my entire life, seen anything sexier. "Hi."

"Good morning," I reply.

"My brother is dropping Charlie off at school so I can swing by and bring you this. She made it as a thank-you and I promised I would give it to you as soon as possible." He hands me the paper he's been holding. It's a homemade card. It has a bunch of flowers she drew on the front and a cute little note inside thanking me for getting rid of her raisin. "And I wanted to thank you for handling her so well and talking her through that life lesson with me."

"I was just doing my job." I take it from him and smile. The flowers Charlie drew are adorable puffs of pale pink and bright blue. "The small stuff is my favorite. No blood, no gore. Just a really cute kid... with a really cute dad. Please tell her thank you from me. She draws really good flowers."

"She does." He nods and tilts his head. The sun loves him. It looks like he's glowing. "She asked me what she should draw for you and I told her wildflowers. I didn't tell her why but you know."

"I remind you of them." My voice is raspy for some reason.

"I know I shouldn't be here. I know this is just going to make things more complicated for both our overly complicated lives." He lifts his sunglasses.

Our eyes meet.

I drop my hand holding the card from Charlie, lift my other one, and touch his cheek with it and brush my lips against his in a chaste kiss. I start to pull back, but his arms wrap around my back, he pulls me closer, and his tongue sweeps into my open mouth. Sweet baby Jesus, it's even better than the first time. My toes curl inside my white sneakers and heat explodes inside me, racing through my veins and warming every part of me. If we don't end this kiss I'm going to start taking his clothes off right here in the hospital parking lot—or faint from the desire to—so even though I hate myself for it, I pull back. I'm panting and I feel sheepish as I step back and cover my mouth with my fingers.

"I have to take you out on a date," he replies, and my eyes widen. "I went home last night and after little Miss Raisin Stuffer went to bed I wrote down all the reasons this is bad timing and not a good idea, and then I lit the list on fire and dropped it in the ocean."

"Are you serious?" I laugh gleefully. This guy is insane...in the most perfect way possible.

"Dead serious." He grins. "So will you give me a second chance at a first date?"

"Yes," I reply. "And for the record, after a kiss like that, I'll give you a third and a fourth and possibly a fifth."

He chuckles and steps closer. "I promise, I won't need one."

He kisses me again. His lips are soft and teasing at first and then more dominant and intense as his tongue meets mine. This time the heat of the kiss burns my willpower to ash, so he has to break the kiss. He does it by gently moving his lips to my cheek where he whispers against it. "Tonight? Eight o'clock?"

I nod.

"Can I give you a lift home?" he asks, and I swear he blushes a little as I notice him subtly adjust the front of his pants. It's fucking hot, and all I want to do is reach out and touch him—feel what I've done to him. I'm so turned on right now my skin feels electric, and I can't for the life of me remember the last time that happened. I know if I let him drive me home I'll probably end up having sex with him in the back of his car.

"I think I need the fresh air to clear my head," I reply and lick my lips slowly. I watch his eyes follow my tongue, and I swear they visibly darken. "Also, if I get in that car with you I might do things that are generally kept for after first dates..."

He laughs, but it's husky and dark with desire. "I am not against bucking convention."

"Neither am I," I reply but take a step back. "But I think I will walk."

"Okay." He looks a little disappointed. "I'll see you tonight. Text me your address."

"Umm...I kind of deleted your number and your texts," I admit.

He looks stunned but grins cheekily as he lifts his hand to his chest like he's been shot. I laugh and step forward and, pressed against him, reach into his back pocket and grab his phone. I hand it to him and try not to overheat at being this close. "Text me. I'll text you back."

He does as he's told.

I start to walk away and hear my phone beep with his text. He's watching me go; I can feel it, and it makes me way more excited than it should. I dig my phone out of my purse and open his text to respond. His two-word text makes me feel lighter than air.

You're beautiful

I glance over my shoulder and see his car pull out of the parking lot. I didn't expect to ever see him again except maybe in passing at another one of Jude's games...if I couldn't avoid him first. And now...I'm kissing him in my work parking lot. And going on a date with him. The universe is all about the U-turns right now.

I float home, my cheeks still tingling from the feel of his scruff and my lips still plump from the intensity of our kiss. I take the stairs up the five floors to our penthouse unit because I'm feeling way too awake and I really have to get some sleep today after that shift, but these butterflies in my stomach are not snoozing anytime soon.

I open the door to the sound of coughing—heavy, bad coughing. I drop my bag and my coat on the floor and rush into the dining room. My mom and my dad's nurse, Maria, are there, bent over my father as he chokes on his breakfast. I run around the table to get a better look at the situation. His face isn't blue, it's red, which is a good sign.

"Randy! Oh, my God!" My mom is freaking out, her voice high and quivering with anxiety.

I don't answer her. Neither does Maria, as she's already got her arms under his armpits and is lifting him out of his chair. I hold his shoulders, to steady him as she wraps her arms around his center and gives him one quick upward thrust.

Then two. A piece of bagel pops out of his mouth and lands with a wet splat on the edge of his plate. My mom quickly picks it up in a napkin and puts it aside.

This is what ALS does—it takes away voluntary muscle control so things like walking, talking, and swallowing become harder and harder and eventually impossible. My dad looks simply horrified. My heart is breaking and pounding at the same time, which makes me feel weak and tired and on the verge of tears. But I give him a quick smile instead of showing it. "Well, that almost went down the wrong pipe."

I act like it's no big deal. I casually walk around the table, grabbing a glass from the buffet and reaching for the orange juice pitcher. I pour myself a glass of juice, impressed that my hand isn't shaking. My whole body wants to shudder, because even though I'm a nurse and deal with far worse than choking on a daily basis, this is my dad. My world.

"No more," my dad says firmly as my mom tries to give him another piece of his bagel and cream cheese. Mom looks stricken.

"Dad, you have to eat," I remind him calmly. "How about a smoothie instead?"

"Okay," he mutters.

I start to stand, but my mom is already up. "I'll make it. Orange and banana with vanilla protein powder?"

My dad nods dejectedly. Mom heads off, and I glance at the nurse and wave at her. She stands up. "I'll be in the den if you need me."

"Thanks, Maria," my dad replies, but it comes out more

like "tansk ma-wee-ah." She smiles at him and heads out of the dining room and down the hall.

Alone, he looks at me and smiles. "How was your night, Sadie?"

"Long. Good. No major traumas," I say and sip my OJ.

"Is that why you were smiling when you walked in?" His body may be betraying him, but his mind is not. He's still the most intuitive person I have ever met. Dixie and Jude have a little of that keen awareness Dad has, but still not as acute as his. My dad could always read moods and catch nonverbal cues like a boss, which made it really hard to be a sneaky teenager.

"Yes, and . . . well, I had one particularly adorable patient," I say vaguely.

His bushy salt-and-pepper eyebrows lift. "Oh . . . ?"

"A six-year-old with a raisin in her nose," I add to throw him off track.

He chuckles. "Jude used to use his nose for storage too."

It takes me a minute to understand what he says, with the slurring, but as soon as I understand I laugh. "I told her dad that—about Jude and the Lego—so she didn't feel too embarrassed. And because ridiculing Jude is always enjoyable."

My father rolls his eyes at that last comment, but he chuckles. Then his face gets serious. "Thank you for helping Maria with the choking."

"You didn't need me. Maria had it under control," I reply, blowing it off because I don't want to get into it. Talking about choking will lead to a bigger conversation about what it means, and the next steps.

"It's happening too much," he says, and my heart constricts

like it's been shoved into a pair of Spanx. It suddenly can't expand to beat properly.

I stare at the oak table between us and the half-eaten bagel on his plate. "We are managing it."

"Barely," he counters.

My mom walks in with a big glass filled with yummy-looking orange smoothie. She puts it down in front of my dad and pops a straw in. He doesn't take a sip, instead staring at me, clearly insistent on continuing the conversation. But I won't—can't—do it.

I stand up. "I love you, Daddy, but I need to catch up on my beauty sleep now." He looks like he's going to insist we continue talking about his choking, which means he wants to talk about the next step, which is a feeding tube, which he has already told us he does not want... which means the end is closer than it would be with a feeding tube... And I can't talk about that. Not now. Maybe never. So I throw out a piece of information I didn't intend to share but that I know will change the subject. "I have a date tonight."

If I could pick a sound effect for my parents' reaction, it would be a record needle being ripped off a turning record player. I actually even laugh at it.

"That's unexpected," my mom says with a curious grin. "With who? The doctor from the diner?"

"Miss Raisin Nose's dad?" Really, truly, my dad should have been a private detective. "Your face lit up when you told me that story."

"Drink your smoothie and I'll tell you more," I say as I stand and walk around the table.

"You're my baby, I'm not yours, pumpkin," my dad warns with a wink. He's jovial about it, but he hates that all his kids are nurturing him now. I nod and he picks up the drink again and takes a long, easy sip. No choking, thank God.

"Yes, with the dad. He's divorced, by the way," I add.

"I assumed that," my dad says, and I lean down and kiss his cheek. He reaches up and rubs my head lovingly as I do it.

I lean down again to kiss my mom's cheek. "I have got to get some rest. Bags under my eyes are not a good accessory on a first date."

I leave them in the dining room and head down the hall, stopping to let Maria know I'm heading for a nap, but to come and get me if she needs help. I also remind her to double-check on his ribs later, to make sure they're not bruised. She nods. God bless the woman, because even I know I'm kind of micromanaging, but she never gets annoyed.

When I get to my room, I'm still a bit panicky and emotionally raw from what just happened and the conversation I skillfully sidestepped that I know is still coming. I strip down to my underwear, leaving my scrubs in a heap, and as I crawl under the covers, I text Griffin with an address. He responds with an emoji of a flower. I smile, turn my phone off, and replay that parking lot kiss in my head until I drift off.

12

SADIE

I toss Dixie's pale pink shirt on her bed and grab a black one with sheer sleeves and a V-neck that's a little deeper than I'm comfortable with. I hold it up to my frame and hesitate. Dixie eyes me from the bed in the corner, stretched out like a cat on top of the pile of colorful throw pillows she insists on covering the bed with.

"Since when are you into shirts like this?" I ask.

"Since always," Dixie replies with a smile as she pulls all her wheat blond hair into a high ponytail and wraps it with the elastic from her wrist. A piece escapes and hangs down the back of her neck, but she doesn't seem to care. "I just never wore stuff like that to work...and I was always working, so you never saw it. Try it on. It's hella flattering."

Despite my initial judgment, I slip it over my head. I stare at my reflection. She's right. It's hot. The neckline shows just enough cleavage but not too much, the material is soft and clingy and cuts in at the waist just right. And the jet black color makes my blue eyes icy and bright and my blond hair look more luminous.

"This one it is," I announce and turn from the mirror to face Dixie. I smooth my hands down my dark jeans. "It's good, right?"

"It's gorgeous," Dixie replies, and I feel instantly more at ease. My sisters and I made a pact long ago not to blow smoke up each other's asses. If she says it looks good, it definitely does. "So do you want to borrow some condoms too?"

I freeze. "First of all, it's not borrowing unless you want them back."

She wrinkles her nose. "Okay. Revising that statement. Do you want to *have* some condoms?"

"I have some in my purse. I bought them on the way over," I admit. She grins and actually claps her hands excitedly like her older sister potentially getting laid is some kind of extraordinary feat, like a Super Bowl touchdown. I should be annoyed, but she's kind of right. "I'm not saying it's definitely going to happen."

"But you want it to," Dixie adds, still smiling, and she pulls herself to a sitting position. "And that's good. That's great, actually. You deserve some fun."

I nod. "I just...don't want to make this a big deal. We'll just see what happens. But we're both consenting adults, and I think we're both willing and able, so..."

I shrug and Dixie nods emphatically, making more hair fall from her ponytail. "I'm so glad he didn't turn out to be a married, cheating dick. I would have had to death-stare him every time I saw him at a Thunder game, and that would've been exhausting."

I grab my purse off the sofa and take my lipstick out of it. "Speaking of the Thunder, you haven't told anyone I'm going on this date with the goalie coach, have you? And by anyone I mean Jude or Eli?"

She shakes her head. "You told me not to, but Mom and Dad might spill it."

"They don't know who the date is with," I say and pause to apply my lipstick. "Which is also why I'm having him pick me up here. I don't want them to meet him or anything."

"Why did you tell them at all?"

"Because they were about to try and discuss a feeding tube," I reply, and Dixie's whole face sinks into darkness. "He choked. Again. And we needed to Heimlich him. He's fine so don't freak out. But next steps are in his thoughts now more than ever."

"What are we going to do?" Dixie lets out a heavy breath and keeps talking before I can answer her. "Sadie, you're a nurse. He'll listen to you. You have to convince him to get a tube."

Why did I bring this up right now? My father wants me to be the buffer, that's why. And I have to talk about this gradually, so they aren't overwhelmed when the time comes. But I realize this isn't putting me in the best head space for a date.

"The next step after that will be a respirator," I murmur softly, as if it will somehow lessen the painful impact of that realization. Dixie and I stare at each other, our expressions mirroring each other's despair. "He won't do that. And I don't want him to."

"But then... he'll die," Dixie argues and pauses. I see her

inner battle, and I feel it too, like it's a jagged knife entering my heart, tearing it in two, because it is. We both want him here as long as possible, by any measure, but we both also don't want him suffering, unable to move or breath or talk, with no quality of life. "That's a long way off. Right?"

"It's not going to happen tomorrow," I reply, hoping the vagueness of that answer will give her some relief.

There's a knock at the door, and the lock turns, and it's cracked open slightly. "Everyone decent?"

Eli has learned, in the time he's been living with my sister, that it's not a good idea to burst into their apartment. Winnie and I are often here, borrowing clothes and half naked. "Come on in!"

His giant frame fills the entry. He gives me a friendly smile as he pulls down the hood to his jacket. Everything is wet, and I realize it must be raining. "Shit. I didn't bring an umbrella."

"You can borrow one of mine." Dixie walks over to her giant closet, the only storage space in their minuscule studio, and disappears inside. "Give me a second."

Eli hangs his jacket on a hook by the door and toes out of his shoes. He walks into the kitchen and pulls a Gatorade out of the fridge. "You look hot, Sadie. Girls' night with Winnie?"

"Something like that," I reply. My phone beeps, and I pull it out of my purse. It's a text from Griffin. He says he should be at my place in a couple minutes.

"Hey, are you still on night shifts?" Eli asks me.

"I'm switching to days soon for a couple weeks. Why?"

"Is Winnie home every night?" he asks, without answering my question.

I glance back to see if Dixie is emerging from the closet yet. She isn't. "She tutors until nine two nights a week. Monday and Wednesday."

"Cool," Eli says. I'm about to ask him what's with the third degree, but then there's a loud thump, followed by a curse word from Dixie, and then she emerges from the closet with a long teal umbrella with a wooden handle carved with daisies.

She hands it to me and leans in to whisper in my ear. "You know if you were wearing a white shirt I wouldn't even give you an umbrella. I'd let you get soaked so you could give him a preview of the merchandise."

"Hysterical, Dix." I use the nickname she doesn't like, and she sticks out her tongue at me while I swipe the umbrella from her.

"So where you going?" Eli asks again.

"Book club," I lie and grin. "Thanks for the top, little D."

"Have fun!" Dixie calls as I fling open her front door and head down the stairs. "I insist!"

I blow her a kiss and push open the door at the bottom of the stairs. It's not raining too badly, more of a mist right now, but I open the umbrella anyway as I stand against the brick wall and wait, since my hair tends to curl when it's wet, and that's not the look I'm going for tonight. It doesn't take long before his Range Rover pulls up at the curb. I see him through the rain-splattered window, and I instantly feel warm. I walk to the passenger door, closing the umbrella as I go. He jumps out and opens my door for me. As I slip by him, he leans in, his full lips grazing my cheek along with his delicious stubble. "God, it's good to see you again."

"You too," I whisper back, and a warm blush blooms from the exact spot he touched with those sexy lips. Thankfully, it's dark enough that he won't see. Jesus, I've dated before—a lot—so why does Griffin make me so loopy?

He gets in the car and eases away from the curb. "You look incredible."

I smile and glance at him. He's wearing a black cashmere sweater with a blue patterned button-down underneath, the cuffs and tails out. "So do you," I reply, which is true, but my other thought is that he has too many layers on. I want to able to feel him when I touch him, and I definitely intend to touch him.

"So..." he starts hesitantly. "I have a plan for tonight but, I'll be honest, this dating stuff isn't like riding a bike. I don't remember the right etiquette, and I probably wasn't very good at it when I was doing it anyway."

"Let me guess...you were either in college or in the juniors," I say. He nods, his expression slightly guarded but still sexy as the raindrops on the windshield catch the street lights and send pretty prisms of light across his rugged features. "You met girls after games, at bars and parties, and they always came up to you sweeter than stevia, and you never even really had to ask them out, it just happened."

"I-I plead the fifth," he stutters, visibly uncomfortable. My stomach drops, because that wasn't my intention.

I reach over and gently touch his biceps, which is solid and wide. He may be retired but his hockey body is still there. "Hey. I'm not judging. If you dated a bunny or two, or even ten, it's not a big deal. I get that there's little time in the world of a pro athlete to meet anyone outside of that life. In case you forgot, my brother used to score more off the ice than on, and I don't hold it against him. I ribbed him to death about it, but I didn't judge him. My sisters and I used to call him the Bunny Wrangler. For like four years the only gifts he got were bunny related. Shirts with bunnies on them, a coffee cup, pajama bottoms, slippers. You name it."

He chuffs out a laugh at that, and I join him. "God, it must have been hell for Jude growing up with the two of you."

"Three of us, the sorority, with my other sister, Winnie. We like to think we keep Jude grounded and humble," I reply in our defense. "So, Mr. Not Great at Dating, where are we headed?"

His expression grows serious again. "I have a couple ideas, but my first...and tell me if this makes you uncomfortable or it's too forward...but my first thought was a charcuterie board and some delicious wine overlooking the ocean."

"That sounds magical," I reply, and I'm truly excited, but he still looks a little concerned as he turns toward the Golden Gate Bridge.

"Great, but the thing is..." He steals a glance at me. "The place I have in mind is my place."

Oh.

"No inappropriate intentions, I swear on my mama," he says, quickly lifting his right hand off the steering wheel to make a cross over his heart to prove his honesty. "It's just I live on the water and have a terrific covered deck on the first floor. It's great to just sit out there and watch the rain on the water. It was the best place I could think of to just hang out and get to know each other."

He's so worried I will think he's picked his home simply so he could transition the date into the bedroom more easily and that will make me think he's a pig. Little does he know I've got a brand-new roll of condoms in my purse. "I think it sounds like a great idea. To be honest, you had me at charcuterie."

His expression relaxes into the sexy smile I am growing very attached to as we head into Marin County. Before I know it we're pulling into the marina, and I'm growing confused. I don't see houses or apartments.

He parks the car, jumps out, and holds out his hand to help me down as soon as I open my door. He doesn't let go of it either as he guides me toward a dock. It's lined with houseboats. "You weren't kidding. You live *on* the water."

"I do," he confirms and stops halfway down the row in front of a gorgeous two-story, modern, dark wood houseboat with black metal accents and a sleek natural cedar deck upstairs and down.

"This place is sexy as fuck," I blurt. I have never seen a dwelling that was just naturally so unique and manly. I know it's just wood and glass floating on water, but it oozes sex appeal. Just like Griffin.

"I don't know what to say to that." He chuckles and dips his head. "I'll make sure to note that on the listing if I ever sell."

"I might buy it from you," I counter as he opens the gate to the lower deck, jumps on, and turns to help me. I make it effortlessly, but purposely land as close to him as possible so our torsos touch. It makes a warm shiver dance up my spine.

He pauses, reaches out, and brushes the back of his fingertips across my cheek to my hairline. Then he dips his head, his lips next to my ear. "You smell incredible."

Heat explodes like a firework in my belly, shooting sparks through my veins. "It's an essential oil called Serenity."

He chuckles. "False advertising. Serenity is not what is happening inside me."

"What is happening?" I can barely hear the words as they come out of my mouth I'm so breathless, so I don't actually expect a response, but I get one.

He steps back, his lips brushing where his fingertips were moments before, and when he looks at me his eyes are hooded and dark with desire. "I'm not entirely sure, but it's good. Great, even."

"I agree."

He grins and grabs my hand again, pulling me toward two oversize black wicker deck chairs filled with crimson pillows and positioned in front of a table that has a place to build a fire in the middle. It really is better than any restaurant he could have chosen.

"If the rain stops I'll turn that on," he tells me and points to the fire pit as I let myself collapse into one of the chairs. Calling it comfortable would be an understatement. "In the meantime there's a throw over the back if you're cold and..."

I watch as he leans over me and flips a switch. The hem of his sweater and shirt lift as he extends his arm, and I can see the slightest sliver of hard abs, wrapped in caramel skin, with a glimpse of a thick, dark treasure trail. It's official—I'm wet. Damn, I have to get a grip on my hormones or I'm going to embarrass myself.

Heat lamps built into the overhang of the deck glow to life as he flips the switch he was reaching for. I'm instantly warm all over instead of just between my legs.

"I'll be back in a flash," he announces and unlocks the front door and steps inside the houseboat.

He returns a couple minutes later, and I realize he wasn't just throwing out an idea. He had planned this whole thing out and done prep. He's carrying a decanter full of wine and a big wood board with an array of meats, cheeses, fruits, and olives and pickles.

Both the wine and food are delicious. As we talk while we enjoy it, I realize how easy it is—like we've known each other forever. I don't remember a first date ever being so easy. I wonder if that kiss in the parking lot is the reason or if it's just because he's perfect for me.

I ask him about how he ended up in hockey. "My younger brother Hunter and I were rambunctious, destructive little kids, always breaking toys, lamps, furniture, windows. My parents put us in every sport they could—hockey, soccer, football, baseball, swimming, just to tire us out. I fell head over heels in love with it."

"And Hunter?"

"Sports made him miserable. By high school he was all about debate club and math club and making nerdism sexy," Griffin says, and I laugh. "His exact words. In fact, he put it in his yearbook blurb as his life goal."

"He sounds like a fun guy," I reply and pop a feta-stuffed olive into my mouth.

Griffin nods. "I wouldn't trade him for anything."

"That's how I feel about Winnie, Dixie, and Jude," I reply and swirl my wine in its glass. "But if you tell any of them, I will deny it."

He grabs a piece of salami. When he's done chewing, he sips his wine and leans back in his chair. "Enough about my kid brother. Tell me what makes Sadie Sadie?"

I wasn't expecting that question. It's so simple and yet...it has me dumbfounded. Of all the men I've met and dated, no one has asked me that. He must realize I've been knocked sideways by that question, because he smiles again. It's soft and kind and not amused or mocking at all, even though he could easily make fun of me since I'm coming off as a young adult who hasn't figured herself out yet.

"I'm sorry," I say sheepishly. "That's not supposed to be a stumper at twenty-seven."

"Don't be sorry," he replies easily and sips his wine. "Let me put it this way...what made Sadie Sadie before she became a rock in someone else's situation?"

My mouth falls open. His smile deepens, and it's so gentle and warm I want to wrap myself in it...in him.

"For me," Griffin says, "I was a stock market nerd who couldn't miss an episode of *The Walking Dead* and loved long, late nights with a good pinot and a true crime book before I had to become a rock for Charlie as she coped with the divorce." He puts his wineglass down as he reaches for the bottle and tops up my glass before refilling his own. "I still manage to sneak in a glass of pinot now and then, but I have to marathon *The Walking Dead* in the summer when she's at day camp. I don't have much time for the stock market anymore, and I'm usually too exhausted to read."

I am truly flabbergasted at how similar his life sounds to mine but for completely different reasons. Instantly—just like that—what I'm feeling for him starts shifting from simple attraction to an actual connection.

I gulp my wine, swallow, and confess. "I loved horses and raising hell at country bars with my sisters and watching reruns Bob Ross's TV show on lazy Sunday afternoons...before my dad was diagnosed."

He nods, without a blink, a hesitation, or a question. He knows what my dad has. I look out at the tranquil bay for a moment. The rain has stopped and the water is as smooth as glass. I inhale the salty air and turn back to him. "But it's not someone else's situation. Just like it isn't for you. My family is my world, and my dad is the center of that world. So I gladly gave up my life in Toronto and my hobbies, because being a rock for my family, while we all collectively lose our rock, is the only option."

He doesn't say anything. He just watches me intently, and I pray I don't look as close to tears as I am. Crying on a first date probably isn't proper etiquette. He tilts his head. Our eyes connect. The weight of his stare is making me breathless. I can't handle it. I feel like I'm in a car and there's a brick on the gas pedal. This attraction—this connection—is moving fast. Too fast for me to control. I'm suddenly searching for a way to slow down. I put my wineglass on the table. "So is there dessert? Please say you're a dessert man."

His expression lightens, and it's like a heavy blanket being pulled off me. I wanted it to happen, but now I'm missing its warmth. "Oh, I am a dessert man," he confirms and starts to stand. "I'll be right back."

Once he's disappeared inside, I can finally take a deep breath. I stand up and walk to the edge of the boat. Away from the warmth of the heat lamps, I grip the railing of the boat and take another breath, trying to clear my head and, more importantly, my heart.

13

GRIFFIN

I take longer than I need to in the kitchen grabbing dessert. I just need a second. This night—this woman—is intense. She isn't trying to be... in fact I think she's trying not to be. But every time our eyes meet it's like we're looking into each other, not at each other. And everything she says reaches me on levels I haven't felt... ever. I feel connected to her without even trying. It's just natural.

I glance at her through the window. She's moved to the railing, and she's looking out at the ocean. Under the moonlight, her hair is luminous and golden, like honey, and her pale skin almost looks like it's glowing. Her round ass is pushed out just a little as she leans on the rail and it is the most perfect thing I have ever seen. My dick is stirring in my pants, just from admiring her silhouette. It's like there's a chemical reaction in my blood from just the sight of her. I have got to rein it in because I don't want to freak her out. Or worse, make her think this is just about one thing. But damn, I do want that one thing...

I adjust the front of my jeans, pull my eyes away from her, and grab the plate on the counter, discarding the plastic wrap I had covered it with, before heading back outside. I place the plate on the table, grab the barbecue lighter, and light the fire pit in the middle of the table. She walks back over from the railing slowly, her blue eyes on the plate.

"S'mores?" she asks in awe, and I nod.

"I brought a bunch of different chocolate to try," I say and reach out to grab the metal skewers with the wood handles that I bought specifically for s'mores since they're Charlie's favorite. "There's dark chocolate, milk chocolate, and this Belgian chocolate that has a vein of peanut butter running through it."

"Oh, yes, please!" she almost squeals as she sits back down on her chair, inching forward to reach for the s'mores makings. I push the plate closer to her. I love that she reaches for the peanut butter chocolate first, because it's my favorite too.

I watch her place the chocolate between the graham crackers and then skewer a marshmallow. Her fingers are long and delicate like an artist's, and I instantly want to know what they would look like wrapped around my shaft. Shit, so much for keeping control. My thoughts are unmanageable.

She holds the marshmallow over the flames. She doesn't pull it back until it's gone from brown to black to on fire. Then she removes it, blows it out, and carefully slides it between the graham crackers next to the chocolate. She looks at me, her face alive with anticipation as she lifts it to her lips and takes a big bite.

"Mmm..." she moans, and the sound runs straight through my core and right to my dick. "This is sooo heavenly sinful."

"That makes no sense." I laugh softly, and she shrugs.

"Yeah, well, it's so good it's nonsensical," she replies and then pauses before holding out what's left of it. "Try."

I want to taste it...I want to taste a lot of things right now, but the s'more isn't the highest thing on this list. Still, I reach out and take her wrist in my hand and gently but firmly tug her up out of her seat and guide her to sit next to me on my chair. I slide over to make room for her and then, with my hand still wrapped around her wrist, I move the s'more toward my mouth and take a big, greedy bite.

It's fucking delicious, but not as delicious as the look of lust on her face. She's as turned on as I am. This current between us runs both ways. Thank the gods.

There's nothing left of the s'more now except a dollop of melted marshmallow on the pad of her thumb. We're both looking at that warm, sticky marshmallow and then...we're both looking at each other.

"You forgot some." She whispers the invitation I was hoping for.

With my fingers still wrapped around her wrist, I lean forward and pull her hand toward me and take her thumb into my mouth. She's moving, so by the time I've licked her thumb clean and released it she's straddling my lap, facing me. Her blue eyes have darkened and are focused on my mouth. Her bottom lip is pushed out, pouty with need. I release her wrist and curl my hand around the back of her neck, guiding her mouth to mine.

Our first kiss was the most passionate, fiery, deep kiss I've ever had. And this one blows it right out of the water. Any re-

maining thoughts of taking this slow or easing up no longer
exist. All that exists is the press of her body on mine, the soft
gasp that escapes her lips as my free hand drops to her ass and
pulls her even closer, and the sweet, sugary taste of her tongue
against mine.

Her hands grip my shoulders and she rolls her hips, pressing herself onto my hardness. I cup her perfect ass as she does
it again and moves her hands up my neck and into my hair.
She laces the short ends through her fingers and tugs on it. I
nip and suck on her bottom lip. "All those inappropriate intentions you were worried about," she whisper-pants against my
ear, and my lips lick and suck my way down her slender neck.
"They're appropriate. And I want them all to happen."

I stand, in one smooth motion, lifting her with me. She
gasps, not expecting it, but quickly adapts, effortlessly wrap-
ping her legs around my waist and her lips around my earlobe.
As I walk us into the boat, she nips my lobe with her teeth,
then whispers, "I have wanted your dick in my mouth since I
first laid eyes on you."

"And I'm all for that, but first I'm going to taste you," I reply gruffly and march through the house and up the stairs. She
wraps a hand more tightly around my neck so that the other
one can slip between our torsos and start undoing my belt. "I
want my lips on your pussy more than I want to breathe air
right now. I bet you're sweeter than that s'more."

"Oh, God..." Her voice is already trembling.

"I want your voice to quiver until it breaks, until you can't
speak, until you can't do anything but pant," I whisper against
her throat, moving my lips along her jugular. Her heart is

pumping so damn hard, and I haven't even gotten her clothes off yet. I pause on the small landing and press her up against the wall, next to the shelves where my hockey trophies are displayed, and I find her lips again with mine as I snap my hips and push my hardest place into her softest.

"Harder," she begs into the kiss, and I do it again, harder. She moans. It's primal and unfeigned and it makes my blood turn to fire.

I pull her off the wall and climb the rest of the stairs so fast I'm almost tripping as I take a sharp right into my bedroom and drop her, and myself, roughly onto the king-size bed. I didn't bother to make it this morning, and there's a full laundry basket in the corner of the room and a towel on the floor in the bathroom because I really, truly, honestly didn't think we'd be here tonight. I was trying to be a gentleman. She doesn't want a gentleman; she wants raw, rough, and dirty. She wants me unfiltered, and I'm going to give it to her.

She makes quick work of the button and fly on my pants, like she did my belt before it. I feel her fingertips, warm and firm, graze my shaft through my underwear, and I bite down on the crook of her neck. She arches her back, and I take the opportunity to finally slip my hands under her clothing, sliding her shirt up her body.

Her belly is taut and her skin is like silk against my lips. My mouth trails my hands, making their way up from her stomach to her ribs to the edge of her black lace bra. She's not timid or hesitant as she grabs the hem of her shirt and pulls it up over her head, letting it fall to my floor. I grab the cups of her bra and dip them down so my fingers can roll her left nipple while my lips cover her right. She sighs and arches her back again. I move my mouth to her other nipple and my hand to the button on her jeans.

Her hands are reaching for my dick again, so I stop to grab them both and push them into the pillows above her head, pressing my body over hers. "You have too many clothes on," she complains.

"Patience, love," I murmur, and she makes a disgruntled sound in her throat, which makes me smile. "Now I'm going to make you wait even longer."

She starts to make the noise again, catches herself, and stops biting her bottom lip. "Don't hurt yourself," I warn as I start to kiss my way down her body again. "I'm going to need those lips later. Around my cock, like you promised."

I don't waste time as I make my way down to those jeans again. I get them undone, and as I nip her hipbone, I command, "Lift."

She raises her hips, and in one hard tug I get her jeans down her thighs. Her black lace underwear stays put. Not what I'd planned, but I can work with it. I use one hand to get her jeans down past her knees and as she kicks her way out of them, I settle between her legs and slide my tongue across the skin next to the lacy edge of her panties.

I run a finger down the center of her panties, and it's not just damp—it's soaked. I quiver with desire, every fucking part of me. I kiss her on top of the lace. "Griffin...please lick me."

"Love, I am going to do more than lick you," I warn and slip two fingers past the lace barrier. "I'm going to worship you."

I pull the lace to the side, and before she can respond, my mouth is on her. Her thighs shake the second I touch her. I thought if and when we ever got to this stage that I would be nervous, tentative because it's been a long time since I've done this to a woman. But any nerves I had have been burned away by desire, along with Sadie's reaction to me. She's pure and visceral, moaning and panting at every pass of my tongue, brush of my lips, press of my fingers. Her legs are splayed, her back is arched, her breath is ragged. And then a tremor ripples through her body, and she pushes her pussy into my mouth and wails my name. No, I'm not nervous. I'm Captain Fucking America.

But I don't get to revel in my achievements, because despite the hot, red flush on her cheeks, the wobbliness of her limbs, she's pulling herself off the bed. I sit back on my knees and watch her, amused and satisfied that the way she's moving, like a baby deer on ice, is because of me. She finally makes it to her own knees, facing me, and starts to pull off my sweater.

"Too many clothes," she repeats her complaint from earlier. I help her on her quest to get me naked, pulling the sweater over my head, but as I reach for the first button on my shirt she's already got three undone, and before I know it, she's shoving it off my body.

"I've got a lot of payback headed your way," Sadie warns, kissing her way down my chest. I've never been happy to be targeted for revenge until now. I'd make a snarky comment about that, but I'm too busy enjoying the feel of her lips as they make their way across my torso. I'm so engrossed in the feel of that, I barely realize that she's gotten my pants down until her lips brush my tip. Oh. My. God. It's like a jolt of electricity through my entire body.

And then she's suddenly got all of me in her warm, soft mouth and I've died and gone to heaven. I know it's been a while since my sexual contact has been anything other than my hand, but this is incredible. And because of that I'm having a hard time holding back...I want to buck my hips, pushing myself deeper into her mouth, and I want to explode—soon. I find myself twisting her hair in my hands, and I worry it's hurting her, so I start to let go, but that just makes her stop moving. Her big blue eyes look up at me from under her thick lashes and her mouth pulls back just long enough for her to whisper, "Don't let go. I like it."

So as she takes me in again, her tongue swirling over my shaft, I grab her hair again. She moves faster and deeper until...yeah, I'm going to come. I pull my hips back, but she grabs my ass with the hand not wrapped around my dick and holds me in place. Then she sucks harder and...I lose it completely. My knees shaking, my cock twitching, and my hips bucking. And I swear, I hear bells.

She pulls back and stands up way quicker than I would like. I force my eyes to focus and my head to clear. Her eyes are darting around the room. She gives me a quick but victorious smile, clearly pleased with herself. "Where are my pants?" she asks, and I'm confused. Is she leaving? "That's my phone."

Oh. Right. The bells I thought were caused in my brain by the earth-shattering orgasm are actually her phone ringing. I turn around and point. She darts over to the foot of the bed and picks up her pants, digging the phone out of the back pocket.

She turns her back to me as she answers, which is fine because she's still naked and I can admire her beautiful body, including that incredible ass, which looks as tight and fine in the moonlight coming in through the open wall of windows as it felt in my hands.

"What?" she says into the phone. Her tone isn't annoyed but definitely terse, like the person on the other end knows they're interrupting something, which makes me think it must be one of her sisters. Probably Dixie, since I know that I picked her up at Dixie's apartment. She doesn't know I know that—she didn't say it outright to me, but I dropped Eli off there after practice once when his car was at the mechanic's.

"Whoa! Slow down!" Sadie says into her phone.

I reach down and grab a pair of shorts on the laundry pile and pull them on. She is listening to a high-pitched voice on the other end of the line. I can hear it, but can't make out the words. "What part of the leg? Compound or stable fracture? Is there a bone protruding? Okay. That's good. Are you sure it's broken? How the hell did this happen? Where was his nurse?"

It's her dad. Shit.

"Okay. I'm on my way. I'll meet you there. Jen is head nurse tonight, and she's a little abrupt," Sadie says as she walks toward the door to my room. I trail behind her. "Drop my name. It will make her nicer. She likes me. I'll be there as soon as I can."

She hangs up and I grab her arm just as she's about to walk into the hall. "What's wrong? Is it your dad?"

She nods and swallows a moment, clearly struggling to be calm. "He tried to walk without help for some reason. He was in the den, and the nurse had left him for a second, and I don't know. I don't know what he was thinking, but he fell and they think he broke his leg. They called an ambulance. I have to meet them at the hospital."

"Okay. I can drive you."

"No I'll call a Lyft." She shakes her head and then tucks some hair behind her ear and turns to my hall again. I refuse to let go of her arm, and when she turns back, her expression is annoyed.

"Sadie. I will drive you," I repeat, and then my eyes drop quickly and lift to hers again. "After you put on clothes."

She glances down, and hot pink color explodes on her apple cheeks. "Shit. Right. Oh, my God, I was actually going to walk out of here."

"You would have felt a draft on the deck and figured it out," I tell her as she walks back toward the bed and grabs her underwear. She dresses at lightning speed.

"Can I use the bathroom?"

"Hallway. First door on the right."

She disappears, and I change back into my jeans and grab a T-shirt, ready to drive her. She emerges from the bathroom a couple moments later, and she's texting on her phone. "My sister Winnie. The ambulance is there, and they're loading him up."

"Okay. That's good," I say and rub her shoulder, trying to be soothing. "Let's get you there."

"I called a Lyft," she replies and shows me the app on her

phone. There's a little black car icon moving toward the marina. "I had a good time. No, wait. I had a great time. But let's just press the pause button here. Let me go and deal with this, and then maybe we can unpause this—right here in this room—again sometime soon?"

She kisses me on the cheek and starts down the stairs before I can even respond, so I follow. She knows I'm right behind her, so she keeps talking. "I'm really sorry, I just..."

"Don't apologize," I reply. "It's your dad. I get it. I just wish you'd let me drive you."

"This..." She stops, turns to face me and points to the ceiling. "That...what just happened. Was...well, it was fucking magical for me, and I am definitely hoping to continue that and see how much more magical we can be. But...this...this thing with my family. My life right now. It's not magical. It's kind of a nightmare, and I'm not ready for you to walk into the nightmare. I need to keep the unicorn away from the darkness."

She turns and keeps walking toward the front door. I follow her. "I don't quite understand all of that, but I think I get it. I guess. It's just I can totally handle the darkness, Sadie. I am not a stranger to it myself. And did you just call me a unicorn?"

"Yes," she confirms and pauses on my deck, as she glances at her app again. Apparently her ride is about to enter the marina. "Because up until tonight I didn't know sexual chemistry like this existed. I thought it was a myth, like the unicorn."

I laugh at that despite the seriousness of the more pressing situation at hand. She looks embarrassed again. "Sorry. I am being blunt, and you're probably thinking I'm insane, but if having a dad dying prematurely has taught me anything, it's say what you mean and don't sugar-coat shit because you might not get a chance to be honest or say how you really feel later."

Headlights glare as a Prius enters the marina. She opens the gate, and I help her onto to dock and follow her up the ramp. "Listen, never apologize for being honest. Or giving me compliments like that."

We reach the car, and I step in front of her to open the door. She gives me a grateful smile, and I take the moment to lean down and kiss her quickly but softly. "For the record, it was fucking magical for me too. And I definitely want to continue this when everything is back on track with your dad."

She nods and kisses me again. "I'll text you."

She slips into the back seat, and the Prius drives away.

14

SADIE

I rush through the doors of the ER and instantly spot Winnie and Dixie. Winnie sees me first and jumps up. Her eyes are bloodshot, and she looks distressed. Dixie jumps up. She's trying to be braver, like she always tries to be, but I can still tell she's been crying, and her hand is shaking as she reaches out to hug me. I hug her and then move on to Winnie, who clings to me like I'm the floating door in *Titanic*.

"Where's everyone?" I ask. I have this weird reaction to my siblings being upset. The more distraught they are, the calmer I become. I think it's a side effect from my trauma training. The ER gets a lot of emotional patients and family, and nurses have to keep their cool.

"Mom is in with Dad, but the room is small, so they asked us to wait here," Dixie explains. "Jude is on his way. Eli is getting us coffee, even though I said I didn't want any."

I nod. Winnie sniffs loudly, her face still buried in the front of my shirt. "Let's sit back down and I'll see what I can find out."

I walk Winnie backward toward the row of plastic chairs and deposit her in one. Dixie sits beside her and takes her hand. I head to the desk at the front. Damn, it's Kina. She's a pediatric nurse but picks up shifts in the ER sometimes to make extra cash. She doesn't do more than she has to, and sometimes you even have to push her to do that. I walk over and smile. "Hey, Kina."

"Oh, hey, Sadie, what are you doing here?"

I blink. "Umm...my dad was admitted."

She looks confused. "Mr. Chang? The guy with the chest pain?"

"No. The man with the same last name as me. Randy Braddock," I reply, trying not to sound annoyed. "Possible broken leg. Can you pull up his file and let me know what's going on?"

"I guess." She shrugs and leans over to type on the keyboard. She turns the monitor a little so I can read it myself.

"Thanks, Kina."

"Hey..." she calls as I start to walk back to my sisters. "Does that mean your brother is coming in tonight?"

"Yes," I reply and frown as I add pointedly, "With his wife and child."

"Oh. Bummer."

I ignore her and rejoin Winnie and Dixie. "They think it's a dislocated hip, not a broken leg. They're going to bring him down for X-rays. Mom should be back out here soon."

Dixie nods. Winnie sniffs. I sigh. Fuck. This isn't good. More times than not what they first think is a dislocated hip, they discover is broken once they do the X-ray. Broken hips are filled with complications for people like my dad who already have compromised health. At the very least it means a prolonged hospital stay. But I'm not going to share that info with my sisters until we know more.

Eli rounds the corner at the other end of the waiting room carrying a tray of coffees. When no one takes them from him, he puts the tray down on the empty seat next to me and drops into the chair across from us. Our eyes meet, and he looks confused. "Where were you?"

"Out for dinner," I reply vaguely.

"In a tornado?" he asks and waves a finger around in front of my face. "Your hair is like...a disaster. And your shirt is on inside out and backward."

I glance down, and I see the little white tag that should be inside my shirt is between my shoulders, staring back at me. Damn. I shrug. "I went to the gym and was rushing to get here."

"Really?" Eli questions, and then he motions to my sisters beside me. "Because judging by the look on Winnie and Dixie's faces you're feeding me bullshit and they know the truth."

I turn and look at my sisters. They're both grinning wildly. I glare at them.

"Where is he?" Jude's deep voice cuts through the room.

Zoey is right beside him with Declan strapped to her chest in a Baby Bjorn. I stand up as he and Zoey walk toward us, and I give him the recap of what I know. He runs a hand roughly through his blond hair, and Zoey lays a hand on his shoulder and squeezes. He reaches up and takes it in his own as I reach for Declan and rub his head. His hair is like peach fuzz, and the feel of it is comforting. God, I want him to know my dad...I want my kids to know...

"Hey," Jude says to me. I look over at him to find his face panicked. "Is this serious? Like more than I think? Because you look like you might cry."

"Is she crying?" Winnie asks, her voice cracking. "Because if Sadie is crying, then someone isn't telling us something. This is a big deal, isn't it? Oh, God..."

I force myself to look relaxed. "I'm not crying. Calm down, Win. I don't know anything more than you told me on the phone. Let's not freak out yet."

"Do you want to call Ty?" Zoey asks.

"No. Things are bad enough," Winnie replies and walks away.

"You know your shirt is on inside out and backward?" Jude asks me. His eyes narrow, and that devious little brain of his starts spinning at a lightning-fast pace. I can virtually see it happen behind his eyes, which are almost identical to mine. "Where were you tonight?"

Thankfully, my mom walks out to join us, and the focus turns to her. Somehow she looks older than she did when I left the house this afternoon. And more frail. We all walk toward her, but Jude and I pull ahead of the pack.

"He's in X-ray," my mom explains. "The first doctor thought his hip was dislocated but the second is thinking it's broken."

"Which doctors?" I ask.

"Dr. Murray thinks dislocated, but he called Dr. Staal for

a consult, and he thinks broken," Mom says. I feel my heart drop from my chest into the soles of my shoes. Murray is just a resident. She's bright but still new, and Dr. Staal is one of our best orthopedic doctors. Chances are he's right. Fuck.

"Okay, well, there's nothing that can be done or decided until he's out of X-ray and we know what we're dealing with, so let's just sit," I say and wrap an arm around my mom's shoulders, guiding her to the chairs.

"I got you a chai tea. I know it's your favorite," Eli says and plucks one of the cups from the cardboard holder. I smile at him approvingly.

"Sweetie," my mom says as she sips the tea. "Your shirt is on wrong."

"Yeah." I nod and grit my teeth. Why does my family have to pick this moment to notice everything about me? I'm a middle child. I'm supposed to be ignored, for crying out loud.

"She's trying a new look," Jude informs her. "I'm calling it 'Hot Mess.' It actually really suits her personality when you think about it."

"You're lucky your child is here or else I would be calling you lots of colorful, accurate names right now," I warn him, and Zoey smiles.

"I can do earmuffs if you'd like," she tells me and covers little Declan's ears with the palms of her hands. Even my mom laughs at that.

Dixie and Jude picked perfect mates. They aren't additions to our family; they're both like members we didn't realize we had. They're perfect. Unlike Ty, Winnie's boyfrenemy. I wonder how Griffin would fit into this crazy family tree. I feel like he'd be the same, just fit right in like a branch that was already a part of our tree. I mean after all, I feel abnormally close and comfortable with him after just one date. I give my head a shake. It's crazy. Thinking about him with my family...how he'd fit in...is getting ahead of myself. It's inappropriate and borderline insane. But so was kissing him in the parking lot and having our first date at his house and ending it with oral sex, but yet...it still feels right.

"Oh, my gosh!" My mom gasps, and it startles me back to reality. Everyone turns toward her, on edge, panicked. She's looking only at me. "You were on your date tonight! Your shirt is on inside out because you were on your date."

Dixie breaks down into giggles. Eli's jaw drops, his mouth a gaping O. Jude's eyes bug out of his head, Zoey looks excited, and Winnie looks confused. I want the floor to open up and swallow me.

"Oh, honey, I'm not judging," my mom whispers. "I know you're a smart woman and you'll always make smart choices...and use protection."

Everyone starts to laugh, and Dixie, who was already laughing, takes it to a new level and snorts. Jude is the only one not laughing. "Who the hell are you dating?"

"Not dating. One date. And it's none of your business," I counter.

"One date and your shirt is on backward," Jude retorts.

"Really? You of all people are going down that road?" Zoey warns him. "Remember how when we met you were on the verge of moving apartments to avoid your hookups?"

"I'm not judging..." he replies with his hands in the air

like he's got a gun pointed at him. He directs his stare at me again. "But Sadie is smarter than me, and I know she doesn't wear backward shirts for just anyone. So we should meet him. I get final approval on all their serious boyfriends."

"Glad I made the cut," Eli pipes up.

"Barely," Jude kids with a grin.

"You'll be lucky if you get an invite to my wedding," I tell my brother.

"We're talking marriage?" Winnie looks horrified. "Already?"

"No. It was just a random statement." I sigh. "You people are exhausting."

"I'm sure it's not us," Dixie mutters. "It's whatever caused you to put your shirt on inside out and backward."

"I hate you," I reply.

"I hate you—because that's my shirt, and now I have to dry-clean it," she retorts.

I am about to dare her to hold it up under a black light first, but then I see Dr. Staal walking toward us. Mom sees him too, and we both stand. The family follows our lead. I can tell by the expression on his face that it's the worst possible outcome.

I'm right. He explains Dad has fractured his hip and will need to surgery. He'll have to stay in the hospital for a while.

"The surgery is fairly routine, but Mr. Braddock's condition does make it a bit more complicated for both the surgery and the recovery," Dr. Staal warns. I reach out and take my mom's hand.

"But he'll recover, right?" Winnie ask, her voice trembling.

"I think it'll be a long road, but I'm hopeful, yes," Dr. Staal says. "Surgery will happen tomorrow morning. I'll be doing it myself."

"Thank you," my mom says as Jude looks over at me. He's wanting confirmation that Staal is the best option. He's not going to let anyone but the best work on our dad. I give him a solid nod, because Staal is the best we have in orthopedics and even one of the best in the state.

"You can see him now," Dr. Staal says. "We've moved him up to the fifth floor. Room fifty-eight."

Everyone walks to the elevators. I pause by the women's restroom. "I'll meet you all up there."

Jude glances at the restroom door. "Fixing your shirt so Dad doesn't notice too?"

"Shut up! And yes," I bark back and disappear into the restroom to sounds of my family laughing their dumb asses off.

15

GRIFFIN

I glance at my phone. It's been two hours since Sadie's dad went in for surgery. Is that long enough to fix a hip? I wonder as I put my bag in the back seat next to Charlie's booster seat and jump into the driver's seat. The team leaves on a seven-day road trip this afternoon. Management has made the decision to send the entire coaching staff, which is rare, but we've been in a losing streak and we're on the verge of falling out of playoff contention, so they're pulling out all the stops.

Of course they didn't tell us until this morning, and so I have to change my schedule with Charlie...which is going to give Lauren fodder for her custody case. Hunter swears it won't be a big deal and that the case is still bullshit, but I still worry. A lot. I pull up in front of Lauren's place and don't see her car in the driveway. I should have called, but if I called she wouldn't let me come over, and I wanted to say goodbye to Charlie myself. I'm at the point where I wonder if my messages to Charlie via Lauren are getting through.

Despite not seeing her car I head up the path to the front door. I ring the doorbell and wait. I'm there so long I'm positive she's not home, so I pull my cell out of my pocket and sit on the swinging bench I installed on the porch for Lauren the day she moved in…when we were on better terms and trying to be actual friends. I start to text her, but then suddenly the front door opens and my daughter is standing there grinning with joy.

"Dad!" she squeals, delighted, and holds open her arms. "Bring it in!"

I laugh despite the fact I'm stunned she opened the front door by herself. I didn't think Lauren let her do that. I don't let her do that. "Hey, Charlie bug! Why are you opening the door by yourself?"

"Because I saw it was you on the security camera," she explains. "I promise I wouldn't do it if it wasn't you. I remember what you told me."

"Oh. Okay." I pick her up, which she normally tells me she's too old for now, but she doesn't complain this time. "I came to say goodbye in person. I have to go on a business trip."

"So I don't get to go to the boat this weekend?" She looks devastated, and the blood pumping through my heart gets thick with guilt.

"Not this weekend. I'm gone until next week," I explain, and her face falls even more. I suddenly wish I were an accountant or a lawyer like Hunter and could have more control over my schedule. Of course I'd be miserable, but maybe that's the tradeoff. "I'm here to talk to Mom and see if I can come get you that night, as soon as I'm back, and we can go to the boat then."

"Mom's not here," she says, still pouting.

I try not to show the concern on my face at her comment. "So Rosa is here?"

She shakes her head and wiggles to be put down. As I place her on the ground I'm struggling to stay calm. We had a rule. A verbal agreement that we both approve all sitters, and Rosa is the only one I've approved. "So who is home with you, nugget face?"

"My face is not a nugget, Dad!" she complains and crosses her arms.

I nudge her back into the house and step into the front hall with her. My eyes sweep what I can see, the front hall, stairs, the door to the kitchen, and a touch of the family room beyond it. "Who's with you, Charlie?"

"Cale."

"You're here alone? With Cale?"

She senses my fury. She thinks she's in trouble. She puts her little left thumb up to her mouth, like she's going to suck it, but she doesn't. "Mommy just went to do her hair and said she would be back soon."

"Okay, baby." I smile at her and run a hand over her head, her curls soft and springy under my hand. "Where is Cale?"

"In the den, but be quiet, Daddy. He's napping," she tells me cautiously.

"Are you f—" The obscenity dies on my lips as her innocent eyes star back at me. "Are you up for some ice cream?"

"Really?"

"Really." I smile. "Let's go. Mommy will meet us there."

"Okay!" She heads back out the front door, bouncing toward my car, gleeful and without a care in the world...because she has no idea I am so upset I could explode right now.

I take her to the closest ice cream place, which is actually gelato, but she doesn't know the difference. She orders a bowl of cookies and cream, and I text her mom as she eats it, explaining to me how she learned in school this week that zebras aren't born with stripes. My text to Lauren is simple:

I'm at Casa Gelato with our daughter. Meet us. NOW.

She doesn't respond, but I know she got it. She can sense the fury and also probably knows she doesn't have a leg to stand on here. By the time Charlie is licking the ice cream bowl, Lauren's Mercedes is parking next to my Rover.

She gets out of the car, fresh blowout catching the breeze, and saunters over to us casually. She smiles at Charlie. "Hey, Charlie! Did Daddy surprise you with ice cream?"

"Best surprise ever!" Charlie proclaims. "Other than a puppy."

Oh, God...I ignore that and look at Lauren. "Let's go to the park across the street for a second."

"Cool!" Charlie jumps up. Today is such an unexpected treat for her but an unwanted, hate-filled battle for her parents. Welcome to divorce.

We follow her to the crosswalk, probably looking like a cute little urban family as we watch her look both ways and then hit the button and start to cross. As soon as we're on the other side, Charlie runs straight for the jungle gym, and I turn to Lauren. She holds her manicured hand up to stop me before I can speak.

"You aren't supposed to pick her up until tonight at six," Lauren snaps. "You don't get to break the arrangement to do spot checks on us. And for the record, I was gone forty minutes. Rosa couldn't come in today and Cale, being the incredible boyfriend he is, volunteered to watch her."

"Cale was passed out in the den," I reply through teeth so gritted my jaw already aches. "He probably doesn't even know we're gone. She answered the door by herself. And I wasn't checking up on you. I came to tell you and Charlie that I have a business trip and can't make it tonight, or any night this week."

"Are you insane?" Lauren's fury now matches my own. "You can't just take her out without telling Cale. He's probably frantic right now looking for her."

I chuff. "Yeah. So he called you? He's worried about her? He's awake? I fucking doubt it. And for the record, I didn't approve him as a caregiver. We both need to approve her caregivers."

"He's not a caregiver, he's my boyfriend. He's part of the family now, whether you like it or not," Lauren barks back. She pauses and puts on a fake smile as Charlie yells at us to watch her go down the slide.

"Good job, kiddo!" I call out, and she gives me a fist pump. God, I love this kid. I turn to Lauren, trying to remember Charlie wouldn't exist without her. "I don't care who you date, but I care who you leave alone with my daughter. I don't want it to be Cale. Not right now. All I know about him is he thinks it's appropriate to fall asleep in the middle of the afternoon while he's tending to a six-year-old. And that doesn't work for me."

"Well, switching our schedule whenever you want doesn't work for me," she snaps back. "Which is why I'm getting sole custody."

"You aren't," I reply. "And you knew, the judge knew, everyone knew that my job would have some challenges. But we also both know your alimony is as high as it is because of this job, so you're either flexible with me or I get a job that doesn't require travel, that pays less. I'll do it, Lauren. If it means you stop trying to take Charlie away. I will fucking do it."

She frowns and turns away, focusing on Charlie as she swings from one monkey bar to the next like a champ. Lauren reaches up and runs a hand through her hair before adjusting her Gucci sunglasses. I know what she's going to say next...because she loves Charlie but she also loves money. "Just go on your hockey trip, and you can see her when you get back. Even though this totally messes with my plans for the week."

"You can have Hunter and Mia take her for a night or two. They'd love it and she'd love it and they're approved caretakers," I tell her calmly. I glance at my watch. Fuck, I have to go or I will miss the team plane.

"Charlie! I've got to fly!" I call out, and she starts to run over.

"I'm going to make a note of this to chat about at the hearing," Lauren whispers, not willing to back the fuck down.

"You do that." I nod. "Don't forget to wake Cale up when you get home. He's a sound sleeper."

She tries to obliterate me with the glare. I bend down and hug my daughter. "Be good, Charlie, and call me whenever you want. I love you."

"Love you too, Dad." She hugs me back as fiercely as she does everything. I swear to God this girl is worth all the drama with her mom and so much more.

"No raisins," I whisper, and she giggles as I squeeze her nose.

"What was that?" Lauren asks.

"Nothing," I mutter and turn and walk away.

I call Hunter on the way to the airport. He's in court so I call his wife, Mia, and update her on the situation. Mia is just as furious as I am that Lauren left Charlie alone with Cale, which makes me feel good. She also reassures me that Lauren pursuing this will do nothing but piss off the judge. Mia is a landscape architect, but I still value her opinion, and she calms me down.

At the airport I check my watch again. The flight doesn't leave for forty minutes, and since we're flying private, we don't have a long security line. I get to the gate and find Jude and Eli instantly. I sigh in relief, because I know that if they're both here, Sadie's dad's surgery went fine. I have been trying not to badger her with texts, but I've been thinking about her nonstop since she left me last night.

I decide now is the time to reach out again, since her dad must be out of surgery. I send her a quick text telling her I'm leaving on the road trip with the team and asking her how she's holding up. By the time we have to board the plane, I haven't gotten a response, and now I have to turn off my phone so I'm worried.

As I settle in my seat, Eli walks down the aisle, talking with his brother and team captain, Levi. I stand up, pretending I have to get something from my bag in the overhead bin. Levi squeezes by me, but as Eli passes I stop him. "Hey, do you have a minute?"

He nods. "Sure, Coach."

I motion for him to sit beside me. I start by talking about the teams we're facing on the road trip. It's not that I don't care about that—I do, and we need a good strategy—but I can talk about that later at practice. I'm only talking about it now so I can segue to something else. "How are you feeling?"

He nods. "One hundred percent."

"No headaches?"

"None," Eli says, and I stare at him, trying to read his face. I think he isn't lying. He's got that scar on his neck to remind him how serious injuries can be. "I'm good, Sully. I swear."

"Speaking of recovery…" I clear my throat, which sounds as awkward as it feels. "How's Dixie's dad doing?"

He looks perplexed. "Mr. Braddock?"

I nod. "I heard he had a fall."

"Yeah. How did you know?"

I shrug, trying to be nonchalant but not quite pulling it off. He looks even more puzzled. "I don't remember. I might have overheard the coach talking about it or Jude or something. Anyway, I was just wondering how he's doing."

"Good," Eli says. "He had surgery this morning, and he's in recovery and didn't have any complications. Jude wanted to stay home, but of course he can't. And Sadie insisted it wasn't necessary. She promised she'd update him daily and keep the rest of the sorority sane."

"Sorority?"

Eli laughs. "That's what Jude calls his sisters. You'd get it if you saw the three of them together. They're like this hive-minded girl gang. They torture him and protect him at the exact same time and, honestly, I'd say it's one of the most dysfunctional functioning families ever. Cracks me up."

"Do you have sisters?" I ask, still trying to cover my curiosity about Sadie's family.

"Nope. Just Levi and my brother Todd, so this sister thing is foreign to me," he says, and luckily his skepticism seems to be quelled now.

"We'll talk more about strategy at the practice when we land," I say, essentially dismissing him. He gets up and makes his way back to a seat next to his brother, but I can't help wondering if he's going to wonder about my invasive questions again.

Damn. I now get to spend the rest of the four-hour flight worrying I might have just made Sadie's life harder...or made my goalie think I'm some kind of weirdo.

16

SADIE

This has been the longest week of my life," I confess to Griffin as I lean back on the gross old couch in the nurses' lounge. It's vinyl and a color that can only be described as baby poop, at least according to the NICU nurses. It's got stains that can't be wiped off and an ugly tear in the left arm. Normally I avoid it and sit in one of the plastic chairs around the long table near the fridge, but I'm just so damn tired. So tired I'm confessing my true feelings to a guy I barely know. I sigh into the phone. "Sorry. I must sound so overdramatic, and I shouldn't be dumping on you."

"You don't and this isn't dumping," he says and his tone is soothing without being patronizing. "Your family is going through something big."

"Yeah, but you don't have to hear about all my family drama."

"I don't have to, but I want to," he replies firmly. "You don't have to keep things bottled up."

"How's Charlie? She must have been happy to see you." I'm very ready to change the subject.

"She was thrilled," Griffin says, and I can hear the relief in his voice. "We had a really fun night. I dropped her off at school this morning and I'll have her back on the weekend," Griffin says. "But for now the team is on a break for a couple days, and I was hoping you might be free tonight?"

"I am." I have never been so excited for a day off before in my life.

"So it's a date then," he confirms.

"Yes." I feel instantly better—happier, more awake, more alive. "When and where?"

"I can pick you up from work if you're down with that, and we can just go grab a bite and a drink and see where the night leads," he replies, and I really like the open-ended way that statement ends.

"That works," I reply. I'm grinning like a lunatic—a horny lunatic. I glance at the industrial clock on the wall. "I have to get back. My break is about to end."

"Tonight, love," he promises. I hang up and take a deep, grounding breath. I'm not sure what's more ridiculous, the fact that he calls me "love" when we've only known each other for a few weeks or the fact that when he says it, I feel euphoric.

Unfortunately the feeling doesn't last. My shift is chaos. The ER is packed with everything from toddlers with stomach bugs to heart attacks and car accidents. If I wasn't on a day shift I would go outside and look for a full moon. I have to call for a neuro doctor twice because of head injuries, and Dr.

Luongo is the one who responds. Bob is friendly and cracks a couple jokes with me, which is great. It's the first I've seen him since he asked me out, and I'm so glad nothing's changed and we really can be friends.

The day is so crazy that I don't have time to run upstairs and say a quick hello to my dad. My shift finally ends, and I'm blissfully off the clock for seventy-two hours. I change into street clothes—boyfriend jeans and an oversize T-shirt with some floral Toms. I normally just come and go in my scrubs, but keep this outfit in my locker as backup for when I have days like this and my scrubs are covered in something gross—in this case, toddler puke—and I can't commute in them. I wish I'd brought something fancier or sexier as a backup outfit, but it is what it is. My excitement over spending time with Griffin trumps my insecurity. I hum to myself as I head out of the nurses' lounge.

"Hey!" I look up from where I've frozen with my purse and my coat in my hand near the nurses' station. Jude is walking toward me. "Have to give any creepy old guys a sponge bath?"

"Yeah, but I like it. Old creepy men turn me on," I tell him and lean forward, darkening my expression. "The more back hair the better. I love to run my hands through it, and sometimes I don't use the sponge to clean them…I use my tongue."

"Stop! You need a better sense of humor," he lectures, and I swear his complexion is green. "Gross is not always funny."

"Really? Then why does your expression when I talk like that make me laugh so hard?" I ask, giggling. "Here to see Dad?"

"I've already seen him," he says. "When I wheeled him over to the diner across the street for dinner with the family."

"What?" My heart stops. I realize how vehemently I don't want to share Griffin with my family. I want to keep him all for myself. I want time to savor this new relationship.

"His doctor gave the okay," Jude explains. "I came back to get you so you could join us."

Oh, shit. I fake a yawn. A big one. He laughs. "Sorry. It's been one hell of a day. I think I need to pass on dinner with you guys."

He makes a face. "It's five o'clock, Sadie. You're going to go home and go to bed?"

"Maybe."

He rolls his eyes and reaches out and tugs on my arm. "Come on. Dad loves it when we're all together."

"I'll meet you there."

"Why? Everyone is waiting for us in the parking lot."

Shit. Shit. Shit. "The whole family is in the parking lot?"

He nods and tilts his head, his eyes narrowing. He's beginning to figure out I'm internally freaking out. So I do the only thing I can think of doing and relent. "Let's go then."

As we walk toward the doors, I dig my phone out of my purse and start to text Griffin to cancel and apologize profusely, but I know in my soul it's too late. He's probably already in the parking lot, and this is about to turn into a family reveal, whether I like it or not. My family is at the other end of the parking lot, waiting by the entrance to the diner. And then I see Griffin's Range Rover a few feet to my left.

He's already stepping out of it—and he's carrying roses. A dozen bright, multicolored roses.

Our eyes meet, and he sees the panic in mine. He glances over at Jude and starts to get back in his car, but it's too late. "Sully?" Jude calls out, stunned. Griffin freezes and slowly turns back toward us. The smile on his face is strained.

"Hey, Braddock!" He waves, and I want to scream when Jude starts toward Griffin instead of continuing toward where our family is waiting... and watching.

"You here to visit someone?" Jude asks.

"Ah... sort of." His eyes slip over to me. He smiles, and this one isn't strained. "Hi, Sadie."

"Hi, Griffin," I reply and lift my hand to my face and pretend to cough when Jude glances over at me, because I can't seem to make my face stop smiling.

"Nice flowers." Jude motions toward the unbelievably beautiful roses. Each one is a kaleidoscope of colors.

"Thanks." Griffin's mahogany eyes find mine again. "Anyway, I should be going, I think."

I nod and mouth the words "I'm sorry," because Jude isn't looking at me.

"Aren't you here to give those to someone?" Jude asks, and then he glances at me with his "this dude is insane" look. I cringe inwardly.

"Coach Sully?" Eli calls, and I turn to see him walking toward us. In fact, everyone is coming toward us. It's a wall of Braddocks marching toward us, sealing my doom.

"Crap," Griffin hisses under his breath, and I bite my lip to keep from laughing. This isn't funny. At all. I am so not ready for this with the emotional week I've had and the stress of knowing my family is about to find out about Griffin and me is clearly making me borderline hysterical. "Hey, Casco."

"Sully as in the goalie coach?" I hear Winnie ask as they all stop beside me. "Oh! It is! This is going to get good."

I glare at her over my shoulder, but no one notices, because Jude and Eli are busy introducing Griffin to everyone. And Winnie is too busy checking him out—blatantly. She gives me an approving nod and I glare back, annoyed. She is not even trying to cover this up.

"Lovely roses," my mom comments as she shakes Griffin's hand. "I've never seen ones like that before."

"They're called unicorn roses," Griffin explains.

"They are not!" I blurt out in disbelief.

"They are."

I burst out laughing, and he joins me. No one else is in on the joke, so they're all staring at us, confused.

"Griffin came here to see me," I finally confess.

He hands me the roses and steps forward and kisses my cheek. My rowdy family is abnormally quiet.

Eli is the first to break out of it, snapping his fingers. "Now it makes sense! I knew something was up with the way you were asking me about the Braddocks on the road trip!"

"Wait...what?"

"I...umm..." Griffin looks like cornered prey.

"Well, we should let you go," my mom says, trying to give the poor guy an exit from the insanity.

"Where are you guys going?" Jude asks like an overprotective dad. I frown at him.

"To a sex club," I snark.

"What? No," Griffin breaks in.

"Well, if you don't have set plans," my dad says, and I hold my breath, "why don't you both join us for dinner?"

His words are so slurred. He tried to say them slowly, but I'm worried Griffin won't understand because he's not used to it. I open my mouth to repeat his offer, but to my surprise and relief, Griffin doesn't need a translator. "I'd love to join you all... if you're sure it's okay."

"It's more than okay," Winnie replies, grinning brightly, and I reach out and shove her.

An hour later I've barely touched my steak sandwich and I want another Perrier, but the waitress is ignoring me, just like everyone else. No one can take their eyes off Griffin. I'm so stressed out about it, my stomach is in knots. My anxiety isn't over how weird this is or how badly it's going—it's over the fact that it isn't weird and it's not going badly at all. My whole family loves him. And Griffin fits. I don't know how else to explain it. He just fits. The teasing, the jokes, the way we all talk at each other like we're re-enacting an episode of the *Gilmore Girls*, none of it seems to faze him. In fact, he somehow gets more charming and funny, like his personality feeds off this bunch of lunatics. I'm in awe. Blissful awe.

"So growing up in Minnesota sounds cold," Winnie tells Griffin.

"Says the Canadian," Griffin replies with a chuckle.

"Touché," Winnie says, smiling at him and then at me. And I can't help but smile back, because I love that he's already comfortable enough to joke around with her.

"Sadie mentioned you have a daughter," my dad says, slowly but clearly.

"Charlie. She's six and nothing short of amazing." I love the way he looks when he talks about his daughter. It's equal parts sweet and sexy and makes my heart swell and my ovaries tingle.

"Daughters are the best," my mom says with a wistful smile.

"Umm…excuse me." Jude clears his throat. "I'm right here."

Everyone laughs.

"You actually have a lot in common with my daughter," Griffin says, turning his gaze to Jude, who is sitting across from him. "She stuffed a raisin up her nose the other day. It's not exactly Lego, but—"

Dixie lets out a whoop that has other customers looking over at us. She turns her eyes to me as Jude groans and my parents laugh. "You told him about the Lego! That's awesome!"

"Not awesome!" Jude grumbles and glances up at Griffin. "You look well adjusted and happy. I assume you don't have sisters."

Griffin laughs. "One brother."

"Is he in Minnesota?" Winnie asks.

"He's here in San Francisco," Griffin says. I love the proud smile that overtakes his face as he talks about his sibling. "He moved here after law school because his wife's from the area. It's been great having him nearby, and Charlie adores him."

"See?" Mom says, looking over at my sisters and me. "Some people actually like their brothers."

The table erupts in laughter again. I glance over at my dad, and he gives me a wink. It's a wink of approval, and it makes me grin. Ten minutes later, when we're back in the parking lot and Mom is wheeling Dad back to his room, and my sisters and Zoey are still fawning all over Griffin, Jude pulls me aside. I face him and want to cross my arms, but it would ruin the bouquet of unicorn roses in my hand, so I settle on a scowl instead. I'm hoping it says "back off," but I know even if it does, he won't.

"Don't get all bitchy about sharing the Lego incident with him," I warn him before he can speak. "He was feeling like a bad dad, and I wanted to make him feel better."

"I don't care about the Lego. I want to know when the hell were you going to tell me you're dating my coach?" he demands, not angry but definitely annoyed.

"Eli's coach," I correct. "And it was one date."

"That ended with your clothes on inside out and backward," Jude reminds me. When I flip him my middle finger, directly in front of his pretty-boy face, he relents. "Not that there is anything wrong with that. You know me, I'm all about removing clothes on a first date. But clearly there's more to it than instant gratification if he's here again. With roses."

I look at the roses, remember the name and smile, which makes Jude's eyes widen in horror, so I bite it back and try to frown. It doesn't work, and I'm fairly certain I now look like I'm having some kind of conniption. "It's no big deal."

"I don't know a single hockey player who has ever given roses to a No Big Deal," Jude proclaims.

"Oh, for crying out loud, you better knock Zoey up again

so you can get a girl and play daddy to her," I snark and turn
to walk away. "Because I'm not letting you do it to me."

I feel his hand on my arm. Winnie is half watching us
from a few yards away where she's standing with Eli, Dixie,
and Griffin. Luckily, Griffin isn't paying attention. He's listening to something Dixie is talking about. I let Jude turn me
back around. He looks less Mad Dad now and more Concerned Friend. "I'm not saying don't do it. I'm just saying
be careful," he says, his voice softer. "You're the one who
told me that you feel like you've got nothing left to give,
and the circumstances that made you feel that way haven't
changed."

"I know." He's right. I just…don't care. No, wait, I do
care. I just can't talk myself out of this thing with Griffin.

"I would just hate for him to get hurt," Jude says quietly,
and I freeze. Wait a minute…His concern is for Griffin.

"He's a big boy, and I'm hardly a man-eater, jackass," I
hiss indignantly.

Jude laughs and grabs me by both shoulders, pulling me
into a hug. "Sadie, I don't mean it that way. I know you'd
never purposely hurt a fly, let alone my coach."

"Eli's coach."

He pulls back, keeping his hands on my shoulders. "He
brought you roses. He looks at you like…like he's not playing around. So don't play around with him. If you really can't
be in something, don't be in something. Get it? Especially
with someone I work with, because I have to see him every
day, and I don't need the drama either right now."

I swallow. Hard. Leave it to Jude to throw all my fears and

concerns in my face when I'd been doing a pretty decent job of ignoring them. He musses my hair like he used to do when I was a teenager, right after I'd spent a stupid amount of time in the bathroom styling it. I take a swing at him, purposely missing, just like I used to do then too. "Okay, they're throwing punches," Griffin remarks, his voice filled with worry. "Is this normal?"

"Totally," Dixie assures him as Jude and I keep swatting at each other as we rejoin the group. "You've played against him; didn't you want to hit him?"

Griffin smiles. It says everything. We all laugh—loudly. Jude looks nothing less than proud. "When you're the best of the best, haters gonna hate."

"Isn't Avery Westwood leading the league in scoring this season?" Winnie asks. "And Jordan Garrison has the most short-handed goals."

"And my brother has the most shoot-out goals in the league," Eli adds.

"And I think it's Alex Larue who has the most penalty minutes," Griffin informs us.

Jude's expression sours. "Stats mean nothing. I have more Cups than all those chumps. And the best wife and cutest kid."

"Well, there's no arguing with that," Zoey exclaims. "Now let's get back to that cute kid. I'm sure my brother and Ned need a break."

Jude takes her hand in his, but before turning away, he looks Griffin in the eye. "You think I was a pain in the ass when you played me? If you play my sister, you ain't seen nothing yet."

"Oh, he's seen something," Winnie remarks tartly. "Remember the wardrobe malfunction."

"Get back under your bridges, trolls!" I holler, exasperated, but everyone just laughs.

"Winnie!" the voice, sharp with frustration, comes from behind me. I recognize it instantly, but am still shocked when I spin around and see Ty, Winnie's boyfriend who lives in Toronto, standing there next to a cab driver with a suitcase next to him.

"Ty?" Dixie says, because she can't believe it either.

He ignores her, and the rest of us, and walks over to Winnie. "You were supposed to pick me up at the airport."

"I am!" Winnie replies defensively. "Tomorrow, when your flight gets in."

Ty's expression is the purest example of exasperation I have ever seen in my life. "Are you kidding me?"

"I'm sorry," she relents. "I honestly thought you were coming tomorrow. I wouldn't leave you there on purpose. In my defense, I have a lot going on, Ty!"

"Why the hell do you think I took time away from work to come here?" he snaps, and I glance over at Griffin. He looks as uncomfortable as I feel.

I walk over to Ty and give him a hug. "Hey, buddy! It's good to see you. Sorry about the mix-up."

"Thanks. Yeah, good to see you too, Sadie." He hugs me back, but it's lackluster, and his jaw is still clenched. "We can give you a lift back to the house. Is that okay, Griff?"

"Yeah, I have a ton of room in the Rover," Griffin agrees easily.

"I'll take them," Jude volunteers. "You two have plans, and I won't feel so bad about driving Zoey's monster truck if it's full of people and luggage."

"It's a hybrid," Zoey reminds him, rolling her eyes. "Drama queen."

"Come on." Jude grabs Ty's suitcase for him and waves goodbye to Griffin and me.

Dixie and Eli head to her Mini, and Jude, Zoey, Winnie, and Ty walk to Zoey's Lexus SUV. Griffin looks down at me when they're all out of earshot. "Who was that?"

"That was Ty. The love of Winnie's life," I say frankly, and he looks like I just told him the world was flat. "I know, right?"

"I'm not here to judge," he says and reaches for my hand that's not holding the roses.

"Sorry about all that," I say as we walk to Griffin's car. "I was hoping to wait a little while before releasing the family on you."

"They're great," he replies without an ounce of hesitation. "I kind of caught on that you were hiding this from them when I asked Eli how your dad was on our road trip. I just wasn't sure why."

"Because they're a lot," I reply, and I feel a little guilty for some reason. "And I wasn't sure if you wanted Jude and Eli to know, since you work with them. I was definitely going to ask you first. Also, I don't know... I guess I just liked having something separate from the rest of my life, you know?"

He thinks about that and then nods. He seems to genuinely get it, thankfully. He glances at the flowers in my hand. "I wanted to get you something because you said you'd had such a rough week, and I originally thought wildflowers, obviously. But they had these, and when the sales lady told me the name I couldn't resist."

"Unicorn roses." I laugh. As he opens the passenger door, I rock up on my tiptoes and kiss his cheek. My lips are still pressed to his cheek when he slowly turns his head, stubble grazing me, until our lips align. Then he wraps an arm around my waist, yanks me closer, and deepens the kiss.

The kiss breaks, and I look up at him with glassy eyes. "Since my family hijacked the first part of our date, can I hijack the second part?

He looks surprised but intrigued. "Why not? I didn't have any solid plans."

I reluctantly leave his lips and climb into the SUV, and he shuts the door for me. A second later he's doing up his own seat belt and starting the engine. "Where to?"

I look out at the inky sky. The sun will set in the next fifteen or twenty minutes.

"Take a left when we get out of the parking lot," I reply.

Griffin follows my directions without questioning me. I find that interesting. I don't think I've dated a guy before who would be so chill about this. It's a sign of confidence and maturity, and it's such a fucking turn-on.

Finally when I tell him to turn on a little street called Bowley, his dark eyes light up. "Are we going to Baker Beach? To watch the sunset?'

"Yeah." I hope he doesn't think it's cheesy or lame.

"Awesome," he says, and I feel at ease again. He parks the

car at the end of the lot, which only has three other cars in it. He picks a spot away from them, nose to the ocean, and turns off the engine. "I've got a blanket in the back."

We get out of the car, and after going into the trunk he comes back with a big gray blanket with Dumbo the elephant all over it. I laugh, and he smiles sheepishly. "It's Charlie's, obviously, but we make her watch *Sesame Street*, so she'll be okay with sharing."

"Ha!" I laugh as he takes the blanket and my hand in his and leads me down to the sand. I kick off my shoes and pick them up, digging my toes deep into the sand.

He lays out the blanket, and I drop onto it, close my eyes, and take a long, slow inhale of the cool, salty air. I feel the stubble on his chin rub my cheek and then his full, firm lips brush my earlobe. "You're a beach girl, I can tell."

I nod as a shiver of desire rolls down my spine. "I grew up spending summers in Maine. My family has a cottage there. We don't go anymore because it's too hard to get my dad there and too hard to go without him. I never seem to find the time to come here."

"We should make a point of coming here," he announces softly, his fingertips dancing along the side of my neck. "I think you have to make a point of it. You look so at peace."

I twist my head to look over at him. "I feel at peace. But I think the company has a lot to do with it."

"I know it does for me," he replies, and then he points to the sky. "But that doesn't hurt either."

I turn to look at the setting sun. Every inch of the sky is a beautiful rose-gold color. The sound of the waves hitting the shore a few feet away immediately makes my shoulders start to loosen. I tilt my neck from side to side, and then I feel his hands on my waist.

"Come here," he whispers and positions me between his legs on the blanket, my back to his front, facing the sinking sun. He starts to rub my shoulders, and it feels so incredible I accidently let out a moan.

"I've heard that sound before," he whispers against the back of my ear. "And I know it means I'm doing something right."

"You do everything right," I sigh back. "You're a unicorn."

You're my unicorn, I think, and it should scare me, but then he hits a knot right between my shoulder blades and digs in, and all I can feel is sweet relief. I moan again.

17

GRIFFIN

I didn't think I would be making out with her on a beach at sunset, but I'm definitely not complaining. Everything between Sadie and me is unpredictable. Not just that, but if you were to make a list of all the dos and don'ts of a successful new relationship, we'd probably tick every item in the don't column—but again, I have no complaints.

She's a fucking fantastic kisser. She holds nothing back. Her lips are needy, her tongue is greedy, and there's this untamed wildness to everything about her when she's kissing me that wakes up parts of me I thought were hibernating for good. She makes me hungry for her touch, for her skin, her lips, her everything, which is why we're still making out long after the sun is gone.

Except for the dim, flickering light of a far-off street lamp, the glow of the moon off the rolling waves, and her cell phone screen occasionally lighting up where she dropped it on the blanket, we're in darkness. I desperately want to take her home and finish what we started more than a week ago.

"If we don't leave here soon, we're going to get slapped with a public nudity charge," she warns me breathlessly. "Because I'm going to take your dick out of your pants and put it in my mouth. Again."

Jesus…this girl's mouth. It alone makes me hard.

"If it's in your mouth, it's not public nudity," I reply cheekily and kiss her again, biting her bottom lip gently.

"You should take me home," Sadie whispers against my cheek, her hand slipping down from my shoulder and to my lap. She purposely presses her palm into my hard-on. Electricity shoots up my spine in a delicious way. "Because this will get out of control if we stay."

I stand up, taking both her hands in mine. I pull her up a little roughly on purpose so she bumps up against me. I reach around and steady her with a hand on her perfect ass. I pull her against me. "Everything about us seems to always be out of control," I tell her.

In the pale light I see her lips part in a guilty smile. "I know. I don't know why. And I feel like we should figure that out but…I just like you."

"I like you too, Sadie Braddock," I confess, and it feels so trite but I swear I have never been so giddy to say something or felt it so genuinely as I do right now. "I feel like myself again with you."

"Me too."

Suddenly we're drowning in bright white light. Headlights. Someone parked in the lot facing the beach not only turned on their headlights but their high beams. We both are instantly blinded as we turn and squint toward the source. I shield my eyes with my hand. "Fuck, buddy."

The driver must realize their mistake because the lights dim to normal and then go out altogether, but then the van peels from the parking lot much more quickly than it should, especially without any lights on now. It drives away so quickly, before my eyes can adjust, and I can't make out anything more than the shape of it and a color—silver.

"That was weird," Sadie remarks, her brow furrowed as she blinks. I nod, grab the blanket off the sand, handing her her cell phone, and then take her hand in mine as we walk back to the car.

I've never been a big hand-holder, but with her it's different. I like to touch her, even innocently; I just like the feel of her. I have this primal instinct when I'm around her to touch her and soothe her. She's a confident, blunt, bold woman who clearly can take care of herself—and others. But yet something in me, something deep, longs to take care of her. It's unnecessary, but it's there, and it's not going away. Every time I see her, my affection for her, my need for her, my urge to soothe her grows stronger.

She's quiet as we get in the car, staring at her phone screen, and the look on her face is changing into something much less relaxed. I reach across the console and cup the side of her face, turning her blue eyes to mine instead of her screen. "What's wrong? And don't say nothing because I can see it's something."

"Jude texted me to say Winnie and Ty fought the whole

way home." I sigh. "God, I wish she would just call time of death on it and save us all more heartache."

"As enjoyable as this unexpected make-out session was, I am happy driving you home and picking up where we left off tomorrow," I volunteer.

"It's not that I don't want to keep this going, because I do," Sadie explains, her expression earnest. "I just know that the thing with Winnie and Ty is probably still blowing up. Those two can fight for hours if no one plays referee, and I don't want that person to be my mom. She's dealing with enough. And she's the only one home with them."

"No explanations necessary," I promise, and I mean it. "Where do you live? I know it's not the place I picked you up at for our first date."

She looks shocked, but she gives me the address.

As I drive I can still sense something is bothering her. I keep glancing over at her, but she's not looking back. Her eyes are on her hands in her lap. I want to coax her into talking again, but for a second I realize this might be a reality check. Maybe I am the only one running too fast here. Maybe she doesn't feel the connection I do and isn't drawn to me as intensely as I am drawn to her.

But then, as I turn into her family's affluent neighborhood, she speaks. It's so soft I have to turn down the radio to hear her. "I'm betting when you decided to jump back into the dating world, you didn't expect to find a woman who still lives at home."

"If you didn't live with your parents here, I wouldn't have met you, because you'd still be in Toronto," I reply. "Also, like you so aptly pointed out, I'm wise enough to know the difference between a woman who still lives at home because she's got valid extenuating circumstances and one who lives at home because she can't stand on her own two feet."

"My extenuating circumstances, valid or not, are kind of a lot to handle," Sadie says, just as softly as before. "Which is why I don't expect anyone to handle it. You can see how well Ty is handling it."

I can't comment on the situation I saw between her sister and this Ty guy. I can tell there's a whole lot of history there I have no idea about. As we pull up in front of the address she gave me, a big, refurbished apartment complex just around the corner from the famous painted ladies, I put the car in park and turn in my seat to face her.

"How about this?" I say and reach for her hand, slowly, deliberately lacing our fingers together. "I'll let you know the second that you being an incredible sister, loving daughter, or dedicated nurse starts annoying me, and you can dump me on my ass. Sound good?"

She blinks. "I mean, I'm not going to be able to—"

I lean forward and silence her with a kiss. "I know what you're going to say. You're not going to be around every time I feel like seeing you. You're not going to be able to just impetuously spend the night at my place or whatever. But that's okay. I've got my own stuff to deal with. This isn't going to be easy, I know that. But I don't want something that's easy, Sadie. I want something that's worth it."

I watch her expression as my words sink in. The worry creasing her brow seems to dissolve, and her lips start to turn up in that incredibly sexy little smirk she does so damn well. Her arm slides around my neck, and she pulls me in for a scorching kiss. And while her tongue slides into my open mouth, she crawls over and into my lap. She is the same way she was from the first kiss—uninhibited and intense. And I react the same way I did before—but getting incredibly turned on and instantly hard. I palm her ass and rub myself against her core. She rolls her hips in rhythm with me.

I groan.

"I just wanted to show you, I'll be worth it," she whispers against my cheek after she breaks the kiss. Then she reaches for the door handle, and before I can stop her—because, damn, do I want to stop her—she's out of the car and walking to the front door of the building, roses in hand, and swinging her perfect ass in a way that is doing nothing to stop my blood from heading south.

I wait until the door closes behind her and I can no longer see her through the glass of the front door, and then I text her before I pull away from the curb.

I'll pick you up tomorrow at four. Dress casual and bring your toothbrush.

I drive toward the marina, but I'm too restless to just go home, so I call Hunter through the car app. "Where are you?" I ask when he answers, because it sounds loud.

"At a thing," he replies vaguely.

"What thing?" Hunter has never been the clubbing type, even when we were in college.

"I'm checking something out with Mia," he says, being just as vague as before.

"Sounds like a club," I tell him, and the sound starts to get more distant. I hear a clang, and then the sounds disappear completely. "Since when do you two go clubbing?"

"Can you meet us?"

Why is he not answering my questions? And why does he sound so tense?

"I was actually calling to see if you two wanted to hang out," I reply. "Where are you? I'll meet you."

"Actually, meet us at our place, okay?"

"On my way." I end the call and drive straight to their place. They live near Golden Gate Park, which means I have to take a million surface streets to get there and traffic is insane. The longer it takes, the more I agitated I get. I don't like the way Hunter evaded every question I asked him. It's not like him at all. Neither is the clipped, tight tone he was using. He's always laid back.

Both Hunter and Mia are standing outside their building when I get there. Hunter stands, and Mia runs over and hugs me. Something is very, very wrong. Hunter doesn't make me wait to find out. "While you were on your road trip and Charlie came to visit us, we took her to the dog park," he begins, and my blood already starts to run cold. "She was telling us how nervous she was to go to a new school next year."

"What?" I'm scrambling to make sense of that. "She's not going to a new school. She's in this one until grade six. Lauren and I looked at every school in the area, and this one is the best and she loves it."

"We were confused too, so we asked her about it," Mia pipes up, her brown eyes clouded with concern. "She said that Lauren said they might be moving."

"What the fuck is she talking about?" I blurt out. I've been really good at curbing my swearing, because I'm worried I'll do it in front of Charlie. But this is swear-worthy. "Is Lauren in-fucking-sane?"

"I think this explains her play for custody," Hunter says, and I feel like the ground under me has given away and is crumbling. Everything is crumbling.

"Is she moving in with that loser musician? Where? Why would she leave Marin? It was her idea to live there to begin with." None of this makes any sense.

Hunter rubs the back of his neck and gets this uncomfortable look on his face. He clears his throat. "See, we didn't want to stress you out until we knew more, and Mia thought maybe if she talked to Lauren, on neutral turf somewhere... They still get along. Mostly."

"I mean not anymore," Mia mutters. "Not if she does this."

"I'm confused. I'm about to punch something, so can you two explain? Please," I beg through gritted teeth, my hands clenched at my side.

"When we dropped Charlie back at Lauren's, Mia tried to find out a little more. But all Lauren wanted to talk about was that loser boyfriend of hers and this gig he had coming up that she was excited to go to," Mia explains, running a hand through her black hair.

"You know I've always though this custody crap had something to do with him," Hunter interjects. Suddenly the inside of my mouth feels like it's filled with sawdust. "So we decided to check out one of his shows ourselves."

"It was tonight, and we skulked in the back so she wouldn't see us," Mia continues. "Anyway, when they introduced Cale's band, they said it was one of his last shows in town before they moved to New York."

"She wants to follow him to New York." The words are so ridiculous, they feel strange coming out of my mouth. She's been dating him less than a year. "What the hell is she thinking? She is not taking my daughter out of state, and she certainly isn't doing it over this asswipe."

"I told you, don't worry," Hunter says, but he looks concerned.

"Where?"

"Where what?" Mia asks, but the quiver in her voice says she knows what I am asking.

"Where is Lauren? Right now. What club? Where is that shithole playing his bullshit music at?" Neither responds. "You can tell me or I can Google it. I'm sure they have a website."

"It's a bar called Skippy's," Hunter confesses, and as I start to Google the address he starts to panic. "But, Griffin, going there and losing your shit on her, in public, is actually going to give her a case for custody. She'll make it seem like you're stalking her, she'll have witnesses to testify that you have anger issues. You will be handing her a case."

"Fuck!" I bellow and shove my phone back into my pocket because he's right. I don't want him to be, but he is. "This can't be happening. Why would she do this to me? To Charlie. We have a great relationship. Our daughter has finally adjusted to the divorce, and she's going to try and rip her away from me?"

"It's selfish, and I will make that case," Hunter promises. I stare at him, unable to speak or move or think of anything but the gut-wrenching possibility that Charlie might move to New York.

"I've got to go," I mutter, running an aggravated hand through my hair as I turn and storm back toward my car parked across the street.

"Griff, do *not* go to that bar!" Hunter calls out.

"I won't," I bark back before getting behind the wheel and slamming the door—hard.

I drive around aimlessly for more than an hour and then to Lauren's house. Hunter said no bar. He didn't say no contact. Here it will be her word against mine in whatever we say to each other. I park across the street and just sit there and wait. Rosa's minivan is in the driveway, and about an hour later a beat-up black Mazda Miata pulls up beside it. That rocker douchebag is driving. Lauren gets out of the passenger side, and I get out of my car.

"Hey!" I call, and she spins to face me, shock all over her face.

"What the hell are you doing here?"

"Are you thinking of moving to New York?" I ask bluntly.

More shock—not shock at the question but shock at the fact that I'm asking it. I know the difference, because this expression is tinged with guilt, and I take that as a good sign. She might actually feel just a little bit bad about ripping my daughter away from me.

"Get out of here, dude," her piece-of-shit boyfriend says as he gets out of the car and walks toward us. "Her life is none of your business now."

I turn toward him, shoulders back, fists clenched, jaw locked. "Listen, Cale...which is a fucking vegetable not a name, by the way. Everything that affects our child is my business for the rest of her life. That's how it works. If you don't like it, get back in the little fucking shitbox car and get the fuck out of here."

"You're a piece of work, man," he hisses back, but he doesn't challenge me. He turns to Lauren. "This isn't my jam. He's killing my post-show buzz. I'm going back to the bar."

"Cale!" she calls in protest, but he gets back in his car and drives away, peeling the tires like the small-dicked douchebag he is. When his car is nothing but taillights at the end of the block, she turns to me with tears in her eyes. "You being here is stalking. I'm telling my lawyer!"

"And I'll say it never happened and bring up that you show up uninvited at my place too." I shrug. "You want to play dirty, I'll play dirty too. You are not taking Charlie to live in New York."

"We're over. You can't control my life anymore," Lauren argues back. "I get to have my own life and be happy. Cale makes me happy. He has to move to New York because it's better for his career. I want to go with him."

"Then go. Leave Charlie with me," I suggest desperately. "She can visit you on holidays and in the summer."

"I can't leave her!" Lauren cries, tears now brimming in her eyes.

"And neither can I!"

"Then move to New York," Lauren replies, and I'm waiting for some kind of hint that she's kidding or being sarcastic, but her hazel eyes are dead serious and her expression is flat.

I'm blown away. "You want me to move to New York?"

She folds her arms across her chest and huffs. "If you care so much about seeing Charlie every week, then that's your only way. Because I am moving to New York."

She turns and storms up the front path to the door. I follow. "I have a job. A career! And a life here!"

"And I want one there!" Lauren spits back. "Now shut up and go away before you wake up Charlie. I swear I will call the police if you don't."

She shuts the door firmly in my face.

18

SADIE

I can't stop smiling. I've been doing it since the second I realized where Griffin was taking me, and I probably won't stop smiling for days. I run my hand over the soft neck of Triscuit, the stunning golden colored horse I'm riding. Griffin is on a bigger mottled gray horse named Zeus.

"Zeus is treating you well," I remark. "And you look less stressed, so you must be getting the hang of it."

"Horseback riding wasn't stressing me out," he replies and gives me a smile, but it's more guarded than his previous smiles. I wonder if he's lying to me to appear tough or cool or sexy or something. The truth is, even if he admitted he was scared of riding, he would still be sexy AF to me. Sitting on top of that horse in a black T-shirt that shows off his tight torso, broad chest, and bulging biceps, he still looks so hot I want to jump him, even with the wrinkled brow and tense jaw.

"I can't believe you planned this," I say, still in awe. I mentioned to him on that very first date that I loved horses and didn't expect him to think twice about it. But he did, and here we are on a ridge over looking the Pacific, riding two beautiful beasts as the sun gets ready to set. Last night at the beach was perfection, but this...this is heaven. "This is the best date I've ever had. Ever."

He moves Zeus closer to Triscuit and leans his body toward mine. "And I'm just getting started," he promises. I lean toward him so our lips can connect.

"Wait a second," I say when our kiss ends and pull my cell out of his pocket. "Let's commemorate this."

If I thought he looked stressed before, I was wrong. Now he's nothing but tension oozing out of every sexy pore on his face. He's clenching his jaw so tightly I'm surprised I can't hear his teeth creak under the pressure. "I don't do social media."

"What?" I ask.

"I just..." He sighs. "I don't put pictures of me on social media. I don't let people. I just...I'm not into that."

"I don't do social media either," I explain, suddenly feeling embarrassed that I might have done something wrong. "I had Instagram for like five minutes and got DM'd by every puck bunny on the planet trying to get my brother's info. So I got rid of it. And Facebook and Twitter."

I watch his shoulders relax just a little. I start to put my phone away. He reaches over and grabs my wrist to stop me. "It's okay. Sorry. I'm just over-cautious. Because of Charlie."

He smiles. It's slightly more relaxed than any smile he's given me all day. "I get it. You don't want her seeing anything that would upset her online. I understand."

"But take it. Of us. For us," he urges and leans closer to me again, letting go of my wrist so I can lift the phone and snap the selfie.

It's the perfect shot of us with the ocean and the setting sun over his shoulder, casting a golden glow on us that no photo filter can replicate. He examines it on my screen. "We look good together."

We do. But I'm feeling a little guarded after his reaction, so I just nod and put my phone back in my pocket. Ten minutes later I'm saying goodbye to Triscuit, and Griffin is chuckling. "What? We formed a real bond."

I go back to nuzzling his nose. With a final pat of his mane, I start to walk away. Impulsively, I reach over and hug Griffin. He's stiff, but he hugs me back. "Thank you for this."

"Seeing your face light up was thanks enough," he replies. "And now for dinner."

We get in his car, and he drives us over the Golden Gate. I wonder if we're going back to his place for dinner. I wouldn't mind that in the least, because I've already decided I'm having him for dessert, and that's how dinner at his place ended last time. Only this time I want more than great oral. I want great sex.

"Want a hint of where we're going?" he asks. I nod, so he turns on the radio and flips the Sirius XM to a country station. I raise my left eyebrow at him, intrigued.

Fifteen minutes later we're pulling to the curb in front of a dilapidated building that looks like a roadhouse—the kind where people go in and don't always come out. But this place has valet parking, so it can't be too sketchy. I look up at the flickering neon sign and laugh. "Pickled Biscuits Brew House."

"I've never been, but it's supposed to be the best honky-tonk in San Francisco," he explains as his full lips part in a wicked grin and he runs his tongue across his bottom lip. "I hope you like barbecue, because they're supposed to have the best in the West."

"I'll be the judge of that," I declare. I almost skip to the entrance I'm so excited.

Inside, the place is a trip. Everything is knotty pine—the walls, the floor, the ceiling, the bar. The only other décor are cowboy hats of all shapes, sizes, and colors hanging on the walls over booths and behind the bar. And as soon as I inhale, I start to salivate. Griffin lets out a grumbling groan. "It smells like heaven. Unless you're a vegan."

I laugh. "This is enough to turn a vegan's mind or at the very least make them weep."

We sit at a booth near the back, because it's the only one available. The place is fairly full, and by the time our food gets here, all the tables are taken and it's standing room only. There's a band setting up on the small stage by the bar as we devour the Road House Sampler we ordered, which has a little bit of everything, including their weird but delicious assortment of pickled vegetables. I eat like it's my last meal, enjoying the hell out of it, and so does he. He also seems to be enjoying me, which I like. His eyes are devouring me while I devour the last rib and then pop another pickled radish in my mouth before licking the rib sauce off my fingers.

"Who knew pickled radish was so delicious?" I ask, trying not to feel self-conscious under the weight of his stare.

He licks his lips slowly. "Who knew watching you eat barbecue would give me a hard-on. But it is."

I blush fiercely. "I'm a slob right now. You're turned on by this?"

I hold up my sticky fingers, and his expression gets darker. He leans forward in the booth and takes me by the wrist. "Everything about you is authentic. You don't pretend, and you're not worried about how you look," he explains. "And it's the biggest turn-on in the world."

He pulls my wrist to his mouth and licks at some of the sauce there. A white-hot flash of desire explodes inside me. He lets go of my wrist, and I almost whimper. "Have you always been so fucking incredible?" he asks softly.

"Do you always make women want to fuck you in public?" I counter, and his eyes get even darker.

"Is that what I'm doing to you?"

"Yes."

"Would you settle for fucking me in private?"

"Yes."

He slides out of the booth and pulls me out of it, while dropping a hundred-dollar bill on the table. "This will more than cover it."

He stalks through the crowded room, grasping my hand so I don't fall behind. People part easily for him, like they know he is on some kind of mission. He's got that kind of presence everywhere he goes, whether he chooses to use it or not. He's commanding. He's imposing. He's impossible to ignore. And he's mine.

We are almost to the door when the band starts up, and it causes me to stutter-step. They're playing one of my favorite songs, "Heartache Tonight" by the Eagles. My dad used to sing it at the top of his lungs on our long summer drives from Toronto to the cottage in Maine. Hearing it now makes me think it's some kind of sign. Like I need another sign to tell me Griffin is perfect for me. He feels my step falter and turns around to face me.

"Sorry. It's just one of my favorite songs," I tell him.

He smiles. "Then we should stay and dance."

"We should?" I blink, stunned. "You dance?"

He laughs and pulls me toward the already crowded dance floor. The man has moves and he isn't afraid to use them, and it's sexy as hell. I dance with abandon for the first time in a long time, and by the end of the song I can't keep my hands off him. He definitely doesn't mind. He grabs me in a searing kiss as the band ends the song and starts another. My body is pressed to his, and he dips me backward a little in the middle of the kiss, and it makes me giggle with delight against his lips.

"More dancing?" he asks softly against the shell of my ear after he breaks the kiss and pulls me upright in his arms.

"Not with our clothes on," I say and grin.

He pulls me off the dance floor.

Outside, he hands the valet his ticket. I lean against the side of the building, under the flashing neon sign, because I'm so turned on I feel light-headed. He smells like spiced rum, leather, and bergamot. Sweet lord, I need him.

I lift the hem of his shirt and press my hands flat against his rippled stomach. "You're the sexiest man I have ever met. You do things to me, to my body, that I don't understand, and I'm a trained professional."

He grins, a deep, rough laugh rumbling up from him as his abs tighten under my palms. He rests his forearms on the wall on either side of my head and then dips his head, his lips ghosting mine. "You do things to me too," he whispers against my lips. As he kisses me, my fingers curl into the waistband of his jeans, just brushing against the tip of his very hard cock.

"I want that in my mouth again," I murmur and then tilt my head and slide my tongue out to touch his bottom lip. He reaches up, cupping the side of my face and curling his fingers into my hair, and he kisses me hard and deep.

"I can't believe I'm saying this, but...no," Did he just turn down a blow job? "I want more this time. I want all of you."

"Sir, your car," the valet calls out.

Griffin bites my bottom lip one last time and then pulls back. As he opens my door and I get in, his phone buzzes. He looks at the screen, and his whole demeanor tightens—his shoulders, his jaw, the way he clutches his phone. "Give me a second..."

He shuts my door. I watch him through the window as he dials a number and turns his back to me. He walks to the edge of the sidewalk, near the alley a few feet away. I can't hear what he's saying, but he's gesturing a lot. He hangs up less than two minutes later and stalks over to the car like a thundercloud about to rain hellfire.

He drops into the driver's seat. I can see him force a change in his disposition. It's literally like watching someone trying to swallow something gross—kind of like how I look trying to swallow Fireball whiskey. But he gets it down and looks at me with a fake but easy smile. "Let's get going."

I put my hand on top of his. "Let's talk about whatever is stressing you out."

His eyebrows pinch together. His mouth opens, then closes, then opens again. "It's nothing. Work crap."

"Griffin, you looked way too stressed for a team that hasn't started playoffs yet," I remark. "And that look on your face is more than work. It's personal. I can tell."

He reaches for his seat belt and as he clicks it, he leans closer and kisses my cheek. The feel of his stubble against my throat as he pulls away makes me tingle. When his eyes meet mine, they hold a raw desperation I fully understand even without the reasoning behind it. "It's not that I'm keeping secrets. It's just that I need tonight to be about something else. Something new. I just want to forget everything for a little while."

With everything I've been through in the last few years with my family and my dad, I get it. This—us—we're something that doesn't get touched by the pain, the mess of our everyday lives.

I put my hand on his thigh and give it a squeeze. "Let's go back to your place and continue this debate about whether I get to put my mouth on your cock again."

He huffs out a surprised laugh. "This is exactly the only kind of conversation I want to have tonight."

He pulls away from the curb, officially leaving our worries on the sidewalk beside the valet.

19

GRIFFIN

From the second I'm inside her, I am teetering on the brink of orgasm. It's more than just how wet she is or how tight she feels. It's the way she tore off my clothing and her own. It's the way she rolled the condom onto me, crawled onto my bed and onto my cock, no timidness, but with confidence and eagerness. And then she drops herself down on me with an arched back, tits on display, hands in her golden hair, moaning in pure abandon. Sadie Braddock is my sexual soul mate.

And shit, that mouth of hers...she says everything I'm thinking. Every hot, dirty thought. "My pussy is so wet," she pants. "I swear you've had me on the verge of coming since I met you."

I reach up and palm those perfect bouncing breasts. "Then let's make you come, love. As many times as you want."

"Oh, God, fuck." She's bouncing on me at a frantic pace, her hips rolling and her pussy tightening with every thrust I give her. Usually I chase orgasm, but with her, I don't want to give in too soon. The tingle in my balls, the pull of her pussy, the sounds she makes...I want it all to last forever.

She grabs my wrist and moves my left hand off her breasts, trailing it down her abdomen. I let her place it over her clit. "Tell me what you want," I command as I lift my hips and slam into her so hard her knees lift off the bed for a second.

She looks down at me, a curtain of golden hair around her flushed face. Her blue eyes are as dark as the ocean at night and just as glassy. "Rub my clit, Griffin. Make me come. Hard."

I move my thumb over her clit. She lets out a gasp that is equal parts relief and anticipation, and it pushes me to the edge of my own release. I can't...I won't go without her. Ladies first. Always. Especially this lady.

"Right there. Harder. Faster. So close," she whispers. I follow her orders and feel my own grip slipping.

She drops forward suddenly, her lips crashing down on mine and there, in the middle of the kiss, I feel her come. She trembles around my dick and whimpers against my mouth. I wrap my arms tightly around her back, pushing her down harder on my dick, and I let my own sweet release take over.

I swear I almost lose consciousness.

She's collapsed on top of me, her head curled into the crook of my neck. I loosen my grip on her but can't bring myself to let go. Seconds turn into minutes, and I know I have to move her, get up, take care of the condom, but right now, with her falling asleep on top of me, flesh to flesh, heartbeat to heartbeat, I am feeling more relaxed and at peace than I have in years. That's not even an exaggeration. She must feel the same, because I realize, after twenty minutes, she's sound asleep.

She doesn't even wake when I gently turn us around to lie on her side on the bed. I roll off the bed and head to the bathroom to clean up. I grab my phone off the nightstand before crawling back into bed and check my messages. Hunter has sent me the court date—two weeks from now. My stomach drops. He keeps reassuring me everything will work out, Charlie isn't gong anywhere, but I can't get rid of the cold knot of fear that forms in my belly when I think about facing the judge. I know I've done nothing wrong. I know I'm a great dad, and I know Charlie is perfectly happy with the current situation. I also know Lauren always gets what she wants. It's been like that since the day I met her. Even the fact that we're here in San Francisco now was her choice. She wanted to settle here after the divorce because her parents live nearby and it was a strong market for freelance graphic designers, which is what she does. I lucked into the perfect job, but the fact is, I would have worked at In-N-Out Burger if it was the only job I could find in the city where my daughter lived.

I text Hunter back and lie back down next to Sadie. She snuggles into me, her head on my bicep and her leg curled over mine, and I instantly start to relax. I run a hand over her long, silky hair, and the lilac scent of her shampoo fills the air. I close my eyes and just enjoy the moment. Nothing else matters right now, but this…the contentment and peace. I close my eyes and, amazingly, I drift off to sleep.

She wakes me up almost six hours later, and I willingly let her win that debate about the blow job. Then I flip her on her back, dip my head between her toned thighs, and return the favor. She falls back asleep, wrapped around me again, but I lie awake and think about how I'm going to tell her about this custody thing. I don't want to make it her problem, but it's going to disrupt my life, and since she's in my life now... I need to tell her.

A few minutes later her phone starts to ring, waking her up. She answers it and doesn't say much after that, but as soon as she hangs up she looks over at me with regret. "I have to go to the hospital."

"You got called into work?" I question.

She shakes her head. "If I tell you something, you have to not tell Eli or Jude."

"Okay."

"It's my dad's doctor. They did some tests, and Dad asked him to give me a preview of the results before my family finds out," she explains, trying to tame her bed head and tuck her wild hair behind her ears. "He didn't want to do it over the phone. That's not a good sign."

"I'm sorry." I know it's lame, but I don't know what else to say.

"I knew it wasn't going to be great. I mean, ALS is incurable," Sadie says quietly. "I'm a nurse. I know how this plays out. I know in excruciating detail, which is why my dad wants me to have the info first. Because everyone else is going to need me to help them come to terms with it."

I stand up and reach for boxer briefs and tug them on. I watch her as she takes an elastic off her wrist I didn't even realize was there and artfully twists her hair up. Then she heads to the bathroom. "Okay if I shower?"

"Of course." I follow her into the bathroom, and as she turns on the water and steps into the shower, I grab a fresh towel from the shelf under the vanity and put it in on sink for her. I walk back into the bedroom and wait for her. I decide now isn't the time to lay my shit at her feet. She's about to get what could be really bad news about her dad. My drama can wait until she's dealt with that, so she doesn't feel overwhelmed. When she emerges ten minutes later, the towel is wrapped around her. She starts getting dressed. She looks good getting ready in my space, and I hope I get to see it happening again...a lot. But now is not the time to bring that up.

"Shit. I have to get to practice," I say with remorse. "I want to drop you off at the hospital but I'll be late."

"It's fine. I'll get a Lyft," she explains, and as she steps out of the bathroom she rocks up on her toes to give me a quick kiss. "And in case I wasn't clear with the moaning and the orgasm-induced tremors, last night and this morning were magical. Almost as magical as the horseback riding and almost as orgasmic as the barbecue."

"Almost?" I repeat in mock indignation.

She giggles and starts down the stairs. I follow her and grab her ass as punishment for that snarky remark. She squeals and swats at me. I follow her right out onto the deck, and as we wait for her Lyft I turn her to face me and lift her so her ass is on the railing.

"I have a question," I say as I part her legs and push my hips between them.

"Is it 'do we have time for a quickie?' Because the answer is technically no, but I'm willing to try anyway," she says with a sly smile as she wraps her arms around my neck.

I laugh softly and step closer. "My question is, who is helping you come to terms with this?"

She looks suddenly flustered. "What?"

"You're clearly there for your sisters and everyone else, but who are you leaning on while everyone leans on you?" It's a loaded question; I think I already know the answer is no one. I want to be that person for her. I don't care how crazy that may seem given that we've known each other less than a month. I want to be her rock.

"I'm fine," she says, but she's not fooling anyone, least of all herself.

I reach up and cup the side of her face, tilting her by the chin so she has to look right at me. "Promise me you'll call if you need anything or want anything. Whether it's to talk, cry, scream, or get naked."

She smiles at that. "You are definitely my go-to for nudity from here on out."

I kiss her. "I want to be your one and only for nudity from here on out. Sound good?"

"Yeah. It sounds good."

I cock my head and scrub my chin like I'm deep in thought. "I think that means we just kind of made this official."

"Nudity clauses usually do that." She winks at me, and I feel myself getting hard over that sexy smirk of hers.

I'm about to kiss her again when a car honks. She glances over her shoulder, and I step back as she drops to her feet.

She looks down. "You're in your underwear," she notes. "And you're half hard."

"Oops." I adjust myself and glance around. The marina is pretty empty except for her Lyft and a few cars in the—

"I'll call you later." She kisses my cheek and gives me a quick hug, which I return, but my eyes are on the van I spotted parked near the end of the lot, sideways across two spots so the tinted driver's side window is aligned with my houseboat.

She jumps in the Lyft, and it turns and drives out of the parking lot, but I don't move. I keep standing on my deck, looking at that van. Is it the same one we saw on the beach a couple of nights ago?

I suddenly don't care that I'm barefoot and in only my underwear. I hop over my deck railing and onto the dock. I start marching toward the parking lot, and as soon as my feet hit the pavement the van roars to life and moves toward the exit. I start to jog and then run, cutting in front of the vehicle. I worry for a split second I'm about to become a speed bump, but, thankfully, the van stops. I slam my hand on the hood with a loud bang.

Through the windshield, which is less tinted than the side windows, I see a terrified dude staring back at me. He's got greasy, long, black hair and beady dark brown eyes. He looks startled and guilty as all hell. Like a raccoon you find raiding your trash bin.

"Open your window!" I bellow, and a second later I hear the hum of the window going down. I walk around the side of the van.

"Look, buddy, I don't want any trouble. Don't make this

worse for you than it already is," he warns, and I frown.

"What the ever-loving fuck are you talking about?" I demand, holding onto his side mirror even though I know, realistically, it's not going to stop him from driving off if he truly wants to. "Were you at the beach last night? Are you following me?"

"I'm doing my job, buddy," he replies. "And no offense, but you're making it incredible easy. I almost feel sorry for you, but I don't know... My boss says your wife is a looker and paying us a ton."

"I don't have a wife," I snap, and every muscle in my body turns to stone. "I have an ex-wife. Holy shit. Did she hire you to follow me?"

He looks confused for a moment, and then he shrugs. "Alls I know is I'm supposed to document your activities with other women and anything else you do that's shady or can be made to look shady."

I don't know what is more shocking, that Lauren would actually do this or that this jackass is stupid enough to confess everything to me. "You're shitty at your job, you know that?"

He smirks smugly. "Nah, dude. I got you looking pretty shady in a lot of photos."

He turns his fancy digital camera around and shows me a series of shots that have my jaw fall open. He's got a picture of me catching Trish when she slipped at the arena. Somehow it looks like we're about to kiss. Then there's also pictures of me with Sadie at the beach, and minutes ago on the deck, and there we are kissing. But the combination of them both make me look like a womanizer for sure. And then there are pictures of me out with Charlie, and in every single photo I'm turned away from her or on my phone. I hardly ever touch my phone when I'm with her, but I've been breaking that rule a lot since Lauren started this custody thing, because I've needed to talk to Hunter a couple times a day. But these photos, out of context, make me look like an uninterested parent.

I reach through the window for the camera, but the guy is quick and yanks it back out of my reach. He looks smug again, and I really want to punch him. If all hope is lost and these photos are going to build Lauren's case, then I have nothing to lose. He sees my balled-up fists and he inches away from the window. "Dude, relax! You break this camera or my face, and your ex definitely wins."

"Do you even know what you're doing? You're fucking up an innocent little girl's life with your bullshit photos," I snarl. His indifferent expression doesn't even flicker.

"You can make this go away," he says simply, and I glare at him in confusion. "All I care about is getting paid…by whoever the fuck wants to give me the most money."

We stare at each other. He's starting to look at me like *I'm* a brainless sleazeball. He inches a little closer and spells it out for me. "She hasn't seen any of the photos yet. You don't want her to, then pay me double what she paid me."

"How much?"

"Fifteen hundred."

I point at him. "Don't fucking move."

I stalk back into my boat and head straight to my room, throwing on a pair of jeans before heading to the small safe in my closet and grabbing my emergency cash supply. I've got two grand. I take out $1,500 and grab my cell phone off the night stand. Just before I step back outside, I turn on my audio recorder app, which I use to mutter notes during games.

When I get back to his van, I hold up the roll of cash. "So I pay you and these pictures go away instead of to my ex?"

"I'll give you the memory card right here and now for fifteen hundred," he replies, a slimy smile on his face. His beady little eyes are glued to the cash. It's exactly why I held it up for him. I don't want him to notice the phone in my other hand.

"And you don't have any copies, because, buddy, I swear if you give them to her anyway..." I don't finish that sentence because I'm not about to threaten him on video.

"No other pics. I don't even back this shit up," he says and pops the memory card out of the camera. "I wouldn't fuck you over, dude. You look like you could fuck me up. What are you, like a personal trainer or bodyguard or something?"

I shove the money at him. He grabs it and hands me the memory card. "Get out of here and don't fucking follow me anymore. If I even see you on the street and you don't turn and walk the other way you will regret it."

"Sure thing, buddy." He gives me a yellow-toothed grin. He starts his van again, and I turn to leave. "But she's got other shit on you too."

I turn back to him. "What?"

"Some injury," he explains. "You took your daughter to the hospital and didn't tell her or something. I don't know. My partner covered the files part, and he already gave them to her. I told him he should see if you'd buy them."

"Go," I growl, and he has the fucking nerve to look offended for a second before he rolls up his window and drives away.

I head back into the houseboat while dialing Hunter.

20

SADIE

It's time to start make the final decision about the—"

"I understand." I cut the doctor off, because if he says the words I will break down. I can't break down. I have to be strong for my family. So he can't say the words *It's time to put in a feeding tube*. Because I will not hold it together. He's just finished giving me the devastating results of my dad's swallowing tests, which in a month have gotten worse, and I think he picks up on the fact I have to absorb that before he continues. After a minute of silence he goes on.

"I know in the past your father has indicated to me that he will not allow a feeding tube," the doctor says. I nod, my heart aching so badly I can barely breathe. "However, that opinion sometimes changes when the decision becomes imminent and not just a hypothetical."

"And it is imminent now." I can't believe my voice isn't shaking.

"It is." Her expression becomes a little softer as she adds, "If he says yes, I would start the process immediately."

"He won't change his mind," I tell her—and there it is. My voice shakes. I swallow and try to calm down. "My father doesn't make snap decisions. He's thought this out. He knew we'd end up here. He's never sugar-coated his illness to us or himself. He won't change his mind, and he knows what that means."

There is a small girl inside me, wailing and sobbing over the unfairness of this. The pure, brutal cruelness of this. I want to run into his hospital room and cry and scream like a child throwing a tantrum until my dad agrees to the feeding tube, but I won't. Instead I'll keep Dixie and Winnie from doing that, because they'll try. And I'll let my mom cry in my arms, and I'll make sure Jude doesn't punch anything. Because if he wasn't my dad, if this man was my patient, I would whole-heartedly get it. This disease has only begun taking away his life. A feeding tube prolongs the inevitable suffering. I under-stand that. I just don't want it to be true.

"Sadie?"

Oh. Apparently she was talking to me. I take a deep breath, but it's ragged. "I'm sorry, Dr. Lack, what was that?"

She stands up and walks around her desk. She sits on the edge of it in front of me. "Your family. When should we have this conversation with them?"

"Today. I'll get them to all come in," I say.

She leans forward and squeezes my shoulder. "I'm really sorry, Sadie."

"I know. I am too. Thank you for everything, especially giving me the chance to know first." I wish my heart would stop aching so damn hard. It's making me feel faint.

"Your dad okayed it. He must know how strong you are," she remarks.

"He knows I'm the only sane one," I joke, but it feels flat. She smiles anyway. I stand up. "I'm going to go check on him and wrangle the family."

"Let me know when they're all here, and I will come down to answer questions and talk about other options," she offers. "Although the feeding tube would be my best recommendation, we have other alternatives that can help a little."

I leave her office and walk slowly down the corridor. Everything feels wrong. The halls are too white, the floor tiles too shiny, the lights too bright, the people walking by too happy. My world is shattering, splintering, and people are just...continuing on. I'm on my way up to see my dad, but I can't make it. I slip into the restroom on his floor and lock myself in a stall and sit on the toilet with my head in my hands as my breathing becomes erratic. I am fighting off tears with every fiber of my being, and instead it's causing a panic attack. I focus on my breathing and will myself to take long, deep breaths even though it physically hurts.

With shaking hands I dial Griffin's number. I need someone, anyone, to talk to. I need to share this information—the weight of it—with someone I won't have to then pick up, emotionally or maybe even physically. But the call goes straight to voicemail. I open my mouth to leave a message but can't. I hang up.

I try again a few minutes later. Still nothing. God, I need him right now.

Stop it, Sadie. Just focus on your breathing and calm down. You can do this.

It takes me about twenty minutes, but I get myself together when I get a text from Dixie. She and Winnie and Mom are on their way over to visit Dad. Eli and Jude are at practice. I send her a text back telling her I will meet them here. She sends back another text saying she wants all the details of my hot night with "Coach Sexy Skates," which I guess is her new nickname for Griffin. Normally it would make me smile, but not today.

I turn off my phone instead of responding and get myself out of the stall and over to the sink, where I splash cold water on my face until the puffy redness brought on by the panic attack is mostly gone. Then I take some deep, cleansing breaths and head to my dad's room. He's sitting in a chair by the window reading *Sports Illustrated* when I knock on the open door. He looks up, and his blue eyes brighten when he sees me. He drops the magazine in his lap.

"Hey, pumpkin," he says. Pumpkin is his nickname only for me. Winnie is Sunshine. Dixie is Little D. Jude is just Jude. "Are you working today? I thought you were off."

He's slurring less than yesterday, less than he has in a while. I wish that could make me hopeful. I wish I didn't know that a good day in this illness is just that—a day. It ultimately changes nothing. I smile at him. "I'm not working. I came by to talk to your doctor and see your silly face."

"Watch it, pumpkin," he warns playfully. "You and Jude look the most like this silly face."

"Ugh. Don't remind me," I joke and drop dramatically onto his empty bed, which makes him laugh. I close my eyes and absorb that sound with every fiber of my being.

"Which doctor were you seeing, Sadie?" he asks as I sit up. "I've got so many these days it's hard to keep track."

"Dr. Lack, your neurologist."

"Aha. So that's why you've been crying." Our eyes meet, and he smiles.

"I haven't," I lie. "It's allergies."

"You're allergic to ALS side effects?" He tries to kid, but when I don't laugh or smile his expression grows solemn. "Honey...Dr. Lack told me the results too."

"Dad..."

"The answer is still no," he replies. His tone reminds me of the time I had a broken arm when I was seventeen but still wanted to go to a water park with my girlfriends, promising that I would wrap my plaster cast in a trash bag. He said no with the same remorse then. He wanted to give me what I wanted, but he couldn't. "We know how this ends, no matter how many tubes they put in me."

I nod.

"Your siblings are going to need you to talk them through this," he says. "You're the only one who can look at this as a professional. I need you, pumpkin."

You're still my dad, I want to cry to him, but that will make it harder on him, and that's not fair. So I just nod again. "They're on their way over now."

"Okay, good." He picks up his magazine again. "Did you know that *Sports Illustrated* wants to put your brother in the body issue?"

"You mean the issue with naked athletes?" I question, and he nods. "Gross."

Dad chuckles and then starts going on about the Thunder's prospects in the upcoming playoffs. I listen, but my brain is elsewhere. I'm planning what I will say to back up Dad's decision and how I will console my sisters. And then, as I run my words over and over in my head, along with every possibility from my family being okay with it to them screaming at the top of their lungs in protest, I remember Griffin's words from this morning.

"My question is, who is helping you come to terms with this?"

Where is he? Why isn't he there for me?

As my dad tries to explain what the Thunder need to do to make it back to the Stanley Cup Finals, I pull out my phone and turn it back on. I've got three more texts from Dixie asking me explicit questions about last night and what happened between Griffin and me. Everything from *Was he good? Did you come?* to *I hope you didn't forget how to do it. It's not like riding a bike.* But nothing from him. I text him.

Can you call me?

My phone buzzes again. My heart leaps and then nosedives when I see it's just Dixie demanding, in all caps, that I answer her immediately. I shove my phone back in my purse.

"Pumpkin, are you listening to me?"

"Sure, Dad." I grin at him, even though it's hard. "You said Thunder blah, blah, blah. Jude blah, blah, blah. Hockey blah, blah, blah."

He laughs.

"Good to see you laughing." My mom's voice fills the room from behind me, and I turn to see her smiling back at my dad. She squeezes my shoulder as she passes by me on her way to my dad.

The look on my dad's face when he sees my mom is utter perfection. It's love, adoration, and elation all whirling together. It's the look every woman deserves to see from the man she spends her life with.

"Sadie won't listen to my predictions for tonight's game," he complains as Winnie and Dixie walk into the room after my mom.

"Ugh. Hockey," Dixie says dramatically. "Can we talk about something else? Like why Sadie doesn't know how to answer text messages suddenly."

Oh, Dix, be careful what you wish for.

Winnie drops down on one side of me on the bed and Dixie on the other. Mom grabs the extra chair and pulls it up next to dad by the window.

"Well, the doctor came by with the results of the tests they did yesterday," Dad starts, and everyone freezes. "Let's all sit down."

Dixie and Winnie both look at me, and I take their each of their hands as I swallow down all the emotions brewing inside of me and almost choke.

21

SADIE

When are you telling Jude?" Winnie asks me from the back seat of Dixie's Mini.

"I'm not. Zoey is," I tell Winnie and try not to be annoyed that she just assumes this is my responsibility. "Dad and Mom told her this afternoon when she visited with Declan while Jude was taking his pregame nap."

"He's going to be devastated." Dixie states the obvious as she pulls into the parking lot of the Thunder arena. "I told Eli earlier. Are you telling Griffin?"

"I tried," I reply, and a wave of something that feels like rejection washes over me. "He didn't answer."

"Are you kidding me?" Winnie ask incredulously. "All day?"

I shrug and dig my phone out of my purse for the first time in hours. I didn't hear it ring or a text message alert go off, but I glance at the screen now to double check. It's black. Oh, my God, I have accidentally turned it off somehow.

"I told Ty," Winnie tells us and sniffs. She's finally stopped crying, but from the moment we left the hospital a couple hours ago, she's been breaking down in little sobbing fits. Surprisingly, neither Dixie nor Winnie argued with Dad about his decision. But since we left him and Mom alone at the hospital and went home to grab some food before the game, they've been begging me to change his mind, hammering me with questions, looking for loopholes in his rationale. Like maybe I hold some kind of extra nurse-only information that would contradict the vicious facts of this illness and make him change his mind. I don't. They know it, yet we talk about it for hours anyway.

I turn my phone back on and curse its slowness as it comes back to life.

"I would rather be anywhere but here," Winnie groans as we get out of the car and walk toward the entrance. There are hoards of fans around us, buzzing with excitement. It's so completely contradictory to our emotions, it almost feels like we're living in an alternate universe.

We walk to the private entrance and swipe our passes at the gate. "We have to go, and we have to pretend to have fun. It's what Dad wants," Dixie mutters. "He explicitly said we have to go to the game and cheer on Jude and Eli."

I stare at my screen. I have four missed calls from Griffin. There's one voicemail, so I type in my password so I can listen to it.

His voice is tense, frustration dripping off of it. "You told me to call, and I'm calling but you aren't answering? Is something wrong? Because I'm in the middle of a crisis myself and I need to talk to you too. Where are you? Call me!"

He's in crisis? That's his message? He sounds more annoyed than concerned, and it makes me angry. But it also makes me hurt. And what the hell is his crisis? I let out a heavy sigh. I started this morning in such a euphoric state, and it all went sideways. Now I feel defeated, broken, and so fucking tired. The last thing I need is to feel worse than I already do, but that's how I feel for not responding to Griffin. And there's this new weight on me, another burden, because he's clearly going through something, and he somehow needs me for that. Everybody fucking needs me.

"Do you know where the coaches are before the game?" I ask Dixie as we approach the friends and family lounge. "Are they in the locker room or their offices or up in a booth?"

"Not sure. When I worked here my only concerns were players and press," Dixie says, and then she waves at Zoey, who is sitting on one of the sofas in the lounge, with Declan passed out in her arms.

"I should put him down to nap, but..." Zoey motions toward the stroller in the corner of the room and then looks up at us with sad eyes. "I just need to snuggle him today, after everything. How are you all holding up?"

Dixie sits beside her and softly runs a hand through the baby's strawberry blond fuzz. Her eyes are visibly watering. "I don't know if he's even going to remember his grandfather."

"I need a drink," Winnie snaps and turns and heads to the bar.

"We'll make sure he does," Zoey promises, and she uses her free arm to side-hug Dixie. I feel my chest get tight and the pressure inside me grow. I feel like a car in one of those crushers, with everything pushing in on me on every side.

"I need to find Griffin," I mutter and walk out of the room. I also just need a break from my family...even though admitting that makes me feel horrible.

I'm walking down the hallway when the hockey team emerges from their dressing room ready to hit the ice.

"Hey, Braddock sister number...?" Duncan Darby, the big red-headed lug of a defenseman says with a dopey smile.

"Two," I finish for him. I look at the rest of the players marching by me. I see Levi next, and he walks right over to me. His expression is grim but that doesn't mean much. I can count on my fingers the number of times I've seen Levi crack a smile and the guy lived with my family for a summer.

"I'm so sorry about your dad, Sadie," he says quietly in that gravelly voice that is only rivaled by his brother Eli's low rumble. "Obviously I'm going to be here for Jude, but if you need anything just reach out, okay?"

I just nod. He tries to give me a hug, but it's awkward because of all the equipment and because it's Levi. Captain Robot, or whatever it is they call him.

Jude walks toward me and comes to a stop in front of me. In his skates, he's towering over me more than usual. "What are we going to do? How do we change his mind?"

Fuck.

"We'll talk after the game," I reply curtly.

"There's got to be something we can say to change his mind," he replies. "I'm going to start calling specialists again and—"

"You're going to get your head in the game and win this," I bark back. "That's what Dad wants right now and you know it."

He steps closer, and now he's right on top of me. It's not menacing, it's desperate. He lowers his voice; it's strained. "You think I give shit about hockey right now? It's taken everything in me not to walk the fuck out of here and go to the hospital and talk some sense into him."

"Braddock!" Levi calls in his captain voice, which is somehow deeper than his regular one. "We gotta go."

"Go. Put it aside and play well, Jude, please. Just do this for me," I beg and turn to leave him. Only now Eli is right in front of me. I know what he's going to say, so I answer him before he can get the words out. "She's trying to stay strong. She's in the lounge with everyone and she's holding it together, so stop worrying."

Thankfully, he nods and follows the rest of his team. Before he turns the corner. I call out. "Where's your coach?"

"Sully?" he questions and I nod. "He's in the owner's booth."

"Eli!" Levi barks.

I know I won't be able to see Griffin now until the first period ends, so I head back to the lounge to watch the game on the monitor in there with my sisters and Zoey and some of the other players' family members. I text him and tell him I'll be in the lounge. He doesn't text back right away, but I understand. His eyes have to be on the ice, not on his phone.

And just when I thought things couldn't get worse, they do. Winnie is still at the bar when I walk back in the lounge, and the bartender is refilling her shot glass. Clearly she's been downing tequila since I left. Dixie has red, puffy eyes, so she's been crying again, and Zoey looks like she joined her. Declan is the only one who isn't falling apart. I start to get a stress headache.

Jude takes two stupid penalties and gets into a fight in the first period. I wish I were at work because I could check my blood pressure there. I'm sure it's through the roof. My phone buzzes three minutes before the intermission. It's Griffin telling me to come to his office.

I jump up. Dixie looks up at me, sniffling. Winnie cracks another beer. Zoey is trying to soothe a fussing Declan, who seems to have started to pick up on the dismal energy of his relatives. "I'm going to meet Griffin. I'll be back."

I don't wait for any kind of response. I just leave the room and head down the hall, past the locker room and toward the offices. Griffin's door is open, and he's pacing behind the desk. Before I'm even in the door he's talking.

"Why haven't you returned my texts or calls?" he demands, and then continues before I can even respond. "We were being followed by a private investigator at the beach and at my house later. And I caught him and bought the images back, but he told me my ex knows about the hospital visit."

"Whoa! Slow down!" I feel like I'm being verbally accosted. "Why would your ex do that?"

"She wants to change our custody agreement. She wants to move to New York to be with her boyfriend, and she wants to take Charlie with her," he blurts out.

"Oh, my God, Griffin, why didn't you tell me?"

"I'm telling you now," he replies, his voice strained, just like his patience, apparently. I can't blame him. It's his daughter. I get it. But I can't help but be a little upset he didn't respond to me when I needed him, and he's not even asking me about it now.

I also feel blindsided and a little crestfallen that he didn't want to confide in me that he's been going through a custody battle. I have been really honest with him about the trials and tribulations in my life, and he either felt like he had to hide his or, worse, that I wasn't someone he wanted to confide in. "My brother is my lawyer, and he said that we're going to need a sworn statement from you since you treated Charlie. I've been trying to get a hold of you all day to tell you this."

"I got some horrible news about my dad today, which is why I was trying to reach you," I reply. Every single emotion flowing through me is raw to the point of almost being physically painful. I feel like I'm made of tissue paper, and all day everything and everyone has dropped a pebble onto me. And now Griffin, the person who promised he would make me stronger, is dropping a piano on me, and I'm tearing apart everywhere.

"Oh, fuck," he breathes, and his face falls. "I'm so sorry. I am such a dick."

"No. You're not." There's not an ounce of conviction behind my words. "You have every right to focus on your own issues."

"No, I know but..." He is struggling to find the words to fix this because I can see by the clouded look in his gorgeous, dark eyes that he sees the rails coming off this new relationship as clearly as I do. "I should have realized. I mean I know you were going to talk to his doctor."

"Yeah, but I understand," I say, because I do. I ignored him completely today because my problems were too big. He has every right to forget about mine when his are big. And losing your child is big. "You did nothing wrong or illegal with that hospital visit. Neither did the hospital."

"Sadie, talk to me about your dad," he says, coming around his desk to get closer to me. I take a step back. I have to because I can't open up to him. I'll break down, and I don't get to break down. I have to be the rock.

"No. Just tell me where I have to go to help you out," I reply.

"Sadie, I'm sorry," he whispers.

"I know. You're not a bad guy, Griffin," I say. I can feel my bottom lip quiver and my eyes start to sting. "I think you're probably the most incredible guy I've ever met. And there's something between us I have never felt before, but let's face it, I can't do this right now."

"What?" He looks as stricken as I feel.

"Give your brother my number. I will give a statement, I promise. I just can't promise anything else. And let's be honest, neither can you. It's not your fault and it's not mine, but I can't anymore." I start to walk toward the door.

I feel his hand wrap around my wrist, and I turn back to him, but I'm going to cry if I stay much longer, and I can't. I won't. Something inside me is starting to splinter. My strength? My sanity? Both? "Griffin, I have a lot to deal with right now. I thought I could handle this. That I had more to give because I would get something back, but...I don't. And neither do you."

"Don't tell me what I have to give," he growls back, frustrated by the truth.

"If, God forbid, your ex gets her way and Charlie moves to New York, what are you going to do?" I ask, and his mouth snaps shut, his jaw clenching. "You're going to quit your job and move to New York. And you should."

I gently pull my wrist back, and he lets it go, a sign of his surrender. I splinter even more inwardly. "I am about to break. If I give you my heart, if I let you in, I'll lose that too, and I can't handle losing anything else. I don't think you can either."

He is giving up. I can see it on his face. My eyes fill with tears despite the fact that it's exactly what he needs to do. Still, he steps closer, grabs my face in his hands and kisses me. It's desperate and passionate and painful. It's goodbye.

I don't let it drag on. I tear my mouth from his and leave, choking on a sob, refusing to let it out. Refusing to break...because no one is there to put me back together.

22

GRIFFIN

Hunter's assistant greets me with a sympathetic smile. "He said to go right in."

"Thanks, Debra." I don't even try to smile back.

Hunter is behind his desk wearing a suit, which means he must have to go to court later. He gives me his trademark laid-back smile as I drop into one of the fancy armless leather chairs across from him. "You look rough, G."

"Great," I mutter, but I know he's right. I threw on an old frayed T-shirt and jeans from the bottom of my closet because I haven't done wash in a while. Plus I drank too much when I got home last night, hoping it would help me sleep, but it didn't. I'm well aware I'm not top-notch this morning.

"I can have Deb make you a coffee. She makes a killer latte," Hunter says. I give him a curt nod, so he calls out, "Deb, two of your magical lattes, stat!"

"Already on it!" Deb calls back.

I glance at my watch. "When is she supposed to be here?"

"In about twenty minutes," Hunter replies and then pauses. "Why are you asking me that? To be honest, I'm a little shocked you didn't come in together."

Our eyes meet, and he groans. "You ended it? What the hell, Griff. Why?"

Shit. He's almost as devastated as I am, and he hasn't even met her. I would feel bad for him if I weren't feeling horrific myself. "It wasn't my decision. It was hers, but I completely agree with it."

"Of course you do." Hunter's sarcasm is undeniable. "Griffin doesn't let Griffin have nice things."

"What the fuck are you talking about?"

"Do you like her?"

I nod.

"So why end it? Why let her talk you out of it? Why not talk her *into* it?" He looks like my mom used to when she didn't like my report card. But unlike with my mom, I can talk back to him.

"Back off. It's complicated."

"Life is complicated. Deal with it or be alone and miserable forever," he gripes.

I lean forward, my elbows on my knees. "I like her. A lot. I feel this connection with her I haven't felt before. Not even with Lauren. I think I was chasing it with Lauren. We were almost there...but we never got there. With Sadie, it's been there since we met."

He leans back in his big black leather chair and lifts his hands as if to say WTF. "You're just making my point, dumbass."

"But she's going through a lot with her family, and she needs someone who can be there for her," I explain and press my fingertips into my temples. "And no, I don't want to be alone, but the fact is the only thing that will make me truly miserable is if I lose Charlie."

"You are not going to lose her," Hunter promises me for the millionth time. "Jesus, Griff. You need to have faith in me. I would never let that happen."

"You know if Lauren gets her custody wish and she moves Charlie to New York that I am moving too, right?" I reply.

Hunter sighs, and his shoulders droop. "Yeah. I know. You didn't even have to say it. But it doesn't matter because that's not happening. And honestly, Charlie is old enough to testify herself and will have a say in this. You know she won't want to leave you."

"I am not making her choose between us." My words are so hard they're almost a growl. I take a breath to calm down. "Lauren and I made a pact about that from the get-go and I am going to stick to it."

There's a knock at the door, so our conversation halts. Debra walks in with two coffee mugs. She places them on Hunter's messy desk and pats my shoulder as she leaves. I grab the latte and take a big, scalding sip before looking at my watch again. "She's late. Maybe she's not coming. Maybe something happened with her dad. Or maybe she just decided not to do it."

Hunter raises both his eyebrows. He just needs a floral dress and he really could pass as our mom. "She would call if something came up, and she won't just bail. You wouldn't be falling in love with a girl who bails on something so important to you."

He's got me there. And as if the universe is proving the point, there's a tap at the door, and I turn to find Debra ushering Sadie into the room. I stand in concern the minute I see her, because she looks worse than I do. Her pale skin is so much paler than normal it's almost translucent. And she's got dark bags under her light blue eyes. She blinks, surprised to see me. "Hi. I didn't know you'd be here."

Hunter stands and walks around his desk. "I like to have him here so he knows what's going down. He's more than a little stressed about this."

"Rightfully so," she replies and extends her hand. "Sadie Braddock."

"Hunter Sullivan." Hunter smiles at her and cracks the joke he always cracks when he meets people when I'm around. "He's the Sullivan brawn and I'm the Sullivan brain."

She doesn't laugh. All she manages is a smile, but it's forced. Luckily, Hunter doesn't take it personally, because I know she doesn't mean it that way. Something is wrong with her and even if it's not my place, I need to know what it is.

"Hunter..."

"I'm going to go get you a latte," Hunter announces, knowing I'm about to ask him for a minute alone with her.

"I don't need coffee," she argues, but her voice has no fight in it. "I just want to get this done."

"You're early. It's fine." Hunter smiles and heads out.

She looks at me, almost desperate, as she runs a hand through her hair and sighs so heavily it's more of a shudder.

"Talk to me, love," I whisper. "How are things with your dad?"

"He came home this morning," she says and walks away from me, over to the chairs, but she doesn't sit down.

"That's good, right?" I prod gently. "Everyone will calm down."

She nods and for a second, I swear I think I see her shudder again. "Everyone in my family is on better emotional ground...except me. I barely slept all night. My heart feels like it's beating erratically. There's a constant pressure in my chest and my stress headache I've had for two days is turning into a migraine. But I don't have time for that because I have to work. It's the only thing that will keep my mind occupied. And I have to get home before I go in for my twelve-hour shift so I can make sure my mom is doing okay and remind Winnie not to cry in front of my dad or fight with Ty in front of my mom."

"I think you need to sit down. Right now. And that's all you need to do," I tell her firmly but with a gentle tone. She looks confused by that command, so I reach out and hold her shoulders and guide her down into the chair. She's resisting me a little at first, but once her butt touches the leather she sags, like a deflating balloon.

"He's not going to get a feeding tube," she whispers so softly I almost don't hear it. "The doctors say it's time, and he said no."

"Is that why Jude was playing like a rabid animal last night?" He spent more time in the penalty box than he had all season. She nods and starts to pull her phone out of her purse. "That reminds me, I have to call Jude. He told me to let him know when Dad got home this morning and if he settled in okay. I forgot. He won't go over there himself because he knows Dad watched him be an idiot on the ice last night, and he wants to avoid the lecture."

I take her phone out of her hand and squat down in front of her. "Sadie... It's time to concentrate on you, not them."

"I can't. We're losing him. The countdown clock just jumped forward. I have to keep them together for his sake. I won't let his last few months with us be filled with Jude's penalty minutes and Winnie's drunken outbursts and Dixie's uncontrollable sobs. He's always strong for us. I'm going to be strong for him."

I don't even think she knows she's crying until I reach out and wipe away the tears with the pads of my thumbs. Her big cornflower blue eyes get bigger, like she's terrified at the realization she's breaking. I do the only thing I can, the thing it feels like I was born to do: I pull her to me and I hold her. She fights it at first, her body rigid and her breath held, but then, all at once, she lets go.

As she sobs in my arms, I rub her back and hold her tight. Over her shoulder I see Hunter walk back in with a latte and immediately turn and walk back out. She doesn't notice, and I don't move. I just let her continue because she needs it desperately, and I know if I don't hold her and comfort her, no one will.

"I'm sorry," she says after about fifteen minutes of crying so hard that the shoulder of my shirt is soaked and stained with her mascara. "I'm here to help you, not weep all over you."

She starts to pull away, and I reluctantly let her. As she wipes at her wet cheeks, embarrassed, I run a hand over her hair, smoothing it down. "It's okay. Everyone in your life needs you to be strong, but I don't. You hold up everyone else. Let me hold you up."

Her eyes are on mine, filled with a pain and sadness that crushes me. "You can't do that. Not now."

She's right. I know she's right. But I don't care about logic. I just care about her.

This time Hunter knocks as he enters. Sadie stands quickly, wiping at her eyes again. I stand too and grab a box of tissue off the bookcase beside Hunter's desk and hold it out to her. Sadie grabs a couple and dabs at her eyes again. "Sorry," my brother says. "I just have to be in court in an hour, so we need to start this."

"Of course." The broken girl is gone and Sadie's back to being the reliable, confident, calm woman way too many people rely on. And here I am relying on her too. Fuck, this sucks.

For the next half hour Hunter takes detailed testimony about what went on the night I brought Charlie into the ER. Sadie praises everything about how I handled the situation and how good I was with Charlie.

"Griffin was kind and gentle but firm with Charlie for her mistake, and he was loving and empathetic to her when she got embarrassed about why it happened," Sadie explains to my brother as the little red light on his tape recorder blinks rhythmically as it records her. "He reminded me of my dad. And my dad is the best."

Hunter asks a few more technical questions about how

Charlie was treated and gets her to explain, on the record, that we followed all policy and procedure, and the hospital was not legally required to tell Lauren. By the time the interview is done, she's composed again. There's no sign she was just broken, sobbing in my arms, except for the slightly puffy look to her eyes and the slightly red tinge to her cheeks and nose.

"Thanks for doing this, Sadie," Hunter says when he shuts off the recorder.

"I hope it helps Griffin," she says, but she won't look at me. It's like she's talking about someone who isn't in the room.

"Thanks. I hope we run into each other again sometime, for a better reason,"

Hunter smiles at her as she stands up and grabs her purse off the floor. I stand with her. "Let me walk you out."

"You shouldn't," she replies quietly but firmly.

"But I'm going to," I counter, and as she starts for the door, I follow.

We pass Debra, and I hold open the door for her to Hunter's small office and we walk down the hall, past other offices, toward the elevator. I stand so close to her that our hands keep brushing. It's on purpose. I can see the struggle on her beautiful face. She wants to step away, so we don't touch, but she doesn't. She knows we're just making things harder on each other, but she can't help but let it happen either.

I hit the call button for the elevator for her. "Thank you. I know you've got a lot on your plate, so the fact that you made time for me—to do this—is incredible." I turn and look at her. "You are incredible."

"You're my unicorn," she says softly with that playful

smile that instantly makes my dick start to get hard. "I can't say no to a unicorn. It's worse than looking a gift horse in the mouth."

"You're a little nuts, you know that?" I chuckle softly under my breath.

Her smile deepens. "Oh, I'm a lot crazy. In the best possible way."

The elevator dings, and the doors slide open. There's an elderly lady inside. Sadie glances up at me.

"Thank you. For being there for that...meltdown." I nod. She just stares up at me. "It won't happen again."

"It's okay if it does," I say.

"I wish that were true."

The doors start to close, and she jumps through them so quickly, they bounce back a bit. The elderly lady frowns. Sadie just gives her a dazzling "I'm sorry" smile. I start to walk on too, but Sadie looks up at me, and her eyes are like a brick wall, right up in my face, telling me no. So I stop and watch the doors close, cutting her off from me physically. Mentally, she's already started to do that too.

23

SADIE

My heart sinks when I open the front door to the house and hear what sounds like a million voices. I had a hard overnight shift after a giant car accident and the vicious flu running rampant through the city right now had our ER overflowing. But it was a bit of a blessing in disguise because I was so busy I could almost ignore that aching in my chest over... well, everything. My life makes me ache. I'm not a psychiatric nurse, but even I know that's not good. Not even close.

"Hey! How was work?" Jude asks. He's the first to notice me as I toe out of my shoes and hang my coat on the rack in the hall. He looks at my scrubs. "Gross. What is that?"

I look down at a yellowish-brown stain on the front of my shirt. "Bodily fluid of some kind. Maybe multiple kinds."

"Okay. Again, gross."

"Kidding. It's mustard from my hot dog at lunch. But stop being a baby. You get blood on your jerseys all the time," I remind him as I walk past him. He turns and follows me as

I go into the kitchen. It's the room farthest away from all the voices. I think the whole family is in the den, and I don't feel like joining them.

"Yeah, but it's like a badge of honor, because I've earned the bloodshed, either mine or someone else's," Jude explains. "Badge of honor, battle wounds and all that."

"I've earned this." I point to the stain and start to sniff. Something smells incredible, and I look to see the oven is on. "Because I saved every life tonight. No flatlines."

Jude lifts his hand, palm out, and I high-five him. "My sister, the real hero."

"Damn fucking right." I smile back and then crack the oven door. "You got Winnie to make her shakshuka?"

He grins. "She volunteered. I guess miracles do exist."

Winnie is an incredible cook, just like our mom, and this savory Middle Eastern egg dish she perfected is a family favorite. But since we moved here, she hasn't even turned on the stove. She also used to love to knit and took Zumba classes every night, but now she doesn't do any of that. She doesn't teach either, because she swears there's no point getting her California credentials when she's heading back to Toronto, and Ty, the guy she can't stop bickering with, eventually. She tutors kids after school with a private company, but she doesn't even have a spark for that anymore like she used to. So this change in her behavior brings me a smidgen of relief.

"Everyone is in the den, and Win said the food will be ready soon," he says. "Why don't you grab one of those gross juices you like and join them and eat with us before you hit the hay?"

Okay. He's acting weird. Normal Jude would make some snarky remark about how I should go straight to bed so I didn't eat all the shakshuka.

"I'm not in the mood for a Braddock family function," I say and yawn. "I have a brutal shift so I'm probably going to grab a kombucha—which FYI isn't gross, and does more good for your body than your stupid salt lamp—and head to bed."

"Come on, Sadie. Give us a little love," Jude begs, and again I'm weirded out. "We're all just relaxing. Nobody's off the rails, needy or bitchy. Give us a chance."

"What the fuck is up with you?" I can't help but ask.

He opens the fridge and hands me a kombucha. Winnie pops up in the doorway from the hall and smiles at me brightly. Too brightly. "Hey! Glad you're home. I just have to warm up the naan and we should be ready to eat."

She pushes us both gently out of the way and starts to zip around the kitchen. I survey the scene, growing more and more skeptical. Out of the corner of my eye I see movement through the arched doorway in the dining room as the rest of the family gathers. Eli and Dixie go to the buffet hutch and start laying out dishes and utensils, and Mom wheels Dad up to his place at the head of the table, and Zoey gets Declan situated in his high chair. They all call out happy greetings when they see me.

"Hey, Sadie, when is your next day off?" Dixie asks.

"Day after tomorrow," I reply.

"I'm booking a girls' day," she replies.

"But it's a Wednesday, and you have work," I remind her. "Winnie has tutoring."

"I can take it off. The other tutors can cover," Winnie replies as she grabs the butter out of the fridge. "I am not passing up a massage and a pedicure. Or time with you."

"Really? Why?"

"Because my toes are in desperate need of attention. And who passes up a massage?" she counters as she pulls the two cast-iron skillets with the delicious egg dishes out of the oven and puts them down on the stovetop.

"I mean, why do you want time with me? I see you every single day." My mouth waters as the heavenly scent of her shakshuka fills the room. My willpower is gone. I'm not going to bed without some of that in my belly.

She shrugs. "I know, but we desperately need a mimosa, massage, pedicure, and shopping day. Like how we used to be."

"Don't question it, Sadie. It's a good idea," my dad advises.

I walk into the dining room and drop down into a chair after nuzzling Declan's cheek and giving him a kiss that makes him grin. He's just like his daddy: he loves female attention. I smile and actually feel myself start to loosen up a bit; the tension I've been carrying like a backpack starts to get lighter. I roll my shoulders.

"We can be normal," Winnie tells me way too enthusiastically, and she carries in one of the cast-iron pans and puts it down on a trivet. "You don't have to worry about us."

"Why would you say that?" Every fiber of my being is tingling. Something happened. I look around the table, and everyone is looking at anything but me.

"Jude . . ." I say.

"It's been too long since we have had this amazing meal. We shouldn't let it get cold," Jude says.

"Jude Jackass Braddock."

"Sadie!" my mom warns.

Jude sighs. Dixie jumps in. "So your boyfriend might have mentioned to Elijah that we need to take it easy on you for a while."

"Yeah, he basically said that we're leaning on you like a wall and you're starting to crumble," Jude adds, and my anger surges so fast I feel light-headed.

"I don't have a boyfriend." My voice is shaking so hard that it makes Zoey's face constrict with concern.

"You prefer the term 'lover'?" Winnie asks and scrunches up her nose.

"Or boy toy?" Eli jokes.

"Man toy," Dixie corrects.

"Senior citizen toy," Jude adds.

"I'm not seeing him anymore," I bark back, and the whole table falls silent instantly. "And he had no right talking to any of you about anything. I'm fine. I don't need you all to act like pod people. It's a hard thing we're dealing with."

I look at my dad. He's looking back at me with such sympathy in his eyes, it makes me shake. He's dying right in front of us, every second of the day, and he's got sympathy for me. That's the last thing I wanted. Ever. I stand up.

"Wait a minute…" Jude's eyes cloud with concern. "Why did you break up with him? What did he do?"

Oh, great. Now my brother wants to punch him. "He didn't do anything. I ended it. He's dealing with some stuff and I'm dealing with stuff, and I can't do it. I just can't. I knew I couldn't. I told you I couldn't and I can't."

I am shaking, from my toes all the way up, like my body is suffering its own personal earthquake. My mom stands up, her hazel eyes wide with fear. "Sadie, sweetheart, come here."

"No, Mom, I need...to sleep." I step away from the table. Every single one of them stands up too. As I walk away from the table, through the kitchen, Jude, Winnie, and Dixie all start to follow.

"Give her space," I hear my dad command as I reach the hall and grab my purse off the floor by the door, where I dropped it when I came in. "Let her go."

I don't turn around, but I'm not surprised when the stampede of footsteps behind me stops. I march all the way down the hall to my room and then close and lock the door before falling facefirst into my bed. How dare Griffin do that! We can't be together. He agreed—easily. So why the hell is he still inserting himself into my life? Why is he looking out for me? How am I supposed to stop myself from falling in love with him if he keeps doing this?

I storm into my bathroom, grab the melatonin out of the medicine cabinet, and take two because I know without it, even after a grueling twelve-hour shift, I won't sleep now, and all I want to do is be unconscious so I can't think about any of this.

I pull off my scrubs and dump them on the floor in the vicinity of the laundry hamper and drop onto my bed, pulling the covers up over my head. I just want to disappear.

* * *

I wake up five and a half hours later. I'm still cocooned under the covers. I was dreaming throughout—chaotic, nonsensical, unrelated dreams—but I only remember random moments of it all. Griffin, shirtless. Winnie crying. And me caught in the ocean, in pitch blackness, fighting wave after wave. That's been my stress dream since I was a kid, so it doesn't surprise me, but as always it leaves me feeling less refreshed than I would normally be after sleeping for so long. I sigh, and my brain is flooded with the memories of what went on with my family, and I suddenly feel tired again.

But I am also hungry and there's no denying it. I have to emerge from my room and face my family or die of starvation. Feeling numb, I walk into my bathroom again. I take a scalding hot shower, washing my hair and body twice because I just feel gross, inside and out. Afterward I towel off and walk, like a robot, over to my dresser and throw on leggings and a T-shirt and reluctantly open the door to my bedroom.

I'm greeted by silence, which is an unexpected relief. I wonder if they've all left, but it seems doubtful, because it takes a lot of effort to take my dad anywhere right now. I walk slowly, almost tentatively, like a skittish mouse, down the main hall of the massive penthouse apartment. I glance into the den, but no one is there. The small home office my mom turned into a craft room: no one. The main hall powder room's door is open, and it's empty too. Winnie's bedroom door is closed so I just scoot by that, praying the very old oak floorboards don't creak. In the kitchen I open the fridge and find a plate with shakshuka and naan, covered in plastic wrap and topped with a Post-It note with my name on it, in my mom's handwriting. I grab the plate, unwrap it, and stick it in the microwave.

When it's heated through, I move to the dining room, which is also empty, and devour my food. It's still fantastic, even reheated. I finish it and even shamelessly lick the plate. Then I stick it in the dishwasher, grab another kombucha out of the fridge, and am about to head back into my room when my dad calls to me from his bedroom.

"Pumpkin, can we talk for a minute?"

I sigh and turn toward his bedroom. From the doorway I can see him lying in his special hospital-style bed, with his head elevated and a book in his lap. "You're alone?"

"No. You're here. Winnie and Dixie took Mom to the movies. Jude and Eli went to practice. Zoey and Declan went home," he explains. "Maria should be here in about twenty minutes to help me shower and do some physical therapy."

"Okay," I say simply and play with a strand of my damp hair while I lean on the doorjamb.

"Can you come in and keep your old man company until she gets here?"

"Depends," I reply and give him a small smile. "Is my old man going to act like a pod person or play psychiatrist or is he just going to be my fantastic old man?"

"Just your dad. I promise."

I walk into the room, and he moves his legs so I can sit at the foot of the bed, facing him. My eyes fall to the book on his lap. Not surprisingly it's a novel about nineteenth-century New England. Historical novels are his favorite. New England is his favorite. I nod toward the book. "Is it any good?"

"It's fascinating," he replies. "This farmer has only daughters, five of them, and is struggling to find them good partners."

"Ah, the good old days when women weren't allowed to make their own decisions." I roll my eyes, and he chuckles.

"It was the good old days," he counters with a wink. "Because at least then I would be able to make sure you didn't become an old maid."

I let out a whoop of amused shock, and it makes him grin so big it warms my heart. "There is not enough time in the world to talk about how annoyingly misogynistic that statement is, Dad."

"You know I was kidding," he replies, his smile still big enough to warm my heart, but it starts to soften. "But I do worry about you. I didn't mean to put too much on you."

"You didn't," I promise, and our eyes connect. That sixth sense of his is seeing right through me. "Okay, it's a lot. It hurts. It's hard, but I want to be here for everyone. I want to be there for you most of all. Whatever you need. Please don't stop relying on me. I need you to rely on me. It's hard because you're dying and I can't change that. So let me be there."

There is a lump in the center of my throat the size of a monster truck tire. I struggle against it. He reaches up and cups the side of my face, and I grab his hand and hold onto it. "You're the only one who has the balls to use the D word. No one else can say I'm dying. That's why I rely on you. But I need you to have someone to rely on too. Like this Griffin fellow. He seems to be looking out for you."

He pauses and takes some labored breathes. Talking is

physically draining for him, but I am so grateful he is making the effort. The day I can no longer hear his voice is too close.

"Griffin is incredible," I admit, and a tiny sharp stab of pain hits me in the chest, like just admitting that is the equivalent of stabbing myself in the heart. "But his life is complicated right now too. He's got a young daughter and he's going through a custody problem with the ex, who wants to move to New York and take the daughter with her. If that happens…he'll quit his job and move too." My father absorbs that information and gives my hand another squeeze. "I don't want to get more involved with him if I'm just going to lose him. I can't willingly set myself up for heartbreak."

"He doesn't feel the same way."

"He agreed with me."

"But he's still looking out for you, making sure someone is there for you since you don't want him there," he replies.

"I want him there. I just can't."

"I'm not trying to pressure you, Sadie, I promise, but consider this," my dad says and pauses until I look up and meet his eye. "If you told me, back when I was a kid, that my life was going to end this way, too soon and in such a shitty way, I would have still let myself fall in love with your mom. I would have still had every single one of you. The only thing I would have changed is I would have enjoyed the hell out of every single second even more than I did and not taken any of them for granted or worried about what-ifs or tried to protect myself."

I want to respond, but I'm choking on my emotions right now and can barely breathe, let alone speak. My dad pauses to rein in his own emotions, his eyes a little more watery than they should be. I panic he's going to cry, but he pulls himself together. "The only reason I'm still here and I haven't given up is because of the love I have for my family and your mother. It's the only thing that's made me fight this disease. Nothing is promised to us forever. But we have to take it when we can get it. Even if we see the expiration date coming."

I hear noise in the hall, and Maria calls out her arrival. I take a shallow, shaky breath because my chest is aching so hard. "In here, Maria!" I call and stand up and walk over to the head of the bed and hug my dad.

"Love you, pumpkin," he says as he rubs my back.

"Afternoon, Mr. Braddock," Maria says as she walks in with a smile.

I give her a wave as I head out of the room to let them do what they need to do. There's a knock at the front door, which stops me dead in the hall. Normally someone would have to buzz to get up to our apartment unless they have keys like Maria does. I look through the peephole and see Eli staring back at me. I unlock and open the door.

"Hey!" he says and gives me a nervous smile. "How ya feeling?"

"I'm good," I say. "How did you get in?"

He holds up Dixie's Cookie Monster key chain. "I used Dixie's keys, but I didn't feel right just barging in."

"She's not here," I reply and open the door wider so he can step into the apartment.

"I know, which is why I came to see your dad, actually." He gives me another nervous smile.

"I'm confused," I say and shake my head.

He kind of rocks on his feet nervously, his hands shoved deep into the pockets of his jeans. "I also wanted to tell you, since I ran into you, that I'm sorry for passing on Griffin's concerns to everyone. I just...well, I kind of agree with him. And I want you to know that you can come to me to vent or whatever if you want. I am kind of an expert on family drama."

Eli and Levi spent most of their lives at odds with their parents. Mr. and Mrs. Casco are not huge fans of their kids playing sports for a living. They even tried to talk Eli into leaving hockey when he was struggling to make the NHL. I give him a halfhearted smile. "Thanks."

"Griffin is a great guy, not just a great coach," Eli tells me with sincerity in his gaze. "I know you know that, but I feel like I should remind you. Levi and I are taken, and so your options for guys this great are limited now."

I laugh, and it sounds so foreign. I haven't done that since...I was with Griffin. I can't think about it. I don't want to right now. I'm already too overwhelmed, so I change the subject. "If you want to see my dad, you'd better get in there now before he gets in the shower."

Eli grins nervously again. What the hell is up with him? I am about to ask, but he heads into my dad's room, knocking on the open door as he enters. I head back to my room, leaving the door open, and pick up my phone. No messages. No missed calls. I pull up the picture of Griffin and me horseback riding. I look happy. Deeply, purely, simply happy. So does he, for that matter.

I don't know how long I'm staring at it, but suddenly I hear my dad whoop, like he does when Jude scores in hockey. What the hell is going on?

By the time I get to my dad's room, Eli is walking out. His nervous grin has turned to one of elation and his trademark cocky swagger is back in full force. "Hey, Spinster Sadie."

"Ouch. Thanks," I say and make a face. "What's going on with my dad?"

"He's just happy."

"Clearly, but why?" I want to know.

"Because he's finally getting a better son than Jude," Eli remarks with a wink, and I laugh again.

"You're getting better with the Jude snark, Eli. I commend you," I say and then the meaning of his words sink in. "Wait...you asked Dixie to marry you?"

He shakes his head. "Not yet. I wanted to get your dad's blessing first."

"Oh, my God!" I almost scream in excitement. Eli shushes me, but I will not be silenced. I pull him into a hug. "This is so great! When are you going to ask her? Where are you going to do it? What if she says no?"

I pull back from the hug and see his entire face fall, and I laugh. "I'm teasing. She'll say yes. She's insane about you. Or just insane. Either way, she will say yes."

"I haven't worked out the details yet. I just wanted to do this first," Eli explains. He starts to look nervous again, like he did when I answered the door. "I think she'll say yes, but I know there's a lot going on right now, and she might want to hold off. You know, until...I know it's going to be hard to plan what's supposed to be a happy thing when something so unhappy is happening."

"Don't wait," I say immediately, my voice thick with conviction. "Do it as soon as you can. It will give us a reason to celebrate again. It'll give my parents hope, and most importantly it will give Dixie happiness, which is something that's going to be hard to come by."

"You're right." His green eyes lock with mine. "Now take your own advice, dumbass."

He turns and head to the door but pauses as he opens it. "Please don't tell her any of this. I want it to be a complete surprise."

"Stop calling me dumbass then," I counter jokingly, but I feel like a lightbulb is turning on inside me and I won't be able to turn it off. "Win your game tonight."

He nods. "You're not coming?"

"Working," I reply, and he turns his big frame, starting to disappear through the front door. "Eli! What time do coaches have to be at the rink for a game?"

He starts to smile. "Griffin usually heads over about an hour before."

He leaves, and I run to my room to get dressed in something presentable. If I'm going to give my heart to someone who might have no choice but to crush it, I'm at least going to look good while I do it.

24

GRIFFIN

I need to get my head into hockey. I need to focus. But I can't stop thinking about Charlie. She stayed over last night, and we had a good time. We watched a movie. I have become an expert in cartoon movies, and I didn't think she'd seen *Brave* yet, but I thought she might like it.

She didn't just like it, she adored it. Her eyes were like saucers the entire movie, and she squealed with delight and cackled with laughter, and it made my heart feel so much better than it has. I asked her what she loved about the movie.

"Merida has hair like me," she said with a ear-to-ear grin. "And she likes tough stuff like I do, not boring stuff. Dad, I wanna bow and arrow."

I'd guessed that was coming. "How about I talk to your mom and find you some archery classes. Nobody's getting arrows and bows without training."

"That would be so cool!" She clapped her hands and then

bounced on the couch as if a thought had just exploded inside her. "Oh! And I love that she has a horse!"

The minute she says it I think of Sadie. Her love of horses. The amazing time we had. How much I miss her. I regret not getting a copy of that picture of us she took. God, she looked so beautiful that evening. Did I tell her that? God, I miss her.

"Daddy?" Charlie prompted because I had zoned out. "I know you can't get me a horse. It can't live on a boat. But I'd be okay with a dog that looks like a horse."

I grinned at her. "Of course you would."

And then I tickled her to change the subject.

But ever since that moment, I haven't been able to shake two strong feelings: how much I miss Sadie and how much I love Charlie—and how cruel it feels that the second thing is causing the first thing. I'll never leave my daughter. It's a simple, undeniable truth that if she moves to New York, I'm moving too. But I know, without a shadow of a doubt, that I'm leaving behind the best relationship I'll never have.

A knock at the door startles me as I'm pulling my suit out of the closet to get ready for tonight's game. I walk over to the glass French doors that open to the balcony and look out. I can't see anyone, so I open the doors and step out. I am leery about just going down and opening the door, worried it's another fucking private detective or some other bullshit. Right now I'm likely to snap at a Girl Scout selling cookies I'm so tense.

I can't see who it is, but what I do see is a giant, inflatable, metallic unicorn balloon. My heart stutters in my chest. The only person who would bring me that is . . .

"Sadie?" I call out tentatively.

Suddenly she's looking up at me. She looks un-fucking-believable in a little flowered summer dress, with her hair wavy and loose around her shoulders, and her lips are a perfect deep shade of red. She gives me a sheepish smile. "Can we talk?"

"Of course." I head back inside and downstairs as fast as I can without losing my towel. As soon as I open the door, I regret not taking a second to throw on real clothing. She looks even better up close, and I am already fighting not to get hard. She hands me the balloon.

"I know. It's stupid, but there was a balloon vendor we passed in the Presidio, and I made the Lyft driver stop and I ran back and got him," she explains, almost tripping over her words. "I know it's silly, but I'm silly. And weird. And wild."

"I know," I reply, taking the balloon from her. "And it's only half of what makes you amazing."

"But I'm actually kind of stupid too," she confesses. "And very, very, very messed up right now. I mean... I'm a daddy's girl. We all are. I stupidly thought he would be around for decades. Because he deserved to see us grow up. We're adults, but not really."

I smile at that, because I can relate. When Charlie was born I was amazed at how young and unprepared I felt. I sometimes still have moments where I feel like I'm not adult enough to babysit a kid, let alone have one of my own. I think about how I've called my parents in those moments and relied on them. How they were there for me during my divorce with kind words and support. "I don't think we're ever adult enough to lose a parent."

"True, and I also think, now, that I'm also never going to be whole enough to ensure I can handle heartbreak," she announces, and my heart sinks like a stone. I have no idea why she is here, but it was beginning to feel like she wanted to be together, but now…"Pushing away someone you're falling in love with because of something that might not happen is stupid. I don't want to be stupid anymore."

"You're falling in love with me?" I whisper roughly as I let the balloon go. Her sky-blue eyes follow it as it rises to the ceiling before she lets them land back on my face.

"You're a unicorn. It's impossible not to," she replies softly, nervousness making her voice tremble a little bit. "Which is terrifying, for the record."

"It's okay, I've got you," I reply and cup the side of her face. "I'll fall with you."

She looks like she might cry, but she doesn't. Instead she jumps me. Literally. Before I can blink she's got her arms wrapped around my neck, her legs wrapped around my waist, and her lips on mine. I stumble but kiss her back with everything in me. This incredible, wild, uncontrollable warrior of a woman is giving herself to me, and I am not going to stop her.

The kiss is exactly what I didn't know I needed. Just like Sadie herself. I walk us toward the living room. My towel is slipping lower and lower and I don't care. I carry her up the staircase and into my bedroom.

"Stop me if you want to," I murmur against the column of her throat. She responds by reaching down and curling her fingers into my towel at my hip and yanking it off. She drops it somewhere on the stairs.

"I don't want you to stop," she says after I lie her down on the bed and slide my hands up her thighs, moving her dress up, revealing inches and inches of glorious skin. But I hesitate. Nothing has changed. She feels my touch falter, and she props herself up on her elbows. "I want this—you—now. Even if I can't have you later. My dad made me realize if it's now or never, I should take now."

"Remind me to thank your dad."

Her hands run down my back to my ass, and she grabs me—hard. "Let's stop talking about my dad."

I am more than willing to oblige.

Her clothes come off, the condom goes on, and we make love at a bruising pace, both of us starving for each other's touch, hungry for the satisfaction we seem to be perfect at giving each other. She comes first, clawing at my back and moaning sweet obscenities in my ear. Her dirty mouth and the pulse of her pussy send me off into my own oblivion.

I collapse on her, burying my face in her neck and kissing my way from her collarbone to her lips. She kisses me back, her fingernails grazing lightly, pleasurably across the back of my neck and into my hair.

"I have to shower again," I say softly, almost apologetically, because I don't want to leave her, but I'm precariously close to being late for work.

"I can help with that," she tells me with a wicked little grin. "I'm trained in bathing people."

I laugh. She carefully pulls herself up, so I slip out of her, and then she wiggles her way out from under me. Hopping out of the bed, she takes my hand and pulls me to my feet and toward the bathroom.

* * *

While we're in the shower, she asks me about the custody hearing. I tell her how nervous I am. She kisses my shoulder and wraps her arms around me, hugging me from behind as the water pours down on us. "No judge in their right mind is going to upset a happy kid. And Charlie is happy, Griffin. That means you're a good dad."

I hold onto her words and let them give me hope. She has to be right. I have a little more than a week to wait until I find out, but now that I have Sadie back in my life, it will be easier. Everything feels better already. After we get out of the shower and get dressed, I drive her home and head straight to the arena. I'm about twenty minutes later than normal, but nobody notices, or if they do, they don't say anything. I head straight to the locker room to check on Eli. He's not there.

"He's in the trainer's room," Jude informs me, and I feel panic. Is something wrong? "He's says his left quad is tight. He told me to tell you it's nothing."

I chuckle. "How considerate. But I'll believe it when I talk to the trainer myself."

I know Eli's history like the back of my hand. I did a lot of research before I took the job. I'm aware he struggled his first season because of PTSD and he butted heads with the goalie coach before me because Eli wouldn't admit what was happening with him and didn't want help. I feel like that might have been an isolated incident now, but I still feel the need to double-check. It's almost playoffs. Players tend to push through stuff they shouldn't right about now.

"He told me you'd say that too," Jude replies as he pulls on his red Under Armour shirt. He meets me with eyes the same color as Sadie's. "I wanted to say thanks. For telling Eli that Sadie was...unraveling."

"You're welcome." Jude isn't turning back to put on the rest of his equipment, so I feel like he has more to say. I wait.

He rubs the back of his neck and looks a little sheepish, and I know he's about to bring up Sadie. More specifically my relationship with Sadie. So I do it for him. I take a couple steps closer, so the guys wandering in and out of the room while they get ready don't overhear too much.

"Sadie means a great deal to me," I tell him honestly. "I will always look out for her and go out of my way to try and help her. She's an incredible woman, and she's going through...fuck, you're all going through a really painful time."

He seems stunned by my candor, and I feel a little bit victorious. I know from playing him on the ice that Jude doesn't get stunned easily. He's usually the one doing the shocking things, not being shocked. "We are," he agrees when he finally manages to speak again. "That's why I have to tell you, if you do anything that puts her in more pain—"

"Oh, good, the older brother speech," I interrupt and give him a cocky grin. "I figured you were the type of guy to threaten your sisters' boyfriends with physical violence. You like to play a douche canoe on the ice, but turns out you're just a big old softie."

Jude laughs, which is exactly the reaction I was hoping for. "First of all, it's 'extremely talented douche canoe.' And secondly...there is no secondly, just don't break her heart."

I pause and grow serious. "I can't promise that. But I can tell you that if I have to, it will also break mine."

He considers my words. "I don't like that."

"Neither do we, but we're going for it anyway," I reply. "And we both think it's worth the risk."

Eli appears in the doorway. "Hey, Coach!"

"How's the quad?" I ask, turning to him.

"A-okay. Just a little tightness from practice," Eli assures me and then looks to Jude and back at me. "What's up with you guys?"

"Jude is just threatening my physical safety for getting back together with Sadie," I reply with a wry grin.

Eli's whole face lights up. "You guys are going to give it a go? That's fucking awesome. Maybe a little awkward because you're my coach and now I'll be seeing you at family dinners, but still awesome."

"Not your family yet," Jude reminds him. "And if you screw up, I'll hit you too."

Eli turns to me, ignoring Jude completely. "You're going to love watching the girls take him down a peg every thirty seconds. It's truly an art form."

I laugh, and Jude rolls his eyes. "I'll let you get to it."

I head out of the locker room, smiling, but the grin and the good feelings that have been building in me evaporate as my phone rings. It's Hunter, and as soon as I say hello he says, "Lauren's lawyer asked for the hearing date to be moved up. It's tomorrow at noon."

And just like that, everything feels dark again.

25

SADIE

The shift is going painlessly. We're not slammed with patients, and everything is manageable. I'm working with Shelda again, whom I adore, and I'm floating on a post-orgasm high.

For the first time in a long time, I chose me. Griffin fills a void in my life, brings me joy. And like my dad said, it already feels way better to know I've made the decision to be with Griffin for as long as I can, regardless of how long that is. And to be there for him and let him be there for me.

Dad was napping when I got home from Griffin's, so I couldn't thank him for his advice, but I decide I'll call him on my break. As soon as I walk into the nurses' lounge, I pull my phone out of the pocket of my scrubs to dial our home number, but I see a text from Griffin and open it instead.

Hunter just called. Somehow Lauren's lawyer got the court date bumped up to tomorrow.

My heart plummets. He may find out tomorrow. I just took a chance at happiness and I might already be getting shot down.

Deep breath, Sadie. Think positive. Or don't think at all and just work. Whatever happens, crying about it now isn't going to change it.

I eat my lunch, but I don't really taste it. As I'm finishing my turkey sandwich, Griffin texts again.

No matter what happens. Even if I end up in NYC, I am not letting you go. Long distance sucks, but it's better than losing you.

I wish he were right, but I look at Winnie and Ty, and I think it's a fate worse than death. Maybe we would be different....

I throw out the rest of my sandwich and start to text him back, but the lounge door bursts open and little Shelda is standing there huffing like she ran a marathon. She puts a hand to her chest dramatically. "Oh, sweet baby Jesus, I am not a sprinter."

"Is something wrong? Did we get a rush of patients?" I ask, standing up. "A car wreck?"

She shakes her head. "Only one new patient. A suspected drug overdose."

That's tragic but not unheard of or worthy of sprinting through the hospital to get me. She struggles to stabilize her breathing, and when she manages it she explains. And it makes my heart clench in fear. "That little girl. The adorable one that belongs to your stud muffin? She's here."

"What?" She's mistaken. It's another kid who looks like

Charlie. Why would Charlie be here in the middle of the night and Griffin doesn't know? She's got to be wrong.

"Came in with her mama, who is here for the overdose guy," Shelda explains. "I know it's her, Sadie. I even said hello to her and she remembered me."

"Oh, God, no." My pulse is racing, and my blood feels cold. "I have to tell Griffin."

"You can't," she argues. "Privacy policy."

My heart plummets so fast I almost gasp. "Shelda, I have to tell him."

She looks at the clock. "That's why you're sick."

"What?"

"There's enough of us on and it's been a slow night, so I've decided, as head nurse, that you should go home and take care of that cough of yours instead of working through it." She drops her voice to a stage whisper, even though no one else is in the room. "If you walk through the ER lobby and see her as a citizen and not an on-duty nurse, you can call him."

I look at the clock. It's almost twelve-thirty in the morning. The game is over and he's home, and I know he's up because he just texted me. I rush over and hug Shelda. "Thank you."

"You're most welcome." Shelda pats my back. "Now get that kiddo with her hot little daddy. Clearly Mommy is making some questionable life choices. Also, she's a bit of a bitch. She yelled at me when I told her she couldn't be in the room while they work on the patient."

Shelda leaves, and I clock out and change into my street clothes so fast that my dress is on inside out, but I don't care. I grab my purse out of my locker and almost run to the waiting room. Seconds before I push open the swinging doors, I take a moment to compose myself so I can look relaxed. I walk into the waiting room, my eyes sweeping the whole area instantly. Charlie is on one of the chairs in the corner playing with the zipper on the jacket she's wearing over her pajamas.

Look up, kiddo. Look up!

I scan the area again, trying to find someone who might be Griffin's ex. There's a tall, pale brunette at the desk arguing with Kina about something. That's got to be her. I glance back at Charlie, and she's finally looking up. She spots me and recognition makes her expression brighten.

I wave enthusiastically, like I have no idea why she's here and I'm just happy to see her. "Hi, Charlie!"

I walk over to her casually, but my legs ache, they want to run to her so badly. I bend down in front of her chair. "I'm Nurse Sadie. Remember me?"

She nods. "My daddy likes you."

"I like him," I reply calmly. "And you. Do you have another raisin problem?"

She shakes her head with gusto. "No. I've been good about ignoring stupid dares from stupid boys. I promise. My dad is going to get me bow and arrow lessons if I stay good. Like Merida in *Brave*."

Oh, my heart. She's a tomboy just like I was. And Griffin embraces it just like my dad did.

"Archery? That's great! You'll be good at that," I tell her and pause, giving her my best silly, overexaggerated perplexed look, and she smiles. "So why are you here tonight so late? Is your dad with you?"

"No," she says sadly. "My mommy's friend got sick so we're here."

"That's too bad," I say and try not to grit my teeth, I'm so angry. Thank God she's naïve about it and isn't overly traumatized—yet. "Have you told your daddy yet?"

"Excuse me!" I twist to look behind me and see the brunette. "Why are you talking to my daughter?"

I stand up and face her. She's pretty. It's one of those stupid things I can't help but notice. Like model pretty. "I've met Charlie before. I just wanted to say hello." I extend my hand. "I'm Sadie Braddock. My brother plays for the Thunder, and I know Griffin."

She blinks—a lot and fast. It's like watching a computer pinwheel spin to process information. "What are you doing here in the middle of the night?"

"I was wondering that about Charlie," I say, sidestepping her question. I look down at Charlie. "We should call your dad."

"She's with her mother. That's all you need to know. Excuse us." She gently takes Charlie's hand and guides her across the waiting area to another row of seats. I head outside to the parking lot and call Griffin.

"Hey," he says, and his voice is low and gravelly, and I worry he was already asleep.

"Griffin...Charlie is fine, one hundred percent, but she is here at the hospital with her mom," I say. "She is perfectly fine," I repeat. "I just talked to her myself."

"What? Why? I'm on my way," he says, and I can hear the panic. "What happened? Is it Lauren? Why didn't anyone call me?"

"Lauren is fine. I'll explain when you get here," I promise. "Just hang up the phone and drive safely. I will meet you in the parking lot."

He gets here way faster than he should have, but I don't call him on it. He jumps from his Range Rover and rushes to me. "Where is she?"

"She's in the waiting room," I explain, holding his biceps because I'm worried he'll just bolt before I can explain everything. "I can't tell you why they are here because it would violate my work rules, but I can tell you neither of them is hurt in any way. They're just in the waiting room."

He's confused and frustrated, but I think he gets it, because he just nods at me, pulls away, and starts stalking toward the building. I chase after him. Everyone in the waiting room looks up as soon as he enters. His energy is dark and fills the room even more than his hulking physical presence. Well, everyone except Charlie, who has curled up on her chair and fallen asleep with her head in her mom's lap. His ex's face falls as soon as she sees him. She looks like a kid who was caught stealing the car. It would be funny except it's so completely not.

Griffin walks right over to her. He starts to scoop up Charlie.

"Daddy!" she says in sleepy elation and wraps her arms around his neck.

"I'm going to take you to the boat, okay, kiddo?" She nods, eyelids still heavy.

The ex opens her mouth, but Griffin's intense stare steals any sound that she might have made. He speaks, calmly. Too calmly. "I'm going to take her to my place to sleep in her bed. You're going to follow me to the parking lot."

"But—"

"Lauren."

She nods. He turns to me and hands me his car key fob.

"Can you help me out and take Charlie and get her settled in the car, please?" I nod, and Lauren makes a face. Griffin sees it. "We need to have a private conversation. Sadie will keep an eye on her at my car while we talk across the lot."

Lauren still has a look of pure hate on her face, but I ignore it, and we all walk out together. Griffin puts Charlie down and squats to her level. "Charlie, honey, Nurse Sadie is going to walk you over to the car and get you settled. Mom and I will be right over there."

He points to a spot a few cars over, and she nods. I take her hand and walk her over to his SUV. A couple minutes later she's strapped into her booster seat and already nodding off. I keep the back door open and lean against the side of the car and keep an eye on her.

I try not to glance over too much, but when I do I see a lot of angry expressions and gesturing arms. Their voices start getting louder and louder as they talk, and I start to hear everything, but Charlie is asleep so she, thankfully, doesn't.

"My boyfriend is sick and you're punishing me by taking away my daughter," she says heatedly. I bristle at the idea that she is turning this around and blaming Griffin.

"What is he sick with, Lauren?" Griffin snaps.

"I don't know why Cale is sick, but I do know you won't get away with this," she yells.

Something in me snaps, and I can't stay silent. I gently close the door to the car and take a step toward Griffin. They notice and both turn to face me at the same time.

"She knows why he was brought in, and so do I," I can't help but interject. My eyes narrow on her face. "And I will tell him if you don't, even if it costs me my job."

Lauren hates my guts. That is clear in the look she gives me. And if I get my way, this woman will be in my life for a very long time, because Charlie will be—because Griffin will be—but if the price I pay is a lifetime of bitchiness and death stares from her, then so be it. "He has to know if it affects his daughter, and clearly it does," I remind her flatly.

"Who the fuck are you?" Lauren hisses.

"Sadie is my girlfriend," Griffin explains.

"How the fuck does she know anything about my life?" Lauren demands.

"Why is my daughter in an emergency room waiting room in the middle of the night?" Griffin asks her in a dark, deep voice so serious it's almost menacing.

"They said Cale overdosed, but I don't believe them," Lauren says, but the quick, furtive way she's talking means that deep down, she does believe them. "I know he's been under a lot of stress, because he wants me to move to New York with him and you're making that harder than it needs to be. But he's not like a serious drug user. It's got to be a mistake. He has the occasional joint but never anything hard. I wouldn't be with him if he had a real drug problem."

Griffin takes a deep breath. He's much calmer looking than

I probably am, and it amazes me. "I'm taking Charlie home. She's spending the two days I'm away for the road trip with Hunter and Mia. You are going to call your lawyer and cancel the custody hearing tomorrow."

"I can't. I won't!"

"Lauren." Griffin's voice suddenly sounds so tired. "She's our baby. She can't move to New York with a drug addict. I know you love her."

"We don't know for sure that's what happened tonight!" She is so desperate that I almost feel bad for her.

"Lauren, it's this plan or I go in there tomorrow and tell the judge all of this," Griffin explains. "And you'll have a lot more to worry about than whether you go to New York."

Lauren starts to cry, but she nods. "Fine. I'm going to need time to deal with this anyway. But I want to see her while she's with Hunter and Mia."

"Of course," Griffin replies. "I will never keep you from your child."

Oh, my God, I love this man. I *love* this man.

Lauren storms past me to the car and opens the door to the back seat. Charlie is still out cold. She strokes her hair and kisses her forehead before glaring at me one last time and turning and heading into the ER without another word. Griffin turns to me, grabs my face in his hands, and kisses me feverishly. When he pulls away I'm breathless.

"I can't tell you what you mean to me," he whispers hoarsely. "Because I can't even process it at this point. But I will never be able to thank you enough."

"Go," I say simply and give him one more quick, soft kiss,

because I am drowning in my own feelings for him. "Get her home."

He nods but it's reluctant. Even with everything going on he still wants to take care of me. "I'll be fine. We'll talk tomorrow."

He nods, kisses me one last time, and drives away.

26

GRIFFIN

The Thunder lost both games on the road, and now we're no longer in a playoff position. We have two more weeks to clinch a spot, which means we're fighting for our life next game and every game until the end of the season. By default that means I didn't get to go straight home when the plane landed. Coach was pissed and called an immediately practice. Not one player was happy about it, but no one dared complain. I was no different, even though for the first time in a long time I have more than Charlie as a reason to want to rush home.

Sadie and I have called and texted throughout the trip. Our bond after the incident in the ER is stronger than ever. She's explained everything to me, and I realize she basically risked her job because she thought my daughter's well-being was in jeopardy. I will never be able to thank her for that. But I will never stop trying.

Practice goes well. Eli looks solid, as always, and the losses weren't on him. Eli let in a total of eight goals over three games, but the defense was a disaster. One of the goals was even tipped in off our own player. I meet with the head coach after practice and reiterate my feelings to him. He's grumpy, but he agrees with me. He just hates losing, because the Thunder aren't used to it, and neither is he. I don't want anyone to get used to it.

Two and half hours after landing, I can finally head home, just in time to hit rush-hour traffic. We have two days before the next game, but there will still be practice. I text Sadie before I get in my car and tell her I'm heading over to get Charlie and that I can't wait to see her tomorrow, since she's working tonight. I make a point to ask her how her dad is and how she's holding up. I know she won't give me the most honest answer, but she's more honest with me than anyone else.

I hop in the SUV and drive straight to Hunter's. They live in the back half of an old Victorian, so you have to walk through the backyard to get to their front door. As I knock I can see into their tiny living room through the half-moon window in the door. Mia is home with Charlie, and Lauren is there too. At first I feel like I must have fallen into a black hole and gone back a decade because Mia and Lauren are sitting on the couch, smiling at each other over cups of tea. They haven't done that since a few years before the divorce. Charlie is plopped down in the middle of the overstuffed bean bag chair, her eyes glued to *Brave,* which is playing on the TV.

Mia waves at me to come in. I use the key they gave me to open the door, and I step inside. Lauren looks completely different from that night in the ER parking lot. She's in brown suede leggings and a white sweater. Her makeup is perfect, and her hair is too. But most important, she's calm and even smiles at me, without contempt. I nod at her and walk over to Charlie. "Hey, honey! I'm back!"

"Hi, Daddy! Missed you," she says, but her eyes don't leave the TV. Oh, God, I've created a monster. I look over at Mia, who stands up and hits the off button on the TV. Charlie looks like someone just murdered her class hamster.

"We have to go pack you up," Mia explains. "Sorry, but I think you know how it ends."

"But I wanted to see the part where she—"

"Charlie, no sass-talking your aunt. Do what she's asking," Lauren says in a quiet but firm voice.

Charlie groans in protest but gets up and follows Mia out of the room. Mia squeezes my arm as she passes. I wait until I know they're out of earshot, and then I face Lauren. "Thank you for canceling the hearing."

She nods and puts her half-empty teacup on the coffee table. "I didn't have a choice."

"No. You didn't."

She stands up. "I'm not moving to New York. Cale and I are done."

I feel a hundred pounds lighter at that declaration. Lauren looks pretty upset by it but also resolved. The one thing I still admire about my ex-wife is that when she makes a decision she follows through on it. She's not the least bit wishy-washy. She looks me square in the eye. "Just to be clear, Cale wasn't at my home when it happened. His roommate called and woke me up to tell me after he called 911, and so I raced to the hospital. I had to bring Charlie with me because I couldn't leave her home alone."

"You could have called me. I would have gone over there and stayed until you got back, and Charlie could have slept through the night," I tell her flatly.

"You were working," she counters. "I still know the Thunder's schedule, Griffin."

After a brief silence of us just staring at each other, she sighs. "I never would have let her near him if I knew what he was into," Lauren tells me, and I can feel the guilt that's radiating off of her. "She is the most important thing in my life."

"I know," I say. "So now what?"

"I'm willing to go back to the original joint custody agreement if you will," Lauren says, and her hazel eyes are filled with fear. She thinks I'm going to make a play for full custody now, and she knows I have reason to. "I made a mistake with Cale, but I've learned from it and I will never do that again."

"We have to do better—with each other," I reply, and I'm including myself in that statement. "Which is why I'm telling you I'm going to officially introduce Charlie to Sadie, because she's my girlfriend and it's serious."

"The girl from the parking lot?" Lauren looks like she is going to start spitting nails any minute.

I stand my ground. "Yes. And she is an amazing person, and you'll have to meet her officially one day too, because she's going to be around for a while."

This takes a few seconds for Lauren to absorb. I use that time to repeat what I said earlier because I meant it. "We need to do better. Be kinder to each other and work as a team, be-

cause we owe that to Charlie. That means complete disclosure
and we talk things out and come to agreements."

"I don't like her."

"You don't have to. You just have to respect her," I explain. "Because she respects your daughter and me, and she'll
respect you too."

"So we can go back to our original agreement?" Lauren's
only real focus right now is keeping ties to Charlie. That's
okay. In fact, it makes me feel better.

"Yes. If Cale is really, truly gone for good."

"He is. I swear on our daughter's life," Lauren says, and I
can see the pure honesty in her expression. "So I can take her
home today?"

I nod. "Yes. But on Wednesday when I get her for my
schedule overnight, I'm going to take her to dinner. With
Sadie."

"Sure," she says, but it looks like she's sucking on lemons.
I can only hope she'll develop a poker face. Lauren nods as
Mia and Charlie come back from the guest bedroom. Lauren's
face relaxes, and she grins at our daughter. "Ready to come
home, sweet pea?"

Charlie nods enthusiastically. "Can I finish watching *Brave*
at home?"

"I don't see why not," Lauren says. Charlie walks over and
lifts her arms to me for a hug.

I pick her off the ground and into a bear hug, which she
wiggles against. "Dad! I'm too old to be picked up!"

"You are never too old!" I argue, and she hugs me anyway,
but she's rolling her eyes.

She wiggles more, so I put her down. She smooths her clothes and hair like she's the queen of England who's just had to endure accolades from the minions. I am in so much trouble with this one. "See you Wednesday."

"Frodo and dog park?" she asks, hope shining in her eyes.

"Okay. After dinner with my friend Sadie," I say and wait for the disappointment. But I don't get any. She hesitates a moment but then nods.

"She was really nice the other night," Charlie remarks. "Does she like dogs?"

"I think she does. And horses."

"She's been on a horse? Cool!"

"Okay, let's get going," Lauren prods lightly, but her shoulders are tense.

I promise myself I will make sure she doesn't feel it's a competition.

I walk out with them and watch them get into the car and wave as they drive off. I'm feeling so much better now. I wasn't sure how things would go down with Lauren. I honestly believe she knows the depths of the mistake she made with the idiot named after a leafy vegetable. I think we are back on track as co-parents.

The next morning I walk into the ER a few minutes before seven a.m. with a bouquet of flowers in one hand and a box in the other. Sadie is behind the desk but already has a sweater on over her scrubs and her purse on her shoulder, so I know she's about to leave. Her face lights up at the sight of me. I will never get sick of that, and I swear I will find a way to make her look like that every day. Her gaze lands on the gifts I'm double-fisting. "Griffin Sullivan, what have you done?" She pauses. "Or more accurately, what have I done to deserve this?"

"You let me in. You gave me a new view of life. You looked out for my daughter," I tell her and lean over the counter to kiss her cheek. "And you know, great sex."

I whisper that last part so no one else hears, but it makes her grin grow devious again, which I fucking love. "But actually only one of these things is for you. The other gifts I have for you can't be experienced in a crowded ER."

The door to the back swings open, and Shelda walks through it. I hand Sadie the box in my left hand and turn to present Shelda with the bouquet in my right. She gapes and smiles. "For me?"

"For looking out for my daughter the other night," I explain. "And for giving Sadie a way to do it too."

"Oh, honey, if you don't lock this man up and throw away the key, I will!" Shelda announces. She sniffs the bouquet. "Thank you. I do believe you've just bumped Idris Elba off the top of my backup husbands list."

I laugh.

"That is serious business, Griffin, and an extreme honor," Sadie tells me in mock seriousness.

Shelda sighs happily and then gets suddenly stern and points at Sadie. "Don't mess this up."

She skips out of the ER. Sadie comes around the desk, and as we walk out together she opens the box I handed her, stops dead, and bursts out laughing. "Unicorn cookies?"

"Of course." I wrap an arm around her shoulders. "And they're delicious. I had to try one, of course."

"You're hysterical." She laughs and bites into one, eating the horn first. "Crap. They are delicious."

"So...I know you're exhausted, so I can just drive you right home," I say as I unlock the SUV with the fob. "Or you can come back to my place and nap there. I promise I won't bug you. You'll have the whole boat to yourself. I'll be at practice from ten until noon anyway."

"Your place," she says as she swallows down the rest of the cookie. "And I am totally going to sleep. Like the dead."

I nod, but a part of me is really disappointed. I start to close her door after she gets in, but she grabs the front of my shirt and pulls me in for a kiss. Then she tells me, "Right after I suck your perfect dick and beg you to fuck me."

"The last thing you need to do is beg, love."

And it takes everything in me not to speed on the way home. But I tell myself I don't need to rush. This amazing wildflower is mine and I'm hers, and this is only the beginning.

27

SADIE

Oh, God..." I feel my clit start to tingle. "Griffin..."

He looks down at me, eyes hooded, the sweat on his brow telling me he's struggling not to come. That makes me belly clench with desire and my clit tingle more. And then he pushes into me, harder than before. The friction of his pelvis against my clit turns tingles into quivers, and I am so close.

"I'm don't want to come yet," I pant, and he huffs out a breath by my ear.

"I'm going to make you," he promises. He drops his hips lower still, swivels them up harder still. "Right..."

He slams into me.

"Fucking..."

He does it again.

"Now." He does it again, once hard and then again, softer, slower, and hard again, and everything inside me melts.

"Oh, fuck," he pants, and I feel him jerk almost violently,

and his head snaps back and his hips snap forward and he comes as hard and as long as I do.

Moments later, when we're back on this earth, he pulls out of me and leans back on his knees to remove the condom. I sit up and watch him drop it in the trash, and then I wrap my arms around his neck and pull him back down on top of me. We make out like teenagers for a few long moments, and then he pulls back and looks down on me with such affection it warms me. He balances on one forearm and runs the pad of his thumb over my lips and chin. "My beard is giving you a rash."

"It also makes you sexy as hell and feels incredible against my thighs, so I don't care," I murmur back.

He kisses me again, but his eyes slip over to the digital clock on the nightstand. "I have to go get Charlie soon."

I nod and kiss his shoulder blade as he rolls off me. He lies on his side, head propped up on his hand, and looks over at me. "You're not nervous? At all?"

"Maybe a little," I admit. "But I've already met her and she likes me. I can only assume that won't change just because she's going to find out we're dating. I mean, why would it? I'm adorable!"

Griffin burst into a grin. "That's definitely the truth."

I sit up, not bothering to cover my exposed breasts with the covers, because he's seen everything before and, quite frankly, I love the way he looks at me naked. "I'm a little more nervous about meeting your brother and his wife."

"You've met Hunter before," he reminds me.

"Yeah, and I was a mess," I say sheepishly, my cheeks

growing warm. "I hope he can forget about that and I can prove to him you're not dating a basket case."

"He doesn't think that, love," Griffin promises me as he untangles himself from the covers and gets out of bed.

Now it's my turn to admire his naked form. He is so tall and so broad, and I swear he's the only guy I know with zero ink. His skin is pure, unmarked...except for a little redness on his back from my nails when I came. His dick is still half hard, or maybe it's hard again. Either way, it makes him even sexier. He reaches for my hand. "Come on, let's get ready."

I let him lead me into the bathroom. As he turns on the water and waits for it to warm up, he turns to me and pulls me into a hug. It's strong and warm and so intimate because we're naked but also because he's the first man I think I have ever been emotionally bare with too. And now I am nervous. I need Charlie to like me. I need his brother and his wife to accept me. Because I want to belong in this man's life forever.

"Come on." He tugs me toward him and the awaiting shower.

Forty-seven minutes later I'm wedged into a booth at an Italian place in the Haight that Mia, Hunter's wife, swears makes the best pizza in San Francisco. Griffin is on one side of me and Charlie is on the other. She insisted on sitting next to me. Across from us, Hunter is telling me a story about when they were kids and the pranks they used to play on each other. He's laughing so hard trying to finish the story that he has tears in his eyes.

"But it turns out it was my dad's toothbrush, not mine,"

Hunter exclaims, and Griffin groans, covering his eyes with his hand at the memory.

I turn and look at him in disbelief. "You soaked your dad's toothbrush in lemon juice?"

"Daddy, that's not nice," Charlie tells him, looking up from her coloring book and making a *tsk* sound that is beyond adorable coming from her tiny mouth.

"It wasn't nice," Griffin agrees. "And you should never do that, because you'll end up grounded for two weeks like your dad did."

Hunter snickers. "It was kind of awesome. I got to watch whatever I wanted on TV and play all the video games without him demanding a turn."

"So, Sadie, was your upbringing as crazy as these two?" Mia asks. "I was an only child so I was spared all this drama."

"It was. Definitely sounds like this," I admit, and I love that we both have great siblings and good families. "There is nothing quite like the joy of terrorizing your teenage brother. But unlike Griffin, I was actually good at it. Still am."

They all burst out laughing.

"I want a brother!" Charlie says out of nowhere, bringing the laughter at the table to a screeching halt. Griffin's staring over at her with shock on his face, completely speechless.

Charlie looks at him, blinking innocently. Hunter jumps in. "I thought you wanted a dog?"

She seems to think about that, her face scrunching up for a moment, and then she bounces in her seat. "Can't I have both?"

Mia snorts.

Hunter looks from Griffin to me and then turns back to

Charlie and smiles. "Not right now, kiddo, but maybe one day."

I feel Griffin's hand wrap around my shoulders. Charlie accepts that answer and runs with it. "So I can have a dog one day? What about a bow and arrow like Merida?"

A sibling seems to have fallen off the radar and an awkward moment has naturally evaporated. I sigh in relief, and Griffin notices, giving my shoulder a squeeze.

The rest of the night goes flawlessly. Mia was right. The pizza is fantastic. And I really hit it off with her and Hunter. Mia and I even make plans to go to the movies together. Charlie asks me questions and tells me stories and seems genuinely content. I don't think she understands I'm her dad's girlfriend, but it doesn't matter. The fact that she seems to like me is all that matters right now. It's the first step. We took it and we're on solid ground so far.

We say goodbye to Mia and Hunter outside the restaurant and start up the hill toward Griffin's car. Charlie begins to complain it's too far. Without a word, Griffin lifts her up and plops her on his shoulders. Her grin lights up the evening sky. My dad used to lift me up like that too whenever I complained about being tired of walking. I used to love it so much that I'd fake complaints. Sometimes he'd give me the slyest smile, as if he knew I was faking, but he'd never deny me. Griffin's grin right now reminds me of my dad's, and it makes everything hurt in the most joyous way. He is so much like my dad with her, and it makes me want his babies. I'm not even scared to admit it to myself, but I'll probably keep that revelation from him for a while.

When we reach the car Griffin puts her in the car in her booster seat. I climb into the passenger seat as he reaches into the pocket in the back seat and pulls out an iPad and clips it to the back of my headrest. "You can watch *Brave* while we drive home."

"Awesome, Dad!"

We drive in comfortable silence to my place. He casually rests his hand over mine on the center console. It's easy and feels so natural, even with Charlie in the back seat and her movie echoing around the car.

Griffin pulls up to the curb next to my building, turns the car off, and looks back at Sadie. "Say goodbye to Sadie, Charlie."

"Bye, Sadie!" she calls out, looking up from her iPad and waving to me enthusiastically.

"I'm going to say goodbye to Sadie now, right next to the car, okay?"

"Sure." Her attention is already back on the movie as she starts to belt out one of the songs.

We get out of the car, and I walk around to his side, so he doesn't have to leave the driver's side unattended. I look up at him, and I can feel that the grin on my face is huge. I reach out and touch his stomach, my hand low on his abdomen as I tug on the fabric of his sweater. "I had fun."

"I can tell," he replies, and his smile matches mine. He reaches out and brushes my hair gently. "Everyone loved you, which I knew would happen."

I tilt my head and give him my best cocky grin. "Because I'm adorable?"

He laughs, his head tipping back a moment. When he looks at me again, though, his expression holds much more than humor in it. "That and because I love you."

My smile softens, and my heart gallops. "I love you too."

He closes the space between us and kisses me. It's not one of our normal kisses. This one is restrained because of Charlie and gentle because we just confessed something so raw and so real to each other that we're both in need of tenderness.

"I have to go," he whispers softly, pulling me in for a hug. The only thing he does better than give orgasms is hugs. They're everything. "She is precariously close to missing her bedtime."

"Drive safe," I tell him as I let him go.

"I'm going to text you later," he says as he opens his car door and starts to get in. "So I can hear you say that again."

I grin and blow him a kiss before silently mouthing the words again. He mouths them back. I head up the walk and into the building and turn to wave to him as he drives away.

I take the elevator up to the apartment, even though I swear I could float there without it. He loves me. And I love him. And even if this world gets harder... somehow it'll always be easier because of that simple truth.

Epilogue

SADIE

Three months later

A week ago, I was woken up in the middle of the night by a phone call. The best type of phone call: Dixie crying tears of joy because Eli had asked her to marry him. And now, tonight, Dixie and Eli's engagement party is in full swing. Half the Thunder team is here, my entire family and even Eli's parents came, and they actually look happy. Jude insisted on hosting it at his place. And Winnie insisted on cooking for it. I sip my wine and glance around the room. Life is good.

"Winnie wants to know if you can help her in the kitchen," Ty says. I hadn't realized he had walked up beside me. "Something about how only you can help her with the secret wing sauce."

I smile at him. "Okay. How are you, Ty?"

"Good." He nods. "Happy to be here."

He smiles at me and wanders off toward the back of the room where Jude is standing with Levi and some of their teammates. Ty's been in town for two weeks, and I haven't caught Winnie and him fighting once. Hopefully this means they're back on track.

I head to the kitchen, where I find Winnie pulling a tray of wings out of the oven. She glances at me. "Oh, good! Can you grab the special sauce?"

I nod and grab the mason jar of sauce she mixed back home this morning. It was on the counter beside the stove and Ty could have easily done it, but she clearly wants me here for something else. I hand her the jar as she carefully slides the wings into a big metal bowl. As she takes it she smiles at me. "Sorry to pull you away from Griffin."

"He's on the front porch with Dad," I explain, and Winnie's head flips up and she looks at me in shock. "I know. Dad said he needed some air and asked Griffin to wheel him out there."

"What do you think that's about?" Winnie asks. "Think he's asking for your hand in marriage like Eli did?"

"God, no," I reply firmly. "It's only been three months. Relax there, Win."

She winks. "Crazier things can happen."

"If you can wait over a decade, I can wait at least a couple of years," I say without thinking. Oh, fuck, I hope this doesn't set her off again with Ty. Luckily, she just shrugs, so I dare to keep going on the subject. "Things are good with you and Ty right now, huh?"

"Yeah." Winnie nods as she tosses the wings in the sauce. "I guess I just...I'm tired of feeling hurt."

I don't know exactly what that means, but I don't have time to ask because Dixie comes bursting into the kitchen. "Why is your boyfriend in a deep conversation with Dad?"

She heads straight for a bottle of red on the counter and refills her glass before turning to me for an answer.

"No idea," I reply. "Mom and Dad met Charlie last week, so maybe it's about that."

"How did that go?" Dixie asks, but Winnie answers before I can.

She turns to Dixie with a big smile on her face. "It was the cutest. Charlie and Griffin came over for dinner, and Charlie was so polite and sweet. Mom and Dad were in love with her and so was I. She wants a skateboard and a dog for her birthday, which is an archery-themed party."

"She sounds fun. When do I get to meet your stepdaughter?" Dixie asks, and my head spins to stare at her, my hair slipping around my face. "Relax. I know I'm jumping the gun. I won't say it in front of Griffin or anything."

"I just want to be careful with this situation," I say quietly. "I mean, you know, Charlie seems to like me, and Lauren and I are civil, but, well, baby steps."

I walk over to the fridge and grab a bottle of white out of the door and refill my own glass. "Anyway, I think I've convinced Griffin it's okay to get her a dog. We've been scouring rescue sites. He really wants one for her, but he's worried about his schedule. I talked to Mom and Dad, and they said they'd be fine if I helped out with the dog and brought him to our place when Griffin's away with the team."

No one is speaking, so I glance up and stare at them staring at me. They've both got goofy grins on their faces. "What?"

"I just fucking love that you are in love," Dixie exclaims.

I blink. "Guess what, weirdo? I love that you're in love too."

"Aww...I feel a group hug coming on!" Winnie turns away from the bowl of wings and opens her arms. Dixie and I walk into them.

"Dixie's right, though, Sadie," Winnie adds as we hug. "You've always been everyone's rock, and it's just nice to know you have a rock now too. You deserve it."

I feel my eyes get watery. Luckily, Jude shows up in the doorway. "Oh, God, did I just walk in on some kind of sorority moment? Gross."

"You ruin everything," Winnie jokes with a dramatic sigh as we pull apart.

"Make with the food, chef," Jude barks back at her. "The supplies are low out there."

"It might be the off-season, but you should probably stick to salad," Winnie snarks back at him, and she swats at his hand when he tries to steal a wing.

He manages to steal a wing anyway. Winnie pours the wings onto a platter and carries them out before he can steal another. Dixie grabs the bottle of wine and follows. I can't help but smile as the cushion-cut solitaire on her finger catches the light. Eli picked a bold, beautiful ring, perfect for bold, beautiful Dixie.

"So Griffin and Dad are on the porch together. Alone," I tell Jude, and he nods as he finishes the wing. "Any idea what that's about?"

"Dad's probably thanking Sully for putting up with you. You know, thanking him for taking you off his hands," Jude replies, reaching for a napkin to wipe his hands. I smile brightly at him but flip him the middle finger. He laughs. "I could tell you what I really think is happening out there, but you'll get all weepy and this is a party."

Now I'm intrigued—and little worried. "What are you talking about?"

Jude opens the fridge and grabs a beer. He turns back around, leans on the closed fridge door, and twists the cap. "He's probably telling Griffin how much he likes him. How well he fits in this family and how well he fits with you, his sweet, good, strong, and beautiful pumpkin."

My eyes are watering again. "He's not."

"You're right he's not saying it," Jude replies and his face grows dark. "The tablet is saying it, but they're Dad's words, even if they can't come out of his mouth anymore."

My dad lost the ability to speak about a month ago. He's been typing what he wants to say into a tablet that speaks for him. Jude sips his beer. I stare out toward the front door. "Should I go rescue him?"

"It's not a crisis situation, Sadie." Jude laughs at me. "It's a good thing. Let them talk."

I glance at the front door again just as it opens and Griffin comes back in, pushing my dad's wheelchair. I watch my mom walk over and take his place, wheeling my dad out of view toward the dining room. Griffin glances around the living room and then glances down the hall, sees me in the kitchen doorway, and he comes straight for me. He bends down and kisses my cheek as he enters. Jude slips by him out of the kitchen, leaving us alone.

"Everything good?"

"Yeah." He smiles at me. "Let's grab more of my guacamole. Supplies look low out there."

He lets go of me and moves to the fridge to pull out a bowl full of guacamole he made for the party. I've learned Griffin is incredible in the kitchen, which is great, because I'm not. I lift one of the giant bags of white corn chips off the counter and pull it open. Griffin takes a chip as soon as I open the bag and dips it into the guacamole, then turns and holds it up in front of my mouth. "Taste test?"

I take a big bite of the chip. The guac is delicious. "Perfect. Just like you."

"Sweetheart, you are way too good for my ego," he replies and drops his head to give me a quick, light kiss when I'm done chewing. He doesn't pull away afterward, though, looking me in the eye. "Are you okay?"

I nod. "Yeah. Today is a good day. I love a party and we need all the reasons possible to create happy moments."

"It's bittersweet," Griffin remarks softly. I bite my bottom lip and nod, and he pulls me into a hug. I rest my cheek on his chest and close my eyes and let the warmth of being in his arms seep into every part of me.

"I'm focusing on the sweet part," I whisper, and I feel his lips on the top of my head. "He might not be here for the wedding, but he knows Eli is the right one. He saw it with his own eyes."

"He just wants you all to be happy," Griffin says. "And he says that I make you happy."

"You do." I lift my head off his chest to stare up into his deep, dark eyes. "I'm glad he knows it."

"I told him I love you," Griffin says softly. "I hope I wasn't supposed to keep that a secret."

I wrap my arms around his neck. "I love you too, and I couldn't hide it even if I wanted to."

He dips his head and kisses me again, long and slow.

"Ew. Gross."

We break apart as Jude is back, standing in the doorway acting like an overdramatic teenager. I roll my eyes and let go of Griffin. "Thank God you interrupted us now, I was just about to ask him for a quickie. A second later and I would have been bent over the—"

"Why do you do that?!" Jude yells, a look of pure horror on his face. "He's my coach!"

"I'm Eli's coach," Griffin corrects but turns to me. "But he's right. Please stop using sex with me to torture your brother."

"I have to use any means possible to torture him," I explain with a shrug as I pour the tortilla chips into a bowl. "It's in my genetic wiring."

"Feel free to beak up with her," Jude tells Griffin in a fake-serious tone. "I can have her banned from Thunder games so you won't ever have to see her again."

"Unfortunately it's too late for that," Griffin tells him as he follows me out of the kitchen, carrying the bowl of guacamole. "I'm in too deep. There's no way out for me. And to be honest, I'm okay with that."

My heart swells at his sweet words despite the fact that Jude is groaning. Griffin has fit into this family like he was always there. I can't even imagine what my life would be like without him. And thankfully, I don't have to.

Look for Winnie's book,
NOW OR NEVER,
coming in early 2019.

ABOUT THE AUTHOR

Victoria Denault loves long walks on the beach, cinnamon dolce lattes, and writing angst-filled romance. She lives in LA but grew up in Montreal, which is why she is fluent in English, French, and hockey.

Learn more at:

VictoriaDenault.com

Facebook.com/AuthorVictoriaDenault

Twitter: @BooksbyVictoria

CPSIA information can be obtained
at www.ICGtesting.com
Printed in the USA
BVHW03s0942030818
523473BV00001B/20/P